LOVE AND MR LEWISHAM

HERBERT GEORGE WELLS was born at Bromley in Kent in 1866. His father was an impecunious shopkeeper and, for a time, a professional cricketer. H. G. Wells's origins and upbringing, like his adolescent vicissitudes and frustrations, profoundly influenced his novels and social attitudes. In 1890 he took degrees in zoology and geology and very soon thereafter tried his hand at scientific journalism and short-story writing. In 1897, with publication of *The Invisible Man*, began a long series of fantastic and imaginative romances which gained him the reputation of a prophet. Alternating with these were his 'real' novels, including *Love and Mr Lewisham, Kipps, Tono-Bungay, Ann Veronica* and *The History of Mr Polly*; and after the First World War he entered upon his encyclopedic phase with books such as *The Outline of History* and *The Science of Life*. His was an emotionally and intellectually turbulent life, at the end of which he felt the frustrations more than he recognized the achievements. He produced over a hundred books, and persisted in writing almost to the end. He died in London in 1946.

BENNY GREEN has been a jazz musician and jazz critic, as well as a literary, film, and television critic. He is well known as a journalist and broadcaster. His most recent publications include *Shaw's Champions, Fred Astaire*, and *P. G. Wodehouse*. He is also a cricket enthusiast and is the editor of the *Wisden Anthology*.

H. G. WELLS

Love and Mr Lewisham

INTRODUCED BY
BENNY GREEN

Oxford   New York
OXFORD UNIVERSITY PRESS
1983

Oxford University Press, Walton Street, Oxford OX2 6DP

London Glasgow New York Toronto
Delhi Bombay Calcutta Madras Karachi
Kuala Lumpur Singapore Hong Kong Tokyo
Nairobi Dar es Salaam Cape Town
Melbourne Auckland
and associated companies in
Beirut Berlin Ibadan Mexico City Nicosia

Oxford is a trade mark of Oxford University Press

Introduction © Benny Green 1983

First published 1900 by Harper
First issued, with a new Introduction, as an Oxford University Press paperback 1983

British Library Cataloguing in Publication Data
Wells, H. G.
Love and Mr Lewisham.
1. Title
823'.912[F] PR5774
ISBN 0-19-281398-6

Library of Congress Cataloging in Publication Data
Wells, H. G. (Herbert George), 1866–1946.
Love and Mr. Lewisham.
(Twentieth century classics) (Oxford paperbacks)
I. Title. II. Series.
PR5774.L6 1983 823'.912 83-7278
ISBN 0-19-281398-6 (pbk.)

Printed in Great Britain by
Richard Clay (The Chaucer Press) Ltd.
Bungay, Suffolk

INTRODUCTION

BY BENNY GREEN

OF THE four Wellsian heroes rooted in the youth of their creator, George Edgar Lewisham is the only one not trapped behind the counter of a drapery emporium. While Hoopdriver, Kipps and Polly, their inchoate sighs muffled behind bales of cretonne at four-and-eleven-three-farthings, seem doomed to go haberdashing haplessly down a predestined path ending in a pensionless cul-de-sac, Lewisham is a sternly dedicated intellectual, a young man on the threshold of dazzling academic honours, a threadbare seeker after truth who digests six impossible irregular verbs before breakfast, whose every waking hour is dedicated to the subtlest of all the taxidermist's arts, the stuffing of his own brain with as many abstruse facts as can be acquired. With his degrees and his diplomas brandished like tilted lances, he will smash his way out of the prison of Class and become master of his fate. He would find little in common with his three spiritual draper-cousins, for although something of a prig and a poseur, his thirst for knowledge and his belief in its power are sincere enough. He really believes he might be able to change the world, where Hoopdriver, Kipps and Polly merely wish to be accepted by it. Compared to them, Lewisham's horizons are vast, his ambitions grandiloquent, his self-confidence rampant.

The differences between them cut deeper. The very furthest limits of Hoopdriver's aspirations represent that condition of a comparative erudition at which

Lewisham has already arrived when we first meet him; Kipps and Polly are even worse, for they harbour no intellectual dreams at all. Their aims are purely negative: not to achieve anything new, but somehow to escape the consequences of the old order. For them, bliss means not being a draper. Indeed, so abject is their quietism as young men that in order to save them from themselves, Wells is obliged to fall back on that hoariest of all Dickensian devices, the mysterious legacy. Were the gods to have arranged an accidental encounter one day between these four projections of the same brain, Lewisham would either have despised his three cousins, or at best felt a sort of condescending pity for the hopelessness of their case. Certainly he would have found no basis for a rational conversation with any of them, except perhaps to have asked sarcastically whether the death of the old Queen had brought about a fall in the price of black bombazine.

And yet Lewisham is the same man as those three fumbling young drapers. He is simply what they become once they are released from their commercial obligations; and if that transition seems remarkable to the brink of incredibility, it is because Wells himself was a character remarkable to the brink of incredibility and far beyond it. When Wells first began attempting to shake off the trammels of retail trade and drifted into that phase of his life reflected in the story of Lewisham, he fell under the benign influence of a certain Horace Byatt, 'a not very brilliant graduate of Dublin University, an animated and energetic teacher', who saw at a glance that here was the student of a life-time, the one-in-a-million born academic. But just as the links were being forged between them, the fifteen-year-old Wells was swept up in yet another family campaign to turn him into a draper's assistant, a condition of life he had already so far outstripped that he records in his autobiography the comical incongruity of the juxtaposition between his daily duties and the speculative philosophic abstractions to which he was becoming increasingly committed. Discussing one day the nebulosities of pantheism and atheism with a fellow-prisoner, his ruminations were received as follows: 'God may be everywhere', said Platt, 'or God may be nowhere. That's HIS look out. It doesn't alter the fact we've got to stack these bloody cretonnes before eleven.'

In his eighteenth year Wells contrived to return to Byatt at Midhurst Grammar School, where the Irishman proceeded to turn his young protégé into a sort of academic performing seal, putting him through the hoop of examinations in physiography, human physiology, vegetable physiology, geology, elementary inorganic chemistry and mathematics. For every first-class pass, Wells received two pounds and Byatt four, a division of the spoils perfectly acceptable to both parties, especially to Wells, who, in addition to these glimmering prizes, was receiving a modest salary as usher-cum-teacher. The Midhurst of Wells's apprenticeship becomes the Whortley of Lewisham's, even down to the landlady who strives so heroically to keep her young boarder sufficiently fed; Lewisham's Mrs Munday makes her contribution to pragmatic theory with 'I'd rather have a good sensible actin' stummik than a full head . . . any day;' Wells's Mrs Walton was a matriarch to whom he not only acknowledged the debt of 'incalculable things', but whose culinary virtuosity gave him guidance as to the name of Lewisham's fictitious town:

I paid her twelve shillings a week and she fed me well. She liked cooking and she liked her food to be eaten. My meals at Midhurst are the first in my life that I remember with pleasure. Her stews were marvellously honest and she was great at junket, custard and whortleberry and blackberry jam. Bless her memory.

Wells was to make a point of describing *Love and*

Mr Lewisham as a very carefully planned and meticulously written book, one of his few attempts to compose a novel artistically instead of assaulting it journalistically. Years later the irrepressible empirical scientist in him regretted all the agonizing over midnight oil and thought that perhaps the outcome might have been better had Jamesian stratagems been thrown to the winds and his muse allowed to let rip. But for better or for worse, *Love and Mr Lewisham* makes a consciously controlled book, full of ironic undertones, not the least bitter of which is to be found in its title. *Love and Mr Lewisham* sounds like a hymn to romance, but that is not at all what is intended, as the reader very soon begins to realize. The story is a cautionary tale in which the two elements of the title are in deadly opposition. Either love or Mr Lewisham will win through, one or the other, not both. Lewisham has set out on his tortuous journey to self-fulfilment as the passionately committed idealist. His resolve has been fanatical. He has lifted himself by his own bootstraps to a position on the very threshold of advancement. He has overcome the handicaps of background, of lack of capital, lack of connections, lack of social polish. He seems certain to triumph. And yet all the fine plans are swept aside like tents in a thunderstorm because of one contingency which has apparently never entered his head, one enemy he has not reckoned with. At the juncture in his affairs where he is poised delicately on the tightrope of his own academic apotheosis, that enemy strikes. George Edgar Lewisham falls in love.

The resultant crash is inevitable, for it is a further irony of his story that believing as he does in certain civilized standards of behaviour, Lewisham is far too honourable a sort to turn his back on his own affections, even though they threaten his entire future career. He could, at least in theory, have walked away from the wreckage and picked up the broken pieces of his plan in an attempt to paste them together again. But he cannot do it. Whatever else he might be, the prig and the pedant is honest enough to remain true to the promptings of his own heart. And, it must be said, his loins, for although Wells is never explicit as to the conjugal aspects of the affair, we are given to understand that the physical attraction is mutual and irresistible. In the context of the mighty issues involved in his attachment to Ethel, Lewisham's old bookish intentions are suddenly made to seem like small beer, an admission which makes him angrier than ever, because he sees it as his betrayal of everything he had always believed he stood for. The symbol of all this is the programme of studies he has so rigorously concocted for himself. His entire destiny is wrapped up in that sad sheet of paper. The first page of the novel begins with it, the last page ends with it, and once again Wells is explicit in his insistence that the story of Lewisham, so far from being the tender moonshine of an aspiring artist, is really something far more urgent, a dispatch from the front line:

In a novel of mine called 'Love and Mr Lewisham' which is about just such a Grammar School teacher as I was, I have described how he pinned up on his wall a 'Schema', planned to make the utmost use of his time and opportunities. I made that Schema, even to the pedantry of calling it that and not calling it plainly a scheme. Every moment in the day had its task. I was never to rest while I was awake. Such things—like my refusal to read novels or play games—are not evidence of an intense and concentrated mind; they are evidence of an acute sense of the need for concentration in a discursive and inattentive brain. I was not attacking the world by all this effort and self-control: I was making my desperate get-away from the shop and the street.

There speaks the voice of Kipps and Polly and Hoopdriver: 'I was making my desperate get-away from the shop and the street.' But Lewisham does not make his get-away. Or at least his escape is into the arms of Ethel, not of the muses—in which sense Lewisham's story is a tragedy of thwarted ambition, which sets out the rival claims of Love and Duty to which Wells was to return time and again in life as well as in art. In *The Sea Lady*, *The New Machiavelli* and *Ann Veronica* in particular, a gifted hero is brought down at the moment of triumph through the irresistible magnetism of romantic love. It is revealing that although he poses this problem so consistently in his work, never once does Wells allow any of his heroes to plump for the hair shirt of Duty. What is wrong with this world, he is saying in effect, is not the irreconcilable contradiction between romance and career, but the piffling Mrs Grundyism of a culture that will discard even the most gifted person with ruthless finality the moment he or she breaches some silly outmoded code of sexual rectitude. In *The Sea Lady* Chatteris, a promising parliamentary candidate, is lost to this world when he succumbs to the blandishments of a distinctly erotic mermaid; in *The New Machiavelli* Remington is brought down within sight of Downing Street because he cannot exist without the embraces of the lovely Isabel; in *Ann Veronica* the scientific lecturer Capes allows his career to crumble rather than deprive himself of the affections of the eponymous heroine. Chatteris, Remington, Capes, these are men of the world. If they are powerless in the face of the old siren-song, what chance has poor, callow, under-nourished, unworldly Lewisham?

And yet his Ethel is anything but a villainess. She is rather the defenceless maiden fortunate enough to win the allegiance of the pimply knight-errant Lewisham—an interpretation of the case which Wells renders irresistible by his introduction of the curious case of Mr Chaffery, Ethel's step-father and a shameless confidence trickster operating out on the credulous rim of the occult, making a living out of the gullibility of the bereaved and cheerfully assuming that Ethel will join the family business, so to speak, the moment she has picked up the tricks of the trade. Any lingering doubts as to where his duty to Ethel lies which still float about at the back of Lewisham's mind are dispelled by this impudent challenge to the bright white integrity of the imminent scientific renaissance. Not only is Ethel desirable, but she is besieged in the Castle of Innocence by the forces of pseudo-scientific deception. It is a typically Wellsian stroke, this confusing of the romantic issues with the red herring of Rationalism, adding as it does, most ingeniously, the cut and thrust of dialectical jousting to the sweet nothings of a conventional courtship.

Not that Lewisham's love affair is exclusively preoccupied with the stern issues of science and duty. There are incidental felicities. The affair of the roses alone—which is at last resolved by the romantic coda, 'The air was heavy with the scent of roses'— suggests that where the pleasures of the flesh are rampant, even the most incongruous partnerships carry their own consolations. Indeed it is this very fluctuation between Lewisham's incidental happiness and his divine discontent which makes his behaviour credible. Ethel loves him, she is true to him with all her heart, she cannot conceive of life without him. Nor is Lewisham altogether regretful. Of course his vanity is badly bruised by the self-discovery that the composition of 'papers in the Liberal interest' is not after all the summit of his life's ambition. But there is consolation in the feeling that in exchanging the paper dreams of the Schema for the realities of the looming struggle with the real world, he has in some obscure way become a 'man', even though the scientist in him remains unsure exactly what that means. It is the very essence of Lewisham's modesty that he is not altogether sorry at the way things have turned out, and even finds subtle pleasure in the sensation of

superiority which his sudden critical ascent to
manhood gives him. There is a particularly exquisite
moment when his chief rival for academic honours
catches him mugging up Whitaker's Almanac, and
wonders 'what valuable tip for a student in botany
might be hidden' in so unexpected a work of reference.
But Lewisham is searching for the practicalities of
marriage, and finds his rival's naïvety as amusing as
we do. Yet we sense that humdrum realities are
catching up with him before he is ready for them. We
sympathize, because we realize that he is in the grip of
an earthly passion which will not be denied. A. T.
Simmons, a fellow-student of Wells in South Kensington days, wrote to him after reading the book: 'Many
of Lewisham's worldly experiences I know by heart,
for haven't I lived them?' And another classmate, the
future Sir Richard Gregory, responded even more
movingly: 'I cannot get that poor devil Lewisham out
of my head, and I wish he had an address, for I would
go to him and rescue him from the miserable life in
which you leave him.'

But Lewisham did have an address—181 Euston
Road—and were we able to peep inside those
long-since vanished premises, we would find the
missing half of the reality behind *Love and Mr
Lewisham*. We know all about him. We know that
like Wells he had only his science scholarship of a
guinea a week on which to survive, know that like
Wells he wore, in the cause of economy, the hated
washable indiarubber detachable shirt-collar, know
that he despised his own puny body just as Wells did,
took solace in the cosy camaraderie of the laboratories
at South Kensington with the lamps lit against the
dusk, just as Wells did. We even know that he was
glib in the identical subjects that Wells had mugged
up under Byatt. So much for Mr Lewisham. But what
of the love which afflicted him? Where is its reality
located? Had Wells appropriated it from his friend

Gregory, who had done in real life what Lewisham does in the book—married a girl on his guinea-a-week grant? Certainly there are overtones of Gregory's experiences in Lewisham's. But this was not a vicarious chronicle that Wells had composed. For the most part it is the story of his own life at the time, and its venue the grimy terraced house in Euston Road. Fortunately Wells, who could be gloriously indiscreet if somewhat partial in his confessionals, has bequeathed the details to posterity.

In that masterpiece of evasive candour, *Experiment in Autobiography*, in the chapter entitled 'Heart's Desire', there is a photographic portrait of a well-proportioned girl with a faintly timorous air and what Wells would have described as a dusky beauty. She stands staring at the camera with slight constraint, hands clasped behind her back, the severity of her dark dress mitigated by a prim lace collar and the white flash of a kerchief at her belt. She is Isabel, Wells's cousin, the daughter of his Aunt Bella, and when, during his stint as a science student he moved into their house in Euston Road he fell instantly in love with her, walking her home from work in the evening just as Lewisham walks Ethel, pouring into her bewildered ear all the scientific and political abstractions with which Lewisham baffles Ethel. Isabel was the diametric opposite of her cousin in every way. Where he was intelligent she was irredeemably unintellectual, passive where he was positive, undemonstrative where he was ardent. He dreamed of one day awakening what he took to be her latent passion, and in acting on that dream committed the first great error of judgement of his adult life:

It was practically inevitable that all this suppressed and accumulating imaginative and physical craving in me should concentrate upon the one human being who was conceivable as an actual lover; my cousin Isabel. She and I had from the outset a subtle sense of kindred that kept us in

spite of differences, marriage and divorce, friendly and
confident of one another to the end of her days, but I think
that from the beginning we should have been brother and
sister to each other, if need, proximity and isolation had not
forced upon us the role of lovers, very innocent lovers. She
was very pleasant to look upon, gentle mannered, kind and
firm, and about her I realised all the pent up imaginations of
my heart. I was devoted to her, I insisted, and she was
devoted to me. We were passionate allies who would
conquer the world together. In spite of all appearances,
there was something magnificent about us. She did her best
to follow me, though something incontrollable in her
whispered that this was all nonsense.

And in the conjugal sense, so it was. And yet after
1890, when the real Lewisham left the real Ethel and
embarked upon that stupefying career of sexual
self-indulgence and the composition of papers in the
Socialist interest, the old tenderness endured. Wells
kept in touch with Isabel through all the breathless
vicissitudes of his life, helped her when she was in
trouble, and grieved over her death in 1931, fifty years
after they had first met. The scent of roses never quite
died. More to the point, when he was struggling to
resolve the problems of *Love and Mr Lewisham*, he
succumbed to a sudden impulse to see her again. In
writing of their romance, the old affections had come
welling up, cutting across subsequent loyalties and
depressing Wells deeply. It had been five years since
they met, but it was as though they had never parted.
They spent the day together at Maidenhead, where
Isabel was running a chicken-farm. Wells tried to
make love to her, but she rejected him, tenderly, in
the words of Lovat Dickson, 'as one would try to hush
a protesting child that would not be restrained'. And
in his autobiography, Wells records his reactions:

I wept in her arms like a disappointed child, and then
suddenly pulled myself together and went out into the
summer dawn and mounted my bicycle and wandered off

southward into a sunlit intensity of perplexity and
frustration, unable to understand the peculiar keenness of
my unhappiness. I felt like an automaton. I felt as though all
purpose had been drained out of me and nothing remained
worth while. The world was dead and I was dead and I had
only just discovered it.

But the world was not dead, and neither was Wells.
The only fatality was his capacity for constancy,
which seems, judging by the long history of his
amours, to have left him never to return after the
break-up of his first marriage.

There remains the curious business of Chaffery. No
writer of the last two hundred years epitomizes more
utterly than Wells the fearless Rationalist intelligence—the disciple of Thomas Huxley and the smiter
of the Fundamentalist philistines, he deploys the mind
of an encyclopaedist and the wit of the creative artist,
just as Lewisham had dreamed of deploying his
diplomas, as so many lances to tilt at the dragons of
superstition and gullibility. Throughout a long and
pugnacious life Wells swept aside with a derisory flick
of his intelligence all the pernicious twaddle of the
supernatural and the occult. He was the exemplary
logician, whose intensity of gaze saw through the
blowsy rhetoric of the politicians, the received
wisdom of the priests, the canting hypocrisy of the
moralists. So far as Wells was concerned the hungry
tigers of mysticism, so dramatically encountered by
Lewisham at the Chelsea seance, were nothing more
than silly sacred cows, and he waded into them with
fine and indiscriminate vigour all through his life.
And yet there remains the curious business of
Chaffery. After taking great care to dispose us against
the man and his impostures, Wells suddenly seems
half-inclined to recant. That the man is an unprin-
cipled rogue there is no question. But he was no fool.
In the chapter called 'Mr Chaffery at Home', we can
perhaps perceive, in the encounter between his

plausibilities and the unworldly rationalism of
Lewisham, the smudged outlines of some real-life
encounter in which the young Wells was bested in
debate by an older hand like Chaffery. But why is the
man let down so lightly, as he dances over the horizon
not only with his feathers unruffled but with the
aureole of magic still undispersed about his head? We
have to assume that Chaffery is allowed to retain his
credibility simply as the surprise device of an aspiring
novelist in search of a piquant ending.

As to that, Wells says nothing, but it is worth
reminding ourselves that, for all its foundations in
truth, *Love and Mr Lewisham* is after all a work of the
imagination, a projection of reality and not a report
upon it, especially in the matter of Lewisham's
ignominious retreat from Whortley. This retreat is
brought about through a failure to meet the exacting
standards required by his academic betters. The real
Lewisham was banished from his Eden for precisely
the opposite reason, because he had conducted
himself not too wildly but too well; when the results of
his hoop-jumping exploits became known to higher
academic authority, he was immediately awarded the
guinea-a-week scholarship which sent him to London
to sit at the feet of Isabel in Euston Road, and of
Thomas Huxley at South Kensington. That moment,
when Darwin's Bulldog is confronted by the young
Wells, is one of the most exhilarating in the
intellectual history of the Victorian age. There is the
vanquisher of Bishop Wilberforce instructing the
creator of the Time Machine and the Invisible Man,
the scientific historian who has perceived the outline
of the past, and the pupil who will describe the shape
of things to come. Wells never forgot the excitement of
that encounter, any more than Lewisham did, and
was proud for the rest of his life to call himself a true
scientist, one who had sat before the great Thomas
Huxley. As for George Edgar Lewisham, who

stumbles at the last academic fence, perhaps we should not think too sadly of him. Had he realized his ambitions, he would have ended as Stephen Leacock did after being awarded his doctorate: 'The meaning of this degree is that the recipient of instruction is examined for the last time in his life, and is pronounced completely full. After this, no new ideas can be imparted to him.'

CONTENTS

CHAPTER I

THE opening chapter does not concern itself with Love—indeed that antagonist does not certainly appear until the third—and Mr Lewisham is seen at his studies. It was ten years ago, and in those days he was assistant master in the Whortley Proprietary School, Whortley, Sussex, and his wages were forty pounds a year, out of which he had to afford fifteen shillings a week during term time to lodge with Mrs Munday, at the little shop in the West Street. He was called 'Mr' to distinguish him from the bigger boys, whose duty it was to learn, and it was a matter of stringent regulation that he should be addressed as 'Sir.'

He wore ready-made clothes, his black jacket of rigid line was dusted about the front and sleeves with scholastic chalk, and his face was downy and his moustache incipient. He was a passable-looking youngster of eighteen, fair-haired, indifferently barbered, and with a quite unnecessary pair of glasses on his fairly prominent nose—he wore these to make himself look older, that discipline might be maintained. At the particular moment when this story begins he was in his bedroom. An attic it was, with lead-framed dormer windows, a slanting ceiling, and a bulging wall, covered, as a number of torn places witnessed, with innumerable strata of florid old-fashioned paper.

To judge by the room, Mr Lewisham thought little of Love but much on Greatness. Over the

I

head of the bed, for example, where good folks
hang texts, these truths asserted themselves,
written in a clear, bold, youthfully florid hand :—
'Knowledge is Power,' and 'What man has done
man can do,'—man in the second instance referring
to Mr Lewisham. Never for a moment were these
things to be forgotten. Mr Lewisham could see
them afresh every morning as his head came through
his shirt. And over the yellow-painted box upon
which—for lack of shelves—Mr Lewisham's library
was arranged, was a '*Schema*.' (Why he should
not have headed it 'Scheme,' the editor of the
Church Times, who calls his miscellaneous notes
'*Varia*,' is better able to say than I.) In this
scheme, 1892 was indicated as the year in which
Mr Lewisham proposed to take his B.A. degree at
the London University, with 'hons. in all subjects,'
and 1895 as the date of his 'gold medal.' Subsequently there were to be 'pamphlets in the Liberal
interest,' and such like things duly dated. 'Who
would control others must first control himself,'
remarked the wall over the wash-hand-stand, and
behind the door against the Sunday trousers was
a portrait of Carlyle.

These were no mere threats against the universe;
operations had begun. Jostling Shakespeare,
Emerson's Essays, and the penny Life of Con-
fucius, there were battered and defaced school
books, a number of the excellent manuals of
the Universal Correspondence Association, exercise
books, ink (red and black) in penny bottles, and
an india-rubber stamp with Mr Lewisham's name.
A trophy of bluish-green South Kensington certificates for geometrical drawing, astronomy, physiology,
physiography, and inorganic chemistry, adorned
his farther wall. And against the Carlyle portrait
was a manuscript list of French irregular verbs.

Attached by a drawing-pin to the roof over the

wash-hand-stand, which—the room being an attic
—sloped almost dangerously, dangled a Time-Table.
Mr Lewisham was to rise at five, and that this was
no vain boasting, a cheap American alarm clock
by the books on the box witnessed. The lumps
of mellow chocolate on the papered ledge by the
bed-head, endorsed that evidence. 'French until
eight,' said the time-table curtly. Breakfast was
to be eaten in twenty minutes; then twenty-five
minutes of 'literature' to be precise, learning
extracts (preferably pompous) from the plays of
William Shakespeare—and then to school and duty.
The time-table further prescribed Latin Composition for the recess and the dinner hour '(literature,'
however, during the meal), and varied its injunctions
for the rest of the twenty-four hours according to
the day of the week. Not a moment for Satan
and that 'mischief still' of his. Only three-score
and ten has the confidence, as well as the time, to
be idle.

But just think of the admirably quality of such
a scheme ! Up and busy at five, with all the world
about one horizontal, warm, dreamy-brained or
stupidly hullish, if roused, roused only to grunt
and sigh and roll over again into oblivion. By
eight, three hours' clear start, three hours' knowledge ahead of every one. It takes, I have been
told by an eminent scholar, about a thousand hours
of sincere work to learn a language completely
—after three or four languages much less—which
gives you, even at the outset, one each a year
before breakfast. The gift of tongues—picked
up like mushrooms ! Then that 'literature'—an
astonishing conception ! In the afternoon mathematics and the sciences   Could anything be simpler
or more magnificent? In six years Mr Lewisham
will have his five or six languages, a sound, all-
round education, a habit of tremendous industry,

and be still but four-and-twenty. He will already have honour in his university and ampler means. One realises that those pamphlets in the Liberal interests will be no obscure platitudes. Where Mr Lewisham will be at thirty stirs the imagination. There will be modifications of the Schema, of course, as experience widens. But the spirit of it—the spirit of it is a devouring flame!

He was sitting facing the diamond-framed window, writing, writing fast, on a second yellow box that was turned on end and empty, and the lid was open, and his knees were conveniently stuck into the cavity. The bed was strewn with books and copygraphed sheets of instructions from his remote correspondence tutors. Pursuant to the dangling time-table he was, you would have noticed, translating Latin into English.

Imperceptibly the speed of his writing diminished. '*Urit me Glyceræ nitor*' lay ahead and troubled him. 'Urit me,' he murmured, and his eyes travelled from his book out of window to the vicar's roof opposite and its ivied chimneys. His brows were knit at first and then relaxed. '*Urit me!*' He had put his pen into his mouth and glanced about for his dictionary. *Urare?*

Suddenly his expression changed. Movement dictionary-ward ceased. He was listening to a light tapping sound—it was a footfall—outside.

He stood up abruptly, and, stretching his neck, peered through his unnecessary glasses and the diamond panes down into the street. Looking acutely downward he could see a hat daintily trimmed with pinkish white blossom, the shoulder of a jacket, and just the tips of nose and chin. Certainly the stranger who sat under the gallery last Sunday next the Frobishers. Then, too, he had seen her only obliquely. . . .

He watched her until she passed beyond the

window frame. He strained to see impossibly round the corner. . . .

Then he started, frowned, took his pen from his mouth. 'This wandering attention!' he said. 'The slightest thing! Where was I? Tcha!' He made a noise with his teeth to express his irritation, sat down, and replaced his knees in the upturned box. 'Urit me,' he said, biting the end of his pen and looking for his dictionary.

It was a Wednesday half-holiday late in March, a spring day glorious in amber light, dazzling white clouds and the intensest blue, casting a powder of wonderful green hither and thither among the trees and rousing all the birds to tumultuous rejoicings, a rousing day, a clamatory, insistent day, a veritable herald of summer. The stir of that anticipation was in the air, the warm earth was parting above the swelling seeds, and all the pine-woods were full of the minute crepitation of opening bud scales. And not only was the stir of Mother Nature's awakening in the earth and the air and the trees, but also in Mr Lewisham's youthful blood, bidding him rouse himself to live—live in a sense quite other than that the Schema indicated.

He saw the dictionary peeping from under a paper, looked up 'Urit me,' appreciated the shining 'nitor' of Glycera's shoulders, and so fell idle again to rouse himself abruptly.

'I *can't* fix my attention,' said Mr Lewisham. He took off the needless glasses, wiped them, and blinked his eyes. This confounded Horace and his stimulating epithets! A walk?

'I won't be beat,' he said—incorrectly—replaced his glasses, brought his elbows down on either side of his box with resonant violence, and clutched the hair over his ears with both hands. . . .

In five minutes' time he found himself watching

the swallows curving through the blue over the vicarage garden.

'Did ever man have such a bother with himself as me?' he asked vaguely but vehemently. 'It's self-indulgence does it—sitting down's the beginning of laziness.'

So he stood up to his work, and came into permanent view of the village street. 'If she has gone round the corner by the post office, she will come in sight over the palings above the allotments,' suggested the unexplored and undisciplined region of Mr Lewisham's mind. . . .

She did not come into sight. Apparently she had not gone round by the post office after all. It made one wonder where she had gone. Did she go up through the town to the avenue on these occasions? . . . Then abruptly a cloud drove across the sunlight, the glowing street went cold, and Mr Lewisham's imagination submitted to control. So 'Mater saeva cupidinum,' 'The untamable mother of desires'—Horace (Book II. of the Odes) was the author appointed by the university for Mr Lewisham's matriculation—was, after all, translated to its prophetic end.

Precisely as the church clock struck five Mr Lewisham, with a punctuality that was indeed almost too prompt for a really earnest student, shut his Horace, took up his Shakespeare, and descended the narrow, curved, uncarpeted staircase that led from his garret to the living room in which he had his tea with his landlady, Mrs Munday. That good lady was alone, and after a few civilities Mr Lewisham opened his Shakespeare and read from a mark onward—that mark, by the bye, was in the middle of a scene—while he consumed mechanically a number of slices of bread and whort jam.

Mrs Munday watched him over her spectacles

and thought how bad so much reading must be for the eyes, until the tinkling of her shop-bell called her away to a customer. At twenty-five minutes to six he put the book back in the window-sill, dashed a few crumbs from his jacket, assumed a mortar-board cap that was lying on the tea-caddy, and went forth to his evening 'preparation duty.'

The West Street was empty and shining golden with the sunset. Its beauty seized upon him, and he forgot to repeat the passage from *Henry VIII.* that should have occupied him down the street. Instead he was presently thinking of that insubordinate glance from his window and of little chins and nose-tips. His eyes became remote in their expression. . . .

The school door was opened by an obsequious little boy with 'lines' to be examined.

Mr Lewisham felt a curious change of atmosphere on his entry. The door slammed behind him. The hall with its insistent scholastic suggestions, its yellow marbled paper, its long rows of hat-pegs, its disreputable array of umbrellas, a broken mortar-board and a tattered and scattered *Principia*, seemed dim and dull in contrast with the luminous stir of the early March evening outside. An unusual sense of the grayness of a teacher's life, of the grayness indeed of the life of all studious souls, came and went in his mind. He took the 'lines,' written painfully over three pages of exercise book, and obliterated them with a huge G. E. L., scrawled monstrously across each page. He heard the familiar mingled noises of the playground drifting into him through the open schoolroom door.

CHAPTER II

'AS THE WIND BLOWS'

A FLAW in that pentagram of a time-table, that pentagram by which the demons of distraction were to be excluded from Mr Lewisham's career to Greatness, was the absence of a clause forbidding study out of doors. It was the day after the trivial window peeping of the last chapter that this gap in the time-table became apparent, a day if possible more gracious and alluring than its predecessor, and at half-past twelve, instead of returning from the school directly to his lodging, Mr Lewisham escaped through the omission and made his way— Horace in Pocket—to the park gates, and so to the avenue of ancient trees that encircles the broad Whortley domain. He dismissed a suspicion of his motive with perfect success. In the avenue—for the path is but little frequented—one might expect to read undisturbed. The open air, the erect attitude, are surely better than sitting in a stuffy, enervating bedroom. The open air is distinctly healthy, hardy, simple. . .

The day was breezy, and there was a perpetual rustling, a going and coming in the budding trees.

The network of the beeches was full of golden sunlight, and all the lower branches were shot with horizontal dashes of new-born green.

> '*Tu, nisi ventis*
> *Debes ludibrium, cave,*'

was the appropriate matter of Mr Lewisham's

thoughts, and he was mechanically trying to keep the book open in three places at once, at the text, the notes, and the literal translation, while he turned up the vocabulary for *ludibrium*, when his attention, wandering dangerously near the top of the page, fell over the edge and escaped with incredible swiftness down the avenue. . . .

A girl wearing a straw hat adorned with white blossom, was advancing towards him. Her occupation, too, was literary. Indeed, she was so busy writing that evidently she did not perceive him.

Unreasonable emotions descended upon Mr Lewisham—emotions that are unaccountable on the mere hypothesis of a casual meeting. Something was whispered; it sounded suspiciously like 'It's her!' He advanced with his fingers in his book, ready to retreat to its pages if she looked up, and watched her over it. *Ludibrium* passed out of his universe. She was clearly unaware of his nearness, he thought, intent upon her writing, whatever that might be. He wondered what it might be. Her face, foreshortened by her downward regard, seemed infantile. Her fluttering skirt was short, and showed her shoes and ankles. He noted her graceful, easy steps. A figure of health and lightness it was, sunlit, and advancing towards him, something, as he afterwards recalled with a certain astonishment, quite outside the Schema.

Nearer she came and nearer, her eyes still downcast. He was full of vague, stupid promptings towards an uncalled-for intercourse. It was curious she did not see him. He began to expect almost painfully the moment when she would look up, though what there was to expect——! He thought of what she would see when she discovered him, and wondered where the tassel of his cap might be hanging—it sometimes occluded one eye. It was, of course, quite impossible to put up a hand and

investigate. He was near trembling with excitement. His paces, acts which are usually automatic,
became uncertain and difficult. One might have
thought he had never passed a human being before.
Still nearer, ten yards now, nine, eight. Would
she go past without looking up? . . .

Then their eyes met.

She had hazel eyes, but Mr Lewisham being
quite an amateur about eyes, could find no words
for them. She looked demurely into his face. She
seemed to find nothing there. She glanced away
from him among the trees and passed, and nothing
remained in front of him but an empty avenue, a
sunlit, green-shot void.

The incident was over.

From far away the soughing of the breeze swept
towards him, and in a moment all the twigs about
him were quivering and rustling and the boughs
creaking with a gust of wind. It seemed to urge
him away from her. The faded dead leaves that
had once been green and young sprang up, raced
one another, leapt, danced, and pirouetted, and then
something large struck him on the neck, stayed for
a startling moment, and drove past him up the
avenue.

Something vividly white ! A sheet of paper—the
sheet upon which she had been writing !

For what seemed a long time he did not grasp
the situation. He glanced over his shoulder and
understood suddenly. His awkwardness vanished.
Horace in hand, he gave chase, and in ten paces
had secured the fugitive document. He turned
towards her, flushed with triumph, the quarry in
his hand. He had, as he picked it up, seen what
was written, but the situation dominated him for
the instant. He made a stride towards her, and only
then understood what he had seen. Lines of a
measured length and capitals ! Could it really

be——? He stopped. He looked again, eyebrows rising. He held it before him, staring now quite frankly. It had been written with a stylographic pen. Thus it ran :—

'*Come! Sharp's the word.*'

And then again,—

'*Come! Sharp's the word.*'

And then,—

'*Come! Sharp's the word.*'

'*Come! Sharp's the word.*'

And so on all down the page, in a boyish hand uncommonly like Frobisher ii.'s.

Surely! 'I say!' said Mr Lewisham, struggling with the new aspect and forgetting all his manners in his surprise. . . . He remembered giving the imposition quite well : Frobisher ii. had repeated the exhortation just a little too loudly—had brought the thing upon himself. To find her doing this jarred oddly upon certain vague preconceptions he had formed of her. Somehow it seemed as if she had betrayed him. That, of course, was only for the instant.

She had come up with him now. 'May I have my sheet of paper, please?' she said, with a catching of her breath. She was a couple of inches less in height than he. Do you observe her half-open lips, said Mother Nature in a noiseless aside to Mr Lewisham—a thing he afterwards recalled. In her eyes was a touch of apprehension.

'I say,' he said, with protest still uppermost, 'you oughtn't to do this.'

'Do what?'

'This. Impositions. For my boys.'

She raised her eyebrows, then knitted them momentarily, and looked at him. 'Are *you* Mr Lewisham?' she asked, with an affectation of entire ignorance and discovery.

She knew him perfectly well, which was one

reason why she was writing the imposition, but pretending not to know gave her something to say.

Mr Lewisham nodded.

'Of all people! Then'—frankly—'you have just found me out.'

'I am afraid I have,' said Lewisham. 'I am afraid I *have* found you out.'

They looked at one another for the next move. She decided to plead in extenuation.

'Teddy Frobisher is my cousin. I know it's very wrong, but he seemed to have such a lot to do and to be in *such* trouble. And I had nothing to do. In fact, it was *I* who offered. . . .'

She stopped and looked at him. She seemed to consider her remark complete.

That meeting of the eyes had an oddly disconcerting quality. He tried to keep to the business of the imposition. 'You ought not to have done that,' he said, encountering her steadfastly.

She looked down and then into his face again. 'No,' she said, 'I suppose I ought not to. I'm very sorry.'

Her looking down and up again produced another unreasonable effect. It seemed to Lewisham that they were discussing something quite other than the topic of their conversation; a persuasion patently absurd and only to be accounted for by the general disorder of his faculties. He made a serious attempt to keep his footing of reproof.

'I should have detected the writing, you know.'

'Of course you would. It was very wrong of me to persuade him. But I did—I assure you. He seemed in such trouble. And I thought——'

She made another break, and there was a faint deepening of colour in her cheeks. Suddenly, stupidly, his own adolescent cheeks began to glow. It became necessary to banish that sense of a duplicate topic forthwith.

'I can assure you,' he said, now very earnestly, 'I never give a punishment, never, unless it is merited. I make that a rule. I—er—*always* make that a rule. I am very careful indeed.'

'I am really sorry,' she interrupted, with frank contrition. 'It *was* silly of me.'

Lewisham felt unaccountably sorry she should have to apologise, and he spoke at once with the idea of checking the reddening of his face. 'I don't think *that*,' he said, with a sort of belated alacrity. 'Really, it was kind of you, you know—very kind of you indeed. And I know that—I can quite understand that—er—your kindness. . . .'

'Ran away with me. And now poor little Teddy will get into worse trouble for letting me . . .'

'Oh, no,' said Mr Lewisham, perceiving an opportunity and trying not to smile his appreciation of what he was saying. 'I had no business to read this as I picked it up—absolutely no business. Consequently. . . .'

'You won't take any notice of it? Really!'

'Certainly not,' said Mr Lewisham.

Her face lit with a smile, and Mr Lewisham's relaxed in sympathy. 'It is nothing—it's the proper thing for me to do, you know.'

'But so many people wouldn't do it. School-masters are not usually so—chivalrous.'

He was chivalrous! The phrase acted like a spur. He obeyed a foolish impulse.

'If you like——' he said.

'What?'

'He needn't do this. The Impot., I mean. I'll let him off.'

'Really?'

'I can.'

'It's awfully kind of you.'

'I don't mind,' he said. 'It's nothing much. If you really think. . . .'

He was full of self-applause for this scandalous sacrifice of justice.

'It's awfully kind of you,' she said.

'It's nothing really,' he explained, 'nothing.'

'Most people wouldn't——'

'I know.'

Pause.

'It's all right,' he said. 'Really.'

He would have given worlds for something more to say, something witty and original, but nothing came.

The pause lengthened. She glanced over her shoulder down the vacant avenue. This interview —this momentous series of things unsaid was coming to an end! She looked at him hesitatingly and smiled again. She held out her hand. No doubt that was the proper thing to do. He took it, searching a void, tumultuous mind in vain.

'It's awfully kind of you,' she said again, as she did so.

'It don't matter a bit,' said Mr Lewisham, and sought vainly for some other saying, some doorway remark into new topics. Her hand was cool and soft and firm, the most delightful thing to grasp, and this observation ousted all other things. He held it for a moment, but nothing would come.

They discovered themselves hand in hand. They both laughed and felt 'silly.' They shook hands in the manner of quite intimate friends, and snatched their hands away awkwardly. She turned, glanced timidly at him over her shoulder, and hesitated. 'Good-bye,' she said, and was suddenly walking from him.

He bowed to her receding back, made a seventeenth-century sweep with his college cap, and then some hitherto unexplored regions of his mind flashed into revolt.

Hardly had she gone six paces when he was at her side again.

'I say, he said, with a fearful sense of his temerity and raising his mortar-board awkwardly as though he was passing a funeral. 'But that sheet of paper . . .'

'Yes,' she said, surprised—quite naturally.

'May I have it?'

'Why?'

He felt a breathless pleasure, like that of sliding down a slope of snow. 'I would like to have it.'

She smiled and raised her eyebrows, but his excitement was now too great for smiling. 'Look here!' she said, and displayed the sheet crumpled into a ball. She laughed—with a touch of effort.

'I don't mind that,' said Mr Lewisham, laughing too. He captured the paper by an insistent gesture and smoothed it out with fingers that trembled.

'You don't mind?' he said.

'Mind what?'

'If I keep it?'

'Why should I?'

Pause. Their eyes met again. There was an odd constraint about both of them, a palpitating interval of silence.

'I really *must* be going,' she said suddenly, breaking the spell by an effort. She turned about and left him with the crumpled piece of paper in the fist that held the book, the other hand lifting the mortar-board in a dignified salute again.

He watched her receding figure. His heart was beating with remarkable rapidity. How light, how living she seemed! Little round flakes of sunlight raced down her as she went. She walked fast, then slowly, looking sideways once or twice but not **back,** until she reached the park gates. Then she looked towards him, a remote, friendly little figure, made a gesture of farewell, and disappeared.

His face was flushed and his eyes bright. Curiously enough, he was out of breath. He stared for a long time at the vacant end of the avenue. Then he turned his eyes to his trophy gripped against the closed and forgotten Horace in his hand.

CHAPTER III

THE WONDERFUL DISCOVERY

On Sunday it was Lewisham's duty to accompany the boarders twice to church. The boys sat in the gallery above the choir, facing the organ loft and at right angles to the general congregation. It was a prominent position, and made him feel painfully conspicuous, except in moods of exceptional vanity, when he used to imagine that all these people were thinking how his forehead and his certificates accorded. He thought a lot in those days of his certificates and forehead, but little of his honest, healthy face beneath it. (To tell the truth there was nothing very wonderful about his forehead.) He rarely looked down the church, as he fancied to do so would be to meet the collective eye of the congregation regarding him. So that in the morning he was not able to see that the Frobishers' pew was empty until the litany.

But in the evening, on the way to church, the Frobishers and their guest crossed the market-square as his string of boys marched along the west side. And the guest was arrayed in a gay new dress, as if it was already Easter, and her face set in its dark hair came with a strange effect of mingled freshness and familiarity. She looked at him calmly! He felt very awkward and was for cutting his new acquaintance. Then hesitated, and raised his hat with a jerk, as if to Mrs Frobisher. Neither lady acknowledged his salute, which may possibly have been a little unexpected. Then young Siddons dropped his hymn-book, stooped to pick it up, and Lewisham almost fell over him. . . . He entered church in a mood of black despair.

But consolation of a sort came soon enough. As *she* took her seat she distinctly glanced up at the gallery, and afterwards as he knelt to pray, he peeped between his fingers and saw her looking up again. She was certainly not laughing at him.

In those days much of Lewisham's mind was still an unknown land to him. He believed among other things that he was always the same consistent intelligent human being, whereas under certain stimuli he became no longer reasonable and disciplined, but a purely imaginative and emotional person. Music, for instance, carried him away, and particularly the effect of many voices in unison whirled him off from almost any state of mind to a fine massive emotionality. And the evening service at Whortley church—at the evening service surplices were worn—the chanting and singing, the vague brilliance of the numerous candle flames, the multitudinous unanimity of the congregation down there, kneeling, rising, thunderously responding invariably inebriated him. Inspired him, if you will, and turned the prose of his life into poetry. And Chance, coming to the aid of Dame Nature, dropped just the apt suggestion into his now highly responsive ear.

The second hymn was a simple and popular one, dealing with the theme of Faith, Hope, and Charity, and having each verse ending with the word 'Love.' Conceive it, long drawn out and disarticulate,—

> Faith will van . . . ish in . . . to sight,
> Hope be emp . . . tied in deli . . . ight,
> Love in Heaven will shine more bri . . . ight
>   There . . . fore give us Love.

At the third repetition of the refrain, Lewisham looked down across the chancel and met her eyes for a brief instant. . . .

He stopped singing abruptly. Then the consciousness of the serried ranks of faces below there, came with almost overwhelming force upon him, and he dared not look at her again. He felt the blood rushing to his face.

Love! The greatest of these. The greatest of all things. Better than fame. Better than knowledge. So came the great discovery like a flood across his mind, pouring over it with the cadence of the hymn and sending a tide of pink in sympathy across his forehead. The rest of the service was phantasmagorial background to that great reality —a phantasmagorial background a little inclined to stare. He, Mr Lewisham, was in Love.

'A . . . men.' He was so preoccupied that he found the whole congregation subsiding into their seats, and himself still standing, rapt. He sat down spasmodically, with an impact that seemed to him to re-echo through the church.

As they came out of the porch into the thickening night, he seemed to see her everywhere. He fancied she had gone on in front, and he hurried up the boys in the hope of overtaking her. They pushed through the throng of dim people going homeward. Should he raise his hat to her again? . . . But it was Susie Hopbrow in a light-coloured dress—a raven in dove's plumage. He felt a curious mixture of relief and disappointment. He would see her no more that night.

He hurried from the school to his lodging. He wanted very urgently to be alone. He went upstairs to his little room and sat before the upturned box on which his Butler's *Analogy* was spread open. He did not go to the formality of lighting the candle. He leant back and gazed blissfully at the solitary planet that hung over the vicarage garden.

He took out of his pocket a crumpled sheet of paper, smoothed and carefully refolded, covered with a writing not unlike that of Frobisher ii., and after some maidenly hesitation pressed this treasure to his lips. The Schema and the time-table hung in the darkness like the mere ghosts of themselves.

Mrs Munday called him thrice to his supper.

He went out immediately after it was eaten and wandered under the stars until he came over the hill behind the town again, and clambered up the back to the stile in sight of the Frobishers' house. He selected the only lit window as hers. Behind the blind, Mrs Frobisher, thirty-eight, was busy with her curl-papers—she used papers because they were better for the hair—and discussing certain neighbours in a fragmentary way with Mr Frobisher, who was in bed. Presently she moved the candle to examine a faint discolouration of her complexion that rendered her uneasy.

Outside, Mr Lewisham (eighteen) stood watching the orange oblong for the best part of half an hour, until it vanished and left the house black and blank. Then he sighed deeply and returned home in a very glorious mood indeed.

He awoke the next morning feeling extremely serious, but not clearly remembering the overnight occurrences. His eye fell on his clock. The time was six and he had not heard the alarm; as a matter of fact the alarm had not been wound up. He jumped out of bed at once and alighted upon his best trousers amorphously dropped on the floor instead of methodically cast over a chair. As he soaped his head, he tried, according to his rules of revision, to remember the overnight reading. He could not for the life of him. The truth came to him as he was getting into his shirt. His head, struggling in its recesses, became motionless, the handless cuffs ceased to dangle for a minute. . . .

Then his head came through slowly with a surprised expression upon his face. He remembered. He remembered the thing as a bald discovery, and without a touch of emotion. With all the achromatic clearness, the unromantic colourlessness of the early morning. . . .

Yes. He had it now quite distinctly. There had been no overnight reading. He was in Love.

The proposition jarred with some vague thing in his mind. He stood staring for a space, and then began looking about absentmindedly for his collar-stud. He paused in front of his Schema, regarding it.

CHAPTER IV

RAISED EYEBROWS

'Work must be done anyhow,' said Mr Lewisham.

But never had the extraordinary advantages of open-air study presented themselves so vividly. Before breakfast he took half an hour of open-air reading along the allotments lane near the Frobishers' house, after breakfast and before school, he went through the avenue with a book, and returned from school to his lodgings circuitously through the avenue, and so back to the avenue for thirty minutes or so before afternoon school. When Mr Lewisham was not looking over the top of his book during these periods of open-air study, then commonly he was glancing over his shoulder. And at last who should he see but—— !

He saw her out of the corner of his eye, and he turned away at once, pretending not to have seen her. His whole being was suddenly irradiated with emotion. The hands holding his book gripped it very tightly. He did not glance back again, but walked slowly and steadfastly, reading an ode that he could not have translated to save his life, and listening acutely for her approach. And after an interminable time, as it seemed, came a faint footfall and the swish of skirts behind him.

He felt as though his head was directed forward by a clutch of iron.

'Mr Lewisham,' she said close to him, and he turned with a quality of movement that was almost convulsive. He raised his cap clumsily.

He took her extended hand by an afterthought, and held it until she withdrew it. 'I am so glad to have met you,' she said.

'So am I,' said Lewisham simply.

They stood facing one another for an expressive moment, and then by a movement she indicated her intention to walk along the avenue with him. 'I wanted so much,' she said, looking down at her feet, 'to thank you for letting Teddy off, you know. That is why I wanted to see you.' Lewisham took his first step beside her. 'And it's odd, isn't it,' she said, looking up into his face, 'that I should meet you here in just the same place. I believe . . . Yes. The very same place we met before.'

Mr Lewisham was tongue-tied.

'Do you often come here,' she said.

'Well,' he considered—and his voice was most unreasonably hoarse when he spoke—'No. No. . . . That is—— At least not often. Now and then. In fact I like it rather for reading and that sort of thing. It's so quiet.'

'I suppose you read a great deal?'

'When one teaches one has to.'

'But you . . .'

'I'm rather fond of reading, certainly. Are you?'

'I *love* it.'

Mr Lewisham was glad she loved reading. He would have been disappointed had she answered differently. But she spoke with real fervour. She *loved* reading! It was pleasant. She would understand him a little perhaps. 'Of course,' she went on, 'I'm not clever like some people are. And I have to read books as I get hold of them.'

'So do I,' said Mr Lewisham, 'for the matter of that. . . . Have you read . . . Carlyle?'

The conversation was now fairly under way.

They were walking side by side beneath the swaying boughs. Mr Lewisham's sensations were ecstatic, marred only by a dread of some casual boy coming upon them. She had not read *much* Carlyle. She had always wanted to, even from quite a little girl—she had heard so much about him. She knew he was a Really Great Writer, a *very* Great Writer indeed. All she *had* read of him she liked. She could say that. As much as she liked anything. And she had seen his house in Chelsea.

Lewisham, whose knowledge of London had been obtained by excursion trips on six or seven isolated days, was much impressed by this. It seemed to put her at once on a footing of intimacy with this imposing Personality. It had never occurred to him at all vividly that these Great Writers had real abiding places. She gave him a few descriptive touches that made the house suddenly real and distinctive to him. She lived quite near, she said, at least within walking distance, in Clapham. He instantly forgot the vague design of lending her his *Sartor Resartus* in his curiosity to learn more about her home. 'Clapham—that's almost in London, isn't it?' he said.

'Quite,' she said, but she volunteered no further information about her domestic circumstances. 'I like London,' she generalised, 'and especially in winter.' And she proceeded to praise London, its public libraries, its shops, the multitudes of people, the facilities for 'doing what you like,' the concerts one could go to, the theatres. (It seemed she moved in fairly good society.) 'There's always something to see even if you only go out for a walk,' she said, 'and down here there's nothing to read but idle novels. And those not new.'

Mr Lewisham had regretfully to admit the lack of such culture and mental activity in Whortley.

It made him feel terribly her inferior. He had only his bookishness and his certificates to set against it all—and she had seen Carlyle's house! 'Down here,' she said, 'there's nothing to talk about but scandal.' It was too true.

At the corner by the stile, beyond which the willows were splendid against the blue with silvery aments and golden pollen, they turned by mutual impulse and retraced their steps. 'I've simply had no one to talk to down here,' she said. 'Not what *I* call talking.'

'I hope,' said Lewisham, making a resolute plunge, 'perhaps while you are staying at Whortley . . .'

He paused perceptibly, and she, following his eyes, saw a voluminous black figure approaching. 'We may,' said Mr Lewisham, resuming his remark, 'chance to meet again, perhaps.'

He had been about to challenge her to a deliberate meeting. A certain delightful tangle of paths that followed the bank of the river had been in his mind. But the apparition of Mr George Bonover, head master of the Whortley Proprietary School, chilled him amazingly. Dame Nature, no doubt, had arranged the meeting of our young couple, but about Bonover she seems to have been culpably careless. She now receded illimitably, and Mr Lewisham, with the most unpleasant feelings, found himself face to face with a typical representative of a social organisation which objects very strongly *inter alia* to promiscuous conversation on the part of the young unmarried junior master.

'——chance to meet again, perhaps,' said Mr Lewisham, with a sudden lack of spirit.

'I hope so, too,' she said.

Pause. Mr Bonover's features, and particularly a bushy pair of black eyebrows, were now very near, those eyebrows already raised, apparently to express a refined astonishment.

'Is this Mr Bonover approaching?' she asked.

'Yes.'

Prolonged pause.

Would he stop and accost them? At any rate, this frightful silence must end. Mr Lewisham sought in his mind for some remark wherewith to cover his employer's approach. He was surprised to find his mind a desert. He made a colossal effort. If they could only talk, if they could only seem at their ease! But this blank incapacity was eloquent of guilt. Ah!

'It's a lovely day, though,' said Mr Lewisham. 'Isn't it?'

She agreed with him. 'Isn't it?' she said.

And then Mr Bonover passed, forehead tight reefed, so to speak, and lips impressively compressed. Mr Lewisham raised his mortar-board, and to his astonishment Mr Bonover responded with a markedly formal salute—mock clerical hat sweeping circuit-ously—and the regard of a searching, disapproving eye, and so passed. Lewisham was overcome with astonishment at this improvement on the nod of their ordinary commerce. And so this terrible incident terminated for the time.

He felt a momentary gust of indignation. After all, why should Bonover or any one interfere with his talking to a girl if he chose? And for all he knew they might have been properly introduced. By young Frobisher, say. Nevertheless, Lewisham's spring-tide mood relapsed into winter. He was, he felt, singularly stupid for the rest of their conversation, and the delightful feeling of enterprise that had hitherto inspired and astonished him when talking to her had shrivelled beyond contempt. He was glad—positively glad—when things came to an end.

At the park gates she held out her hand. 'I'm afraid I have interrupted your reading,' she said.

'Not a bit,' said Mr Lewisham, warming slightly. 'I don't know when I've enjoyed a conversa tion. . . .

'It was—a breach of etiquette, I am afraid, my speaking to you, but I did so want to thank you. . . .'

'Don't mention it,' said Mr Lewisham, secretly impressed by the etiquette.

'Good-bye.' He stood hesitating by the lodge, and then turned back up the avenue in order not to be seen to follow her too closely up the West Street.

And then, still walking away from her, he remembered that he had not lent her a book as he had planned, nor made any arrangement ever to meet her again. She might leave Whortley any-when for the amenities of Clapham. He stopped and stood irresolute. Should he run after her? Then he recalled Bonover's enigmatical expression of face. He decided that to pursue her would be altogether too conspicuous. Yet. . . . So he stood in inglorious hesitation, while the seconds passed.

He reached his lodging at last to find Mrs Munday half-way through dinner.

'You get them books of yours,' said Mrs Munday, who took a motherly interest in him, 'and you read and you read, and you take no account of time. And now you'll have to eat your dinner half cold and no time for it to settle proper before you goes off to school. It's ruination to a stummik— such ways.'

'Oh, never mind my stomach, Mrs Munday, said Lewisham, roused from a tangled and appar-ently gloomy meditation; 'that's *my* affair.' Quite crossly he spoke for him.

'I'd rather have a good sensible actin' stummik than a full head,' said Mrs Munday, 'any day.'

'I'm different, you see,' snapped Mr Lewisham, and relapsed into silence and gloom.

('Hoity, toity!' said Mrs Munday under her breath.)

CHAPTER V

HESITATIONS

MR BONOVER, having fully matured a hint suitable
for the occasion, dropped it in the afternoon, while
Lewisham was superintending cricket practice.
He made a few remarks about the prospects of the
first eleven by way of introduction, and Lewisham
agreed with him that Frobisher i. looked like shaping
very well this season.

A pause followed, and the head master hummed.
'By the bye,' he said, as if making conversation
and still watching the play : 'I, ah—understood
that you, ah—were a *stranger* to Whortley.'

'Yes,' said Lewisham, 'that's so.'

'You have made friends in the neighbourhood?

Lewisham was troubled with a cough and his
ears—those confounded ears—brightened. 'Yes,'
he said, recovering. 'Oh, yes. Yes. I have.'

'Local people, I presume.'

'Well, no. Not exactly.' The brightness spread
from Lewisham's ears over his face.

'I saw you,' said Bonover, 'talking to a young
lady in the avenue. Her face was somehow quite
familiar to me. Who *was* she?'

Should he say she was a friend of the Frobishers?
In that case Bonover, in his insidious, amiable way,
might talk to the Frobisher parents and make things
disagreeable for her. 'She was,' said Lewisham,
flushing deeply with the stress on his honesty
and dropping his voice to a mumble, 'a . . a . . .
an old friend of my mother's. In fact, I met her
once at Salisbury.'

29

'Where?'

'Salisbury.'

'And her name?'

'Smith,' said Lewisham, a little hastily and repenting the lie even as it left his lips.

'Well *hit*, Harris!' shouted Bonover, and began to clap his hands. 'Well *hit*, sir.'

'Harris shapes very well,' said Mr Lewisham.

'Very,' said Mr Bonover. 'And—what was it? Ah! I was just remarking the odd resemblances there are in the world. There is a Miss Henderson—or Henson—stopping with the Frobishers—in the very same town, in fact, the very picture of your Miss . . .'

'Smith,' said Lewisham, meeting his eye and recovering the full crimson note of his first blush.

'It's odd,' said Bonover, regarding him pensively.

'Very odd,' mumbled Lewisham, cursing his own stupidity and looking away.

'*Very*—very odd,' said Bonover.

'In fact,' said Bonover, turning towards the schoolhouse, 'I hardly expected it of you, Mr Lewisham.'

'Expected what, sir?'

But Mr Bonover feigned to be already out of earshot.

Damn!' said Mr Lewisham. 'Oh!—*damn!*'— a most objectionable expression and rare with him in those days. He had half a mind to follow the head master and ask him if he doubted his word. It was only too evident what the answer would be.

He stood for a minute undecided, then turned on his heel and marched homeward with savage steps. His muscles quivered as he walked, and his face twitched. The tumult of his mind settled at last into angry indignation.

'Confound him!' said Mr Lewisham, arguing the matter out with the bedroom furniture. 'Why the *devil* can't he mind his own business?'

'Mind your own business, sir !' shouted Mr Lewisham at the wash-hand-stand. 'Confound you. sir, mind your own business !'

The wash-hand stand did.

'You overrate your power, sir,' said Mr Lewisham, a little mollified. 'Understand me ! I am my own master out of school.'

Nevertheless, for four days and some hours after Mr Bonover's Hint, Mr Lewisham so far observed its implications as to abandon open-air study and struggle with diminishing success to observe the spirit as well as the letter of his time-table pre-scriptions. For the most part he fretted at accumu-lating tasks, did them with slipshod energy or looked out of window. The Career constituent insisted that to meet and talk to this girl again meant reproof, worry, interference with his work for his matriculation, the destruction of all 'Dis-cipline,' and he saw the entire justice of the insistence. It was nonsense this being in love; there wasn't such a thing as love outside of trashy novelettes. And forthwith his mind went off at a tangent to her eyes under the shadow of her hat brim, and had to be lugged back by main force. On Thursday when he was returning from school he saw her far away down the street, and hurried in to avoid her, looking ostentatiously in the opposite direction. But that was a turning-point. Shame overtook him. On Friday his belief in love was warm and living again, and his heart full of remorse for laggard days.

On Saturday morning his preoccupation with her was so vivid that it distracted him even while he was teaching that most teachable subject, algebra, and by the end of the school hours the issue was decided and the Career in headlong rout. That afternoon he would go, whatever happened, and see her and speak to her again. The thought of Bonover arose only to be dismissed. And besides——

Bonover took a siesta early in the afternoon.

Yes, he would go out and find her and speak to her. Nothing should stop him.

Once that decision was taken his imagination became riotous with things he might say, attitudes he might strike, and a multitude of vague fine dreams about her. He would say this, he would say that, his mind would do nothing but circle round this wonderful pose of lover. What a cur he had been to hide from her so long ! What could he have been thinking about? How *could* he explain it to her, when the meeting really came? Suppose he was very frank——

He considered the limits of frankness. Would she believe he had not seen her on Thursday?— if he assured her that it was so?

And, most horrible, in the midst of all this came Bonover with a request that he would take 'duty' in the cricket field instead of Dunkerley that afternoon. Dunkerley was the senior assistant master, Lewisham's sole colleague. The last vestige of disapprobation had vanished from Bonover's manner; asking a favour was his autocratic way of proffering the olive branch. But it came to Lewisham as a cruel imposition. For a fateful moment he trembled on the brink of acquiescence. In a flash came a vision of the long duty of the afternoon—she possibly packing for Clapham all the while. He turned white. Mr Bonover watched his face.

'*No*,' said Lewisham bluntly, saying all he was sure of, and forthwith racking his unpractised mind for an excuse. 'I'm sorry I can't oblige you, but . . . my arrangements . . . I've made arrangements, in fact, for the afternoon.'

Mr Bonover's eyebrows went up at this obvious

lie, and the glow of his suavity faded. 'You see,' he said, 'Mrs Bonover expects a friend this afternoon, and we rather want Mr Dunkerley to make four at croquet. . . .'

'I'm sorry,' said Mr Lewisham, still resolute, and making a mental note that Bonover would be playing croquet.

'You don't play croquet by any chance?' asked Bonover.

'No,' said Lewisham, 'I haven't an idea.'

'If Mr Dunkerley had asked you? . . .' persisted Bonover, knowing Lewisham's respect for etiquette.

'Oh! it wasn't on that account,' said Lewisham, and Bonover, with eyebrows still raised and a general air of outraged astonishment, left him standing there, white and stiff, and wondering at his extraordinary temerity.

CHAPTER VI

THE SCANDALOUS RAMBLE

As soon as school was dismissed Lewisham made a jail-delivery of his outstanding impositions, and hurried back to his lodgings, to spend the time until his dinner was ready—Well? . . . It seems hardly fair, perhaps, to Lewisham, to tell this; it is doubtful, indeed, whether a male novelist's duty to his sex should not restrain him, but, as the wall in the shadow by the diamond-framed window insisted, '*Magna est veritas et prevalebit.*' Mr Lewisham brushed his hair with elaboration, and ruffled it picturesquely, tried the effect of all his ties and selected a white one, dusted his boots with an old pocket-handkerchief, changed his trousers because the week-day pair was minutely frayed at the heels, and inked the elbows of his coat where the stitches were a little white. And, to be still more intimate, he studied his callow appearance in the glass from various points of view, and decided that his nose might have been a little smaller with advantage. . . .

Directly after dinner he went out, and by the shortest path to the allotment lane, telling himself he did not care if he met Bonover forthwith in the street. He did not know precisely what he intended to do, but he was quite clear that he meant to see the girl he had met in the avenue. He knew he should see her. A sense of obstacles merely braced him and was pleasurable. He went up the stone steps out of the lane to the stile that overlooked

the Frobishers, the stile from which he had watched
the Frobisher bedroom. There he seated himself
with his arms folded, in full view of the house.

That was at ten minutes to two. At twenty
minutes to three he was still sitting there, but his
hands were deep in his jacket pockets, and he
was scowling and kicking his foot against the step
with an impatient monotony. His needless glasses
had been thrust into his waistcoat pocket—where
they remained throughout the afternoon—and his
cap was tilted a little back from his forehead and
exposed a wisp of hair. One or two people had gone
down the lane, and he had pretended not to see
them, and a couple of hedge-sparrows chasing each
other along the side of the sunlit, wind-rippled field
had been his chief entertainment. It is unaccountable, no doubt, but he felt angry with her as the
time crept on. His expression lowered.

He heard some one going by in the lane behind
him. He would not look round—it annoyed him
to think of people seeing him in this position.
His once eminent discretion, though overthrown,
still made muffled protests at the afternoon's enterprise. The feet down the lane stopped close at
hand.

'Stare away,' said Lewisham between his teeth.
And then began mysterious noises, a violent rustle
of hedge twigs, a something like a very light foot-
tapping.

Curiosity boarded Lewisham and carried him
after the briefest struggle. He looked round, and
there she was, her back to him, reaching after the
spiky blossoming blackthorn that crested the
opposite hedge. Remarkable accident! She had
not seen him!

In a moment Lewisham's legs were flying over
the stile. He went down the steps in the bank
with such impetus that it carried him up into

the prickly bushes beside her. 'Allow me,' he said, too excited to see she was not astonished.

'Mr Lewisham!' she said in feigned surprise, and stood away to give him room at the blackthorn.

'Which spike will you have?' he cried, overjoyed. 'The whitest? The highest? Any!'

'That piece,' she chose haphazard, 'with the black spike sticking out from it.'

A mass of snowy blossom it was against the April sky, and Lewisham, struggling for it—it was by no means the most accessible—saw with fantastic satisfaction a lengthy scratch flash white on his hand, and turn to red.

'Higher up the lane,' he said, descending triumphant and breathless, 'there is blackthorn. . . . This cannot compare for a moment. . . .'

She laughed and looked at him as he stood there flushed, his eyes triumphant, with an unpremeditated approval. In church, in the gallery, with his face foreshortened, he had been effective in a way, but this was different. 'Show me,' she said, though she knew this was the only place for blackthorn for a mile in either direction.

'I *knew* I should see you,' he said, by way of answer. 'I felt sure I should see you to-day.'

'It was our last chance almost,' she answered, with as frank a quality of avowal. 'I'm going home to London on Monday.'

'I knew,' he cried in triumph. 'To Clapham?' he asked.

'Yes. I have got a situation. You did not know that I was a shorthand clerk and typewriter, did you? I am. I have just left the school, the Grogram School. And now there is an old gentleman who wants an amanuensis.'

'So you know shorthand?' said he. 'That accounts for the stylographic pen. Those lines were written. . . . I have them still.'

She smiled and raised her eyebrows. 'Here,' said Mr Lewisham, tapping his breast-pocket.

'This lane,' he said—their talk was curiously inconsecutive—'some way along this lane, over the hill and down, there is a gate, and that goes—I mean, it opens into the path that runs along the river bank. Have you been?'

'No,' she said.

'It's the best walk about Whortley. It brings you out upon Immering Common. You *must*—before you go.'

'*Now*?' she said, with her eyes dancing.

'Why not?'

'I told Mrs Frobisher I should be back by four,' she said.

'It's a walk not to be lost.'

'Very well,' said she.

'The trees are all budding,' said Mr Lewisham, 'the rushes are shooting, and all along the edge of the river there are millions of little white flowers floating on the water. *I* don't know the names of them, but they're fine. . . . May I carry that branch of blossom?'

As he took it their hands touched momentarily . . . and there came another of those significant gaps.

'Look at those clouds,' said Lewisham abruptly, remembering the remark he had been about to make and waving the white froth of blackthorn. 'And look at the blue between them.'

'It's perfectly splendid. Of all the fine weather the best has been kept for now. My last day. My very last day.'

And off these two young people went together in a highly electrical state—to the infinite astonishment of Mrs Frobisher, who was looking out of the attic window—stepping out manfully and finding the whole world lit and splendid for their entertainment. The things they discovered and told each other that afternoon down by the river !—that spring was wonderful, young leaves beautiful, bud scales astonishing things, and clouds dazzling and stately !—with an air of supreme originality ! And their naïve astonishment to find one another in agreement upon these novel delights ! It seemed to them quite outside the play of accident that they should have met each other.

They went by the path that runs among the trees along the river bank, and she must needs repent and wish to take the lower one, the towing path, before they had gone three hundred yards. So Lewisham had to find a place fit for her descent, where a friendly tree proffered its protruding roots as a convenient balustrade, and down she clambered with her hand in his.

Then a water-vole washing his whiskers gave occasion for a sudden touching of hands and the intimate confidence of whispers and silence together. After which Lewisham essayed to gather her a marshmallow at the peril, as it was judged, of his life, and gained it together with a bootful of water. And at the gate by the black and shiny lock, where the path breaks away from the river, she overcame him by an unexpected feat, climbing gleefully to the top rail with the support of his hand, and leaping down, a figure of light and grace, to the ground.

They struck boldly across the meadows, which were gay with lady's smock, and he walked, by special request, between her and three matronly cows—feeling as Perseus might have done when he fended off the sea-monster. And so by the mill, and up a steep path to Immering Common. Across the meadows Lewisham had broached the subject of her occupation. 'And are you really going away from here to be an amanuensis?' he said, and started her upon the theme of herself, a theme she treated with a specialist's enthusiasm. They dealt with it by the comparative method, and neither noticed the light was out of the sky until the soft feet of the advancing shower had stolen right upon them.

'Look!' said he. 'Yonder! A shed,' and they ran together. She ran laughing, and yet swiftly and lightly. He pulled her through the hedge by both hands, and released her skirt from an amorous bramble, and so they came into a little black shed in which a rusty harrow of gigantic proportions sheltered. He noted how she still kept her breath after that run.

She sat down on the harrow and hesitated. 'I *must* take off my hat,' she said, 'that rain will spoil it,' and so he had a chance of admiring the sincerity of her curls—not that he had ever doubted them. She stooped over her hat, pocket-handkerchief in hand, daintily wiping off the silvery drops. He stood up at the opening of the shed and looked at the country outside through the veil of the soft vehemence of the April shower.

'There's room for two on this harrow,' she said.

He made inarticulate sounds of refusal, and then came and sat down beside her, close beside her, so that he was almost touching her. He felt a fantastic desire to take her in his arms and kiss her, and overcame the madness by an effort. 'I don't even know your name,' he said, taking refuge from his whirling thoughts in conversation.

'Henderson,' she said.

'*Miss* Henderson?'

She smiled in his face—hesitated. 'Yes—*Miss* Henderson.'

Her eyes, her atmosphere were wonderful. He had never felt quite the same sensation before, a strange excitement, almost like a faint echo of tears.

He was for demanding her Christian name. For
calling her 'dear' and seeing what she would say.
He plunged headlong into a rambling description
of Bonover and how he had told a lie about her
and called her Miss Smith, and so escaped this
unaccountable emotional crisis. . . .

The whispering of the rain about them sank and
died, and the sunlight struck vividly across the
distant woods beyond Immering. Just then they
had fallen on a silence again that was full of daring
thoughts for Mr Lewisham. He moved his arm
suddenly and placed it so that it was behind her on
the frame of the harrow.

'Let us go on now,' she said abruptly. 'The
rain has stopped.'

'That little path goes straight to Immering,'
said Mr Lewisham.

'But, four o'clock?'

He drew out his watch and his eyebrows went
up. It was already nearly a quarter past four.

'Is it past four?' she asked, and abruptly they
were face to face with parting. That Lewisham
had to take 'duty' at half-past five seemed a thing
utterly trivial. 'Surely,' he said, only slowly
realising what this parting meant. 'But must you?
I—I want to talk to you.'

'Haven't you been talking to me?'

'It isn't that. Besides—no.'

She stood looking at him. 'I promised to be
home by four,' she said. 'Mrs Frobisher has
tea. . . .'

'We may never have a chance to see one another
again.'

'Well?'

Lewisham suddenly turned very white.

'Don't leave me,' he said, breaking a tense silence
and with a sudden stress in his voice. 'Don't leave

me. Stop with me yet—for a little while. . . .
You . . . you can lose your way.'

'You seem to think,' she said, forcing a laugh,
'that I live without eating and drinking.'

'I have wanted to talk to you so much. The
first time I saw you. . . . At first I dared not . . .
I did not know you would let me talk. . . And
now, just as I am—happy, you are going.'

He stopped abruptly. Her eyes were downcast.
'No,' she said, tracing a curve with the point of
her shoe. 'No. I am not going.'

Lewisham restrained an impulse to shout. 'You
will come to Immering?' he cried, and as they
went along the narrow path through the wet grass,
he began to tell her with simple frankness how he
cared for her company. 'I would not change this,'
he said, casting about for an offer to reject, 'for—
anything in the world. . . . I shall not be back for
duty. I don't care. I don't care what happens so
long as we have this afternoon.'

'Nor I,' she said.

'Thank you for coming,' he said in an outburst
of gratitude. 'Oh, thank you for coming,' and held
out his hand. She took it and pressed it, and so
they went on, hand in hand, until the village street
was reached. Their high resolve to play truant at
all costs had begotten a wonderful sense of fellow-
ship. 'I can't call you Miss Henderson,' he said.
'You know I can't. You know . . . I must have
your Christian name.'

'Ethel,' she told him.

'Ethel,' he said, and looked at her, gathering
courage as he did so. 'Ethel,' he repeated. 'It is
a pretty name. But no name is quite pretty
enough for you, Ethel . . . *dear*.' . . .

The little shop in Immering lay back behind a
garden full of wallflowers, and was kept by a very
fat and very cheerful little woman, who insisted

on regarding them as brother and sister, and calling them both 'dearie.' These points conceded, she gave them an admirable tea of astonishing cheapness. Lewisham did not like the second condition very much, because it seemed to touch a little on his latest enterprise. But the tea and the bread and butter and the whort jam were like no food on earth. There were wallflowers, heavy scented, in a jug upon the table, and Ethel admired them, and when they set out again the little old lady insisted on her taking a bunch with her.

It was after they left Immering that this ramble, properly speaking, became scandalous. The sun was already a golden ball above the blue hills in the west—it turned our two young people into little figures of flame—and yet, instead of going homeward, they took the Wentworth road that plunges into the Forshaw Woods. Behind them the moon, almost full, hung in the blue sky above the tree-tops, ghostly and indistinct, and slowly gathered to itself such light as the setting sun left for it in the sky.

Going out of Immering, they began to talk of the future. And for the very young lover there is no future but the immediate future.

'You must write to me,' he said, and she told him she wrote such *silly* letters. 'But I shall have reams to write to you,' he told her.

'How are you to write to me?' she asked, and they discussed a new obstacle between them. It would never do to write home—never. She was sure of that with an absolute assurance. 'My mother——' she said, and stopped.

That prohibition cut him, for at that time he had the makings of a voluminous letter-writer. Yet it was only what one might expect. The whole world was unpropitious—obdurate indeed. . . . A splendid isolation *à deux*.

Perhaps she might find some place where letters might be sent to her? Yet that seemed to her deceitful.

So these two young people wandered on, full of their discovery of love, and yet so full too of the shyness of adolescence that the word 'Love' never passed their lips that day. Yet as they talked on, and the kindly dusk gathered about them, their speech and their hearts came very close together. But their speech would seem so threadbare, written down in cold blood, that I must not put it here. To them it was not threadbare.

When at last they came down the long road into Whortley, the silent trees were black as ink and the moonlight made her face pallid and wonderful, and her eyes shone like stars. She still carried the blackthorn, from which most of the blossoms had fallen. The fragrant wallflowers were fragrant still. And far away, softened by the distance, the Whortley band, performing publicly outside the vicarage for the first time that year, was playing with unctuous slowness a sentimental air. I don't know if the reader remembers it, that favourite melody of the early eighties :—

'Sweet dreamland faces, passing to and fro (pum, pum)
Bring back to Mem'ry days of long ago-o-o-oh,'

was the essence of it, very slow and tender and with an accompaniment of pum, pum. Pathetically cheerful that pum, pum, hopelessly cheerful indeed against the dirge of the air, a dirge accentuated by sporadic vocalisation. But to young people things come differently.

'I *love* music,' she said.

'So do I,' said he.

They came on down the steepness of West Street.

They walked athwart the metallic and leathery tumult of sound into the light cast by the little circle of yellow lamps. Several people saw them and wondered what the boys and girls were coming to nowadays, and one eye-witness even subsequently described their carriage as 'brazen.' Mr Lewisham was wearing his mortar-board cap of office—there was no mistaking him. They passed the Proprietary School and saw a yellow picture framed and glazed, of Mr Bonover taking duty for his aberrant assistant master. And outside the Frobisher house at last they parted perforce.

'Good-bye,' he said for the third time. 'Good-bye, Ethel.'

She hesitated. Then suddenly she darted towards him. He felt her hands upon his shoulders, her lips soft and warm upon his cheek, and before he could take hold of her she had eluded him, and had flitted into the shadow of the house. 'Good-bye,' came her sweet, clear voice out of the shadow, and while he yet hesitated an answer, the door opened.

He saw her, black in the doorway, heard some indistinct words, and then the door closed and he was alone in the moonlight, his cheek still glowing from her lips. . . .

So ended Mr Lewisham's first day with Love.

CHAPTER VII

THE RECKONING

AND after the day of Love came the days of Reckoning. Mr Lewisham was astonished—overwhelmed almost—by that Reckoning, as it slowly and steadily unfolded itself. The wonderful emotions of Saturday carried him through Sunday, and he made it up with the neglected Schema by assuring it that She was his Inspiration, and that he would work for Her a thousand times better than he could possibly work for himself. That was certainly not true, and indeed he found himself wondering whether the interest had vanished out of his theological examination of Butler's *Analogy*. The Frobishers were not at church for either service He speculated rather anxiously why?

Monday dawned coldly and clearly—a Herbert Spencer of a day—and he went to school sedulously assuring himself there was nothing to apprehend. Day boys were whispering in the morning apparently about him, and Frobisher ii. was in great request. Lewisham overheard a fragment. 'My mother *was* in a wax,' said Frobisher ii.

At twelve came an interview with Bonover, and voices presently rising in angry altercation and audible to Senior-assistant Dunkerley through the closed study door. Then Lewisham walked across the schoolroom, staring straight before him, his cheeks very bright.

Thereby Dunkerley's mind was prepared for the news that came the next morning over the exercise books. 'When?' said Dunkerley.

'End of next term,' said Lewisham.

'About this girl that's been staying at the Frobishers?'

'Yes.'

'She's a pretty bit of goods. But it will mess up your matric next June,' said Dunkerley.

'That's what I'm sorry for.'

'It's scarcely to be expected he'll give you leave to attend the exam. . . .'

'He won't,' said Lewisham shortly, and opened his first exercise book. He found it difficult to talk.

'He's a greaser,' said Dunkerley. 'But there! —what can you expect from Durham?' For Bonover had only a Durham degree and Dunkerley, having none, inclined to be particular. Therewith Dunkerley lapsed into a sympathetic and busy rustling over his own pile of exercises. It was not until the heap had been reduced to a book or so that he spoke again—an elaborate point.

'Male and female created He them,' said Dunkerley, ticking his way down the page. 'Which (tick, tick) was damned hard (tick, tick) on assistant masters.'

He closed the book with a snap and flung it on the floor behind him. 'You're lucky,' he said. 'I *did* think I should be first to get out of this scandalising hole. You're lucky. It's always acting down here. Running on parents and guardians round every corner. That's what I object to in life in the country : it's so confoundedly artificial. *I* shall take jolly good care *I* get out of it just as soon as ever I can. You bet !'

'And work those patents?'

'Rather, my boy. Yes. Work those patents. The Patent Square Top Bottle ! Lord ! Once let me get to London. . . .'

'I think *I* shall have a shot at London,' said Lewisham.

And then the experienced Dunkerley, being one of the kindest young men alive, forgot certain private ambitions of his own—he cherished dreams of amazing patents—and bethought him of agents. He proceeded to give a list of these necessary helpers of the assistant master at the gangway—Orellana, Gabbitas, The Lancaster Gate Agency, and the rest of them. He knew them all—intimately. He had been a 'nix' eight years. 'Of course, that Kensington thing may come off, said Dunkerley, 'but it's best not to wait. I tell you frankly—the chances are against you.'

The 'Kensington thing' was an application for admission to the Normal School of Science at South Kensington, which Lewisham had made in a sanguine moment. There being an inadequate supply of qualified science teachers in England, the Science and Art Department is wont to offer free instruction at its great central school and a guinea a week to select young pedagogues who will bind themselves to teach science after their training is over. Dunkerley had been in the habit of applying for several years, always in vain, and Lewisham had seen no harm in following his example. But then Dunkerley had no green-gray certificates.

So Lewisham spent all that 'duty' left him of the next day composing a letter to copy out and send the several scholastic agencies. In this he gave a brief but appreciative sketch of his life, and enlarged upon his discipline and- educational methods. At the end was a long and decorative schedule of his certificates and distinctions, beginning with a good-conduct prize at the age of eight. A considerable amount of time was required to recopy this document, but his modesty upheld him. After a

careful consideration of the time-table, he set
aside the midday hour for 'Correspondence.'

He found that his work in mathematics and
classics was already some time in arrears, and a
'test' he had sent to his correspondence Tutor
during those troublous days after the meeting with
Bonover in the Avenue, came back blottesquely
endorsed: 'Below Pass Standard.'   This last
experience was so unprecedented and annoyed him
so much that for a space he contemplated retorting
with a sarcastic letter to the tutor.   And then came
the Easter recess, and he had to go home and tell
his mother, with a careful suppression of details,
that he was leaving Whortley. 'Where you have
been getting on so well!' cried his mother.

But that dear old lady had one consolation. She
observed he had given up his glasses—he had
forgotten to bring them with him—and her secret
fear of grave optical troubles—that were being
'kept' from her—was alleviated.

Sometimes he had moods of intense regret for
the folly of that walk. One such came after the
holidays, when the necessity of revising the dates
of the Schema brought before his mind, for the
first time quite clearly, the practical issue of this
first struggle with all those mysterious and powerful
influences   the   springtime   sets   astirring.   His
dream of success and fame had been very real and
dear to him, and the realisation of the inevitable
postponement of his long anticipated matriculation,
the doorway to all the other great things, took
him abruptly like an actual physical sensation in
his chest.

He sprang up, pen in hand, in the midst of his
corrections, and began pacing up and down the
room. 'What a fool I have been!' he cried. 'What
a fool I have been!'

He flung the pen on the floor and made a rush at

an ill-drawn attempt upon a girl's face that adorned
the end of his room, the visible witness of his
slavery. He tore this down and sent the fragments
of it scattering. . . .

'Fool !'

It was a relief—a definite abandonment. He
stared for a moment at the destruction he had
made, and then went back to the revision of the
time-table, with a mutter about 'silly spooning.'

That was one mood. The rarer one. He watched
the posts with far more eagerness for the address
to which he might write to her than for any reply
to those reiterated letters of application, the writing
of which now ousted Horace and the higher mathematics (Lewisham's term for conics) from his
attention. Indeed he spent more time meditating
the letter to her than even the schedule of his
virtues had required.

Yet the letters of application were wonderful
compositions; each had a new pen to itself and
was for the first page at least in a handwriting far
above even his usual high standard. And day after
day passed and that particular letter he hoped for
still did not come.

His moods were complicated by the fact that,
in spite of his studied reticence on the subject, the
reason of his departure did in an amazingly short
time get 'all over Whortley.' It was understood
that he had been discovered to be 'fast,' and
Ethel's behaviour was animadverted upon with
complacent indignation—if the phrase may be
allowed—by the ladies of the place. Pretty looks
were too often a snare. One boy—his ear was
warmed therefor—once called aloud 'Ethel,' as
Lewisham went by. The curate, a curate of the
pale-faced, large-knuckled, nervous sort, now passed
him without acknowledgment of his existence.
Mrs Bonover took occasion to tell him that he was

a 'mere boy,' and once Mrs Frobisher sniffed quite
threateningly at him when she passed him in the
street. She did it so suddenly she made him jump.

This general disapproval inclined him at times
to depression, but in certain moods he found it
exhilarating, and several times he professed himself
to Dunkerley not a little of a blade. In others, he
told himself he bore it for *her* sake. Anyhow, he
had to bear it.

He began to find out, too, how little the world
feels the need of a young man of nineteen—he
called himself nineteen, though he had several
months of eighteen still to run—even though he
adds prizes for good conduct, general improvement,
and arithmetic, and advanced certificates signed by
a distinguished engineer and headed with the Royal
Arms, guaranteeing his knowledge of geometrical
drawing, nautical astronomy, animal physiology,
physiography, inorganic chemistry, and building
construction, to his youth and strength and energy.
At first he had imagined head masters clutching at
the chance of him, and presently he found himself
clutching eagerly at them. He began to put a
certain urgency into his applications for vacant
posts, an urgency that helped him not at all. The
applications grew longer and longer, until they
ran to four sheets of note-paper—a pennyworth,
in fact. 'I can assure you,' he would write, 'that
you will find me a loyal and devoted assistant.'
Much in that strain. Dunkerley pointed out that
Bonover's testimonial ignored the question of moral
character and discipline in a marked manner, and
Bonover refused to alter it. He was willing to do
what he could to help Lewisham, in spite of the way
he had been treated, but unfortunately his conscience. . . .

Once or twice Lewisham misquoted the testimonial—to no purpose. And May was half-way

through, and South Kensington was silent. The future was gray.

And in the depths of his doubt and disappointment came her letter. It was typewritten on thin paper. 'Dear,' she wrote simply, and it seemed to him the most sweet and wonderful of all possible modes of address, though, as a matter of fact, it was because she had forgotten his Christian name, and afterwards forgotten the blank she had left for it.

'Dear, I could not write before because I have no room at home now where I can write a letter, and Mrs Frobisher told my mother falsehoods about you. My mother has surprised me dreadfully —I did not think it of her. She told me nothing. But of that I must tell you in another letter. I am too angry to write about it now. Even now you cannot write back, for *you must not send letters here.* It would *never* do. But I think of you, dear'—the 'dear' had been erased and rewritten—'and I must write and tell you so, and of that nice walk we had, if I never write again. I am very busy now. My work is rather difficult and I am afraid I am a little stupid. It is hard to be interested in anything just because that is how you have to live, is it not? I dare say you sometimes feel the same of school. But I suppose everybody is doing things they don't like. I don't know when I shall come to Whortley again, if ever, but very likely you will be coming to London. Mrs Frobisher said the most horrid things. It would be nice if you could come to London, because then perhaps you might see me. There is a big boys' school at Chelsea, and when I go by it every morning I wish you were there. Then you would come out in your cap and gown as I went by. Suppose some day I was to see you there suddenly ! !'

So it ran, with singularly little information in it,

and ended quite abruptly, 'Good-bye, dear. Good-bye, dear,' scribbled in pencil. And then, 'Think of me sometimes.'

Reading it, and especially that opening 'dear,' made Lewisham feel the strangest sensation in his throat and chest, almost as though he was going to cry. So he laughed instead, and read it again, and went to and fro in his little room with his eyes bright and that precious writing held in his hand. That 'dear' was just as if she had spoken—a voice suddenly heard. He thought of her farewell, clear and sweet, out of the shadow of the moonlit house.

But why that 'If I never write again,' and that abrupt ending? Of course he would think of her.

It was her only letter. In a little time its creases were worn through.

Early in June came a loneliness that suddenly changed into almost intolerable longing to see her. He had vague dreams of going to London, to Clapham, to find her. But you do not find people in Clapham as you do in Whortley. He spent an afternoon writing and re-writing a lengthy letter, against the day when her address should come. If it was to come. He prowled about the village disconsolately, and at last set off about seven and retraced by moonlight almost every step of that one memorable walk of theirs.

In the blackness of the shed he worked himself up to the pitch of talking as if she were present. And he said some fine brave things.

He found the little old lady of the wallflowers with a candle in her window, and drank a bottle of ginger beer with a sacramental air. The little old lady asked him, a trifle archly, after his sister, and he promised to bring her again some day. 'I'll certainly bring her,' he said. Talking to the little old lady somehow blunted his sense of desolation. And then home through the white indistinctness in a state of melancholy that became at last so fine as to be almost pleasurable.

The day after that mood a new 'text' attracted and perplexed Mrs Munday, an inscription at once mysterious and familiar, and this inscription was :—

Mizpah.

It was in Old English lettering and evidently very carefully executed.

Where had she seen it before?

It quite dominated all the rest of the room at first, it flaunted like a flag of triumph over 'discipline' and the time-table and the Schema. Once, indeed, it was taken down, but the day after it reappeared. Later a list of scholastic vacancies partially obscured it, and some pencil memoranda were written on the margin.

And when at last the time came for him to pack up and leave Whortley, he took it down and used it with several other suitable papers—the Schema and the time-table were its next-door neighbours— to line the bottom of the yellow box in which he packed his books; chiefly books for that matriculation that had now to be postponed.

CHAPTER VIII

THE CAREER PREVAILS

THERE is an interval of two years and a half and the story resumes with a much maturer Mr Lewisham, indeed no longer a youth, but a man, a legal man, at any rate, of one-and-twenty years. Its scene is no longer little Whortley embedded among its trees, ruddy banks, parks, and common land, but the gray spaciousness of West London.

And it does not resume with Ethel at all. For that promised second letter never reached him, and though he spent many an afternoon during his first few months in London, wandering about Clapham, that arid waste of people, the meeting that he longed for never came. Until at last after the manner of youth, so gloriously recuperative in body, heart, and soul, he began to forget.

The quest of a 'crib' had ended in the unexpected fruition of Dunkerley's blue paper. The greenblue certificates had, it seemed, a value beyond mural decoration, and when Lewisham was already despairing of any employment for the rest of his life, came a marvellous blue document from the Education Department promising inconceivable things. He was to go to London and be paid a guinea a week for listening to lectures—lectures beyond his most ambitious dreams! Among the names that swam before his eyes was Huxley—Huxley and then Lockyer! What a chance to get! Is it any wonder that for three memorable years the Career prevailed with him?

54

You figure him on his way to the Normal School of Science at the opening of his third year of study there. (They call the place the Royal College of Science in these latter days.) He carried in his right hand a shiny black bag, well stuffed with text-books, notes, and apparatus for the forthcoming session; and in his left was a book that the bag had no place for, a book with gilt edges, and its binding very carefully protected by a brown paper cover.

The lapse of time had asserted itself upon his upper lip in an inaggressive but indisputable moustache, in an added inch or so of stature, and in his less conscious carriage. For he no longer felt that universal attention he believed in at eighteen; it was beginning to dawn on him indeed that quite a number of people were entirely indifferent to the fact of his existence. But if less conscious, his carriage was decidedly more confident—as of one with whom the world goes well.

His costume was—with one exception—a tempered black—mourning put to hard uses and 'cutting up rusty.' The mourning was for his mother, who had died more than a year before the date when this story resumes, and had left him property that capitalised at nearly a hundred pounds, a sum which Lewisham hoarded jealously in the Savings Bank, paying only for such essentials as university fees, and the books and instruments his brilliant career as a student demanded. For he was having a brilliant career, after all, in spite of the Whortley check, licking up paper certificates indeed like a devouring flame.

(Surveying him, Madam, your eye would inevitably have fallen to his collar—curiously shiny, a surface like wet gum. Although it has practically nothing to do with this story, I must, I know, dispose of that before I go on, or you will be inattentive.

London has its mysteries, but this strange gloss
on his linen ! 'Cheap laundresses always make
your things blue,' protests the lady. 'It ought to
have been blue-stained, generously frayed, and
loose about the button, fretting his neck. But this
gloss . . .' You would have looked nearer, and
finally you would have touched—a charnel house
surface, dank and cool ! You see, Madam, the collar
was a patent waterproof one. One of those you
wash overnight with a tooth-brush, and hang on
the back of your chair to dry, and there you have
it next morning, rejuvenesced. It was the only
collar he had in the world, it saved threepence a
week at least, and that, to a South Kensington
'science teacher in training,' living on the guinea
a week allowed by a parental but parsimonious
Government, is a sum to consider. It had come to
Lewisham as a great discovery. He had seen it
first in a shop window full of india-rubber goods, and
it lay at the bottom of a glass bowl in which gold-
fish drifted discontentedly to and fro. And he told
himself that he rather liked that gloss.)

But the wearing of a bright red tie would have
been unexpected—a bright red tie after the fashion
of a South-Western railway guard's ! The rest of
him by no means dandiacal, even the vanity of
glasses long since abandoned. You would have
reflected. . . . Where had you seen a crowd—red
ties abundant and in some way significant? The
truth has to be told. Mr Lewisham had become a
Socialist !

That red tie was indeed but one outward and
visible sign of much inward and spiritual develop-
ment. Lewisham, in spite of the demands of a
studious career, had read his Butler's *Analogy*
through by this time, and some other books; he
had argued, had had doubts, and called upon God
for 'Faith' in the silence of the night—'Faith' to

be delivered immediately if Mr Lewisham's patronage was valued, and which nevertheless was not so delivered. . . . And his conception of his destiny in this world was no longer an avenue of examinations to a remote Bar and political eminence 'in the Liberal interest (D. V.)' He had begun to realise certain aspects of our social order that Whortley did not demonstrate, begun to feel something of the dull stress deepening to absolute wretchedness and pain, which is the colour of so much human life in modern London. One vivid contrast hung in his mind symbolical. On the one hand were the coalies of the Westbourne Park yards, on strike and gaunt and hungry, children begging in the black slush, and starving loungers outside a soup kitchen; and on the other, Westbourne Grove, two streets farther, a blazing array of crowded shops, a stirring traffic of cabs and carriages, and such a spate of spending that a tired student in leaky boots and graceless clothes hurrying home was continually impeded in the whirl of skirts and parcels and sweetly pretty womanliness. No doubt the tired student's own inglorious sensations pointed the moral. But that was only one of a perpetually recurring series of vivid approximations.

Lewisham had a strong persuasion, an instinct it may be, that human beings should not be happy while others near them were wretched, and this gay glitter of prosperity had touched him with a sense of crime. He still believed people were responsible for their own lives; in those days he had still to gauge the possibilities of moral stupidity in himself and his fellow-men. He happened upon " Progress and Poverty" just then, and some casual numbers of the " Commonweal," and it was only too easy to accept the theory of cunning plotting capitalists and landowners, and faultless, righteous, martyr workers. He became a Socialist forthwith.

The necessity to do something at once to manifest the new faith that was in him was naturally urgent. So he went out and (historical moment) bought that red tie !

'Blood colour, please,' said Lewisham meekly to the young lady at the counter.

'*What* colour?' said the young lady at the counter sharply.

'A bright scarlet, please,' said Lewisham, blushing. And he spent the best part of the evening and much of his temper in finding out how to tie this into a neat bow. It was a plunge into novel handi-craft—for previously he had been accustomed to made-up ties.

So it was that Lewisham proclaimed the Social Revolution. The first time that symbol went abroad a string of stalwart policemen were walking in single file along the Brompton Road. In the opposite direction marched Lewisham. He began to hum. He passed the policemen with a significant eye and humming the *Marseillaise.* . . .

But that was months ago, and by this time the red tie was a thing of use and wont.

He turned out of the Exhibition Road through a gateway of wrought iron, and entered the hall of the Normal School. The hall was crowded with students carrying books, bags, and boxes of instru-ments, students standing and chattering, students reading the framed and glazed notices of the Debating Society, students buying notebooks, pencils, rubber, or drawing pins from the privileged stationer. There was a strong representation of new hands, the paying students, youths, and young men in black coats and silk hats or tweed suits, the scholar contingent, youngsters of Lewisham's class, raw, shabby, discordant, grotesquely ill-dressed and awestricken; one Lewisham noticed with a sailor's peaked cap gold-decorated, and one with mittens and very genteel gray kid gloves; and Grummett the perennial Official of the Books was busy among them.

'Der Zozalist!' said a wit.

Lewisham pretended not to hear and blushed vividly. He often wished he did not blush quite so much, seeing he was a man of one-and-twenty. He looked studiously away from the Debating Society notice board, whereon 'G. E. Lewisham on Socialism' was announced for the next Friday, and struggled through the hall to where the Book awaited his signature. Presently he was hailed by name, and then again. He could not get to the Book for a minute or so, because of the hand-shaking and clumsy friendly jests of his fellow-'men.'

He was pointed out to a raw hand, by the raw hand's experienced fellow-townsman, as 'that beast Lewisham—awful swat. He was second last year on the year's work. Frightful mugger. But all these swats have a touch of the beastly prig. Exams—Debating Society—more Exams. Don't seem to have ever heard of being alive. Never goes near a Music Hall from one year's end to the other.'

Lewisham heard a shrill whistle, made a run for the lift and caught it just on the point of departure. The lift was unlit and full of black shadows; only the sapper who conducted it was distinct. As Lewisham peered doubtfully at the dim faces near him, a girl's voice addressed him by name.

'Is that you, Miss Heydinger?' he answered. 'I didn't see. I hope you have had a pleasant vacation.'

CHAPTER IX

ALICE HEYDINGER

WHEN he arrived at the top of the building he stood aside for the only remaining passenger to step out before him. It was the Miss Heydinger who had addressed him, the owner of that gilt-edged book in the cover of brown paper. No one else had come all the way up from the ground floor. The rest of the load in the lift had emerged at the 'astronomical' and 'chemical' floors, but these two had both chosen 'zoology' for their third year of study, and zoology lived in the attics. She stepped into the light, with a rare touch of colour springing to her cheeks in spite of herself. Lewisham perceived an alteration in her dress. Perhaps she was looking for and noticed the transitory surprise in his face.

The previous session—their friendship was now nearly a year old—it had never once dawned upon him that she could possibly be pretty. The chief thing he had been able to recall with any definiteness during the vacation was, that her hair was not always tidy and that even when it chanced to be so, she was nervous about it; she distrusted it. He remembered her gesture while she talked, a patting exploration that verged on the exasperating. From that he went on to remember that its colour was, on the whole, fair, a light brown. But he had forgotten her mouth, he had failed to name the colour of her eyes. She wore glasses, it is true. And her dress was indefinite in his memory—an amorphous dinginess.

60

And yet he had seen a good deal of her. They were not in the same course, but he had made her acquaintance on the committee of the school Debating Society. Lewisham was just then discovering Socialism. That had afforded a basis of conversation—an incentive to intercourse. She seemed to find something rarely interesting in his peculiar view of things, and, as chance would have it, he met her accidentally quite a number of times, in the corridors of the schools, in the big Education Library, and in the Art Museum. After a time those meetings appear to have been no longer accidental.

Lewisham for the first time in his life began to fancy he had conversational powers. She resolved to stir up his ambitions—an easy task. She thought he had exceptional gifts and that she might serve to direct them; she certainly developed his vanity. She had matriculated at the London University and they took the Intermediate Examination in Science together in July—she a little unwisely—which served, as almost anything will serve in such cases, as a further link between them. She failed, which in no way diminished Lewisham's regard for her. On the examination days they discoursed about Friendship in general, and things like that, down the Burlington Arcade during the lunch time— Burlington Arcade undisguisedly amused by her learned dinginess and his red tie—and among other things that were said she reproached him for not reading poetry. When they parted in Piccadilly, after the examination, they agreed to write, about poetry and themselves, during the holidays, and then she lent him, with a touch of hesitation, Rossetti's poems. He began to forget what had at first been very evident to him, that she was two or three years older than he.

Lewisham spent the vacation with an unsympathetic but kindly uncle who was a plumber and builder. His uncle had a family of six, the eldest eleven, and Lewisham made himself agreeable and instructive. Moreover, he worked hard for the culminating third year of his studies (in which he had decided to do great things) and he learnt to ride the Ordinary Bicycle. He also thought about Miss Heydinger, and she, it would seem, thought about him.

He argued on social questions with his uncle, who was a prominent local Conservative. His uncle's controversial methods were coarse in the extreme. Socialists, he said, were thieves. The object of Socialism was to take away what a man earned and give it to 'a lot of lazy scoundrels.' Also rich people were necessary. 'If there weren't well-off people, how d'ye think I'd get a livin'? Hey? And where'd *you* be then?' Socialism, his uncle assured him, was 'got up' by agitators. 'They get money out of young Gabies like you, and they spend it in champagne.' And thereafter he met Mr Lewisham's arguments with the word 'Champagne' uttered in an irritating voice, followed by a luscious pantomime of drinking.

Naturally Lewisham felt a little lonely, and perhaps he laid stress upon it in his letters to Miss Heydinger. It came to light that she felt rather lonely too. They discussed the question of True as distinguished from Ordinary Friendship, and from that they passed to Goethe and Elective Affinities. He told her how he looked for her letters, and they became more frequent. Her letters were indisputably well written. Had he been a journalist with a knowledge of '*per thou.*' he would have known each for a day's work. After the practical plumber had been asking what he expected to make by this here science of his, re-reading her letters was balsamic. He liked Rossetti—the exquisite sense of separation in *The Blessed Damozel* touched him. But, on the whole, he was a little surprised at Miss Heydinger's taste in poetry. Rossetti was so sensuous . . . so florid. He had scarcely expected that sort of thing.

Altogether he had returned to the schools decidedly more interested in her than when they had parted. And the curious vague memories of her appearance as something a little frayed and careless, vanished at sight of her emerging from the darkness of the lift. Her hair was in order, as the light glanced through it it looked even pretty, and she wore a well-made, dark-green and black dress, loose-gathered as was the fashion in those days, that somehow gave a needed touch of warmth to her face. Her hat, too, was a change from the careless lumpishness of last year, a hat that, to a feminine mind, would have indicated design. It suited her—these things are past a male novelist's explaining.

'I have this book of yours, Miss Heydinger,' he said.

'I am glad you have written that paper on Socialism,' she replied, taking the brown-covered volume.

They walked along the little passage towards the biological laboratory side by side, and she stopped at the hat pegs to remove her hat. For that was the shameless way of the place, a girl student had to take off her hat publicly, and publicly assume the holland apron that was to protect her in the laboratory. Not even a looking-glass !

'I shall come and hear your paper,' she said.

'I hope you will like it,' said Lewisham at the door of the laboratory.

'And in the vacation I have been collecting evidence about ghosts—you remember our arguments. Though I did not tell you in my letters.'

'I'm sorry you're still obdurate,' said Lewisham. 'I thought that was over.'

'And have you read *Looking Backward*?'

'I want to.'

'I have it here with my other books, if you'd care for me to lend it to you. Wait till I reach my table. My hands are so full.'

They entered the laboratory together, Lewisham holding the door open courtly-wise, Miss Heydinger taking a reassuring pat at her hair. Near the door was a group of four girls, which group Miss Heydinger joined, holding the brown-covered book as inconspicuously as possible. Three of them had been through the previous two years with her, and they greeted her by her Christian name. They had previously exchanged glances at her appearance in Lewisham's company.

A morose elderly young demonstrator brightened momentarily at the sight of Lewisham. 'Well, we've got one of the decent ones anyhow,' said the morose elderly young demonstrator, who was apparently taking an inventory, and then brightening at a fresh entry. 'Ah! and here's Smithers.'

CHAPTER X

As one goes into the South Kensington Art Museum from the Brompton Road, the Gallery of Old Iron is overhead to the right. But the way thither is exceedingly devious and not to be revealed to everybody, since the young people who pursue science and art thereabouts set a peculiar value on its seclusion. The gallery is long and narrow and dark, and set with iron gates, iron-bound chests, locks, bolts, and bars, fantastic great keys, lamps, and the like, and over the balustrade one may lean and talk of one's finer feelings and regard Michelangelo's horned Moses, or Trajan's Column (in plaster) rising gigantic out of the hall below and far above the level of the gallery. And here, on a Wednesday afternoon, were Lewisham and Miss Heydinger, the Wednesday afternoon immediately following that paper upon Socialism, that you saw announced on the notice board in the hall.

The paper had been an immense success, closely reasoned, delivered with a disciplined emotion, the redoubtable Smithers practically converted, the reply after the debate methodical and complete, and it may be there were symptoms of that febrile affection known to the vulgar as 'swelled 'ed.' Lewisham regarded Moses and spoke of his future. Miss Heydinger for the most part watched his face.

'And then?' said Miss Heydinger.

'One must bring these views prominently before people. I believe still in pamphlets. I have thought . . . Lewisham paused, it is to be hoped through modesty.

65

'Yes?' said Miss Heydinger.

'Well—Luther, you know. There is room, I think, in Socialism, for a Luther.'

'Yes,' said Miss Heydinger, imagining it. 'Yes —that would be a grand way.'

So it seemed to many people in those days. But eminent reformers have been now for more than seven years going about the walls of the Social Jericho, blowing their own trumpets and shouting —with such small result beyond incidental displays of ill-temper within, that it is hard to recover the fine hopefulness of those departed days.

'Yes,' said Miss Heydinger. 'That would be a grand way.'

Lewisham appreciated the quality of personal emotion in her voice. He turned his face towards her, and saw unstinted admiration in her eyes. 'It would be a great thing to do,' he said, and added, quite modestly, 'if only one could do it.'

'*You* could do it.'

'You think I could?' Lewisham blushed vividly —with pleasure.

'I do. Certainly you could set out to do it. Even to fail hopelessly would be Great. Sometimes . . .'

She hesitated. He looked expectation. 'I think sometimes it is greater even to fail than to succeed.'

'I don't see that,' said the proposed Luther, and his eyes went back to the Moses. She was about to speak and changed her mind.

Contemplative pause.

'And then, when a great number of people have heard of your views?' she said presently.

'Then I suppose we must form a party and . . . bring things about.'

Another pause—full, no doubt, of elevated thoughts.

'I say,' said Lewisham quite suddenly. 'You

do put—well—courage into a chap. I shouldn't
have done that Socialism paper if it hadn't been
for you.' He turned round and stood leaning with
his back to the Moses, and smiling at her. 'You do
help a fellow,' he said.

That was one of the vivid moments of Miss
Heydinger's life. She changed colour a little.
'Do I?' she said, standing straight and awkward
and looking into his face. 'I'm . . . glad.'

'I haven't thanked you for your letters,' said
Lewisham. 'And I've been thinking . . .'

'Yes?'

'We're first-rate friends, aren't we? The best of
friends.'

She held out her hand and drew a breath. 'Yes,'
she said, as they gripped. He hesitated whether to
hold her hand. He looked into her eyes, and at
that moment she would have given three-quarters
of the years she had still to live, to have had eyes
and features that could have expressed her. Instead,
she felt her face hard, the little muscles of her mouth
twitching insubordinate, and fancied that her self-
consciousness made her eyes dishonest.

'What I mean,' said Lewisham, 'is—that this
will go on. We're always going to be friends, side
by side.'

'Always. Just as I am able to help you—I will
help you. However I can help you, I will.'

'We two,' said Lewisham, gripping her hand.

Her face lit. Her eyes were for a moment touched
with the beauty of simple emotion. 'We two,' she
said, and her lips trembled and her throat seemed
to swell. She snatched her hand back suddenly
and turned her face away. Abruptly she walked
towards the end of the gallery, and he saw her
fumbling for her handkerchief in the folds of the
green and black dress.

She was going to cry !

It set Lewisham marvelling—this totally inappropriate emotion.

He followed her and stood by her. Why cry? He hoped no one would come into the little gallery until her handkerchief was put away. Nevertheless he felt vaguely flattered. She controlled herself, dashed her tears away, and smiled bravely at him with reddened eyes. 'I'm sorry,' she said, gulping.

'I am so glad,' she explained.

'But we will fight together. We two. I *can* help you. I know I can help you. And there is such Work to be done in the world!'

'You are very good to help me,' said Lewisham, quoting a phrase from what he had intended to say before he found out that he had a hold upon her emotions.

'No!

'Has it ever occurred to you,' she said abruptly 'how little a woman can do alone in the world?'

'Or a man,' he answered, after a momentary meditation.

So it was Lewisham enrolled his first ally in the cause of the red tie—of the red tie and of the Greatness that was presently to come. His first ally; for hitherto—save for the indiscretion of his mural inscriptions—he had made a secret of his private ambitions. In that now half-forgotten love affair at Whortley even, he had, in spite of the considerable degree of intimacy attained, said absolutely nothing about his Career.

CHAPTER XI

MANIFESTATIONS

Miss Heydinger declined to disbelieve in the spirits of the dead, and this led to controversy in the laboratory over Tea. For the girl students, being in a majority that year, had organised Tea between four o'clock and the advent of the extinguishing policeman at five. And the men students were occasionally invited to Tea. But not more than two of them at a time really participated, because there were only two spare cups after that confounded Simmons broke the third.

Smithers, the square-headed student with the hard gray eyes, argued against the spirits of the dead with positive animosity, while Bletherly, who displayed an orange tie and lank hair in unshorn abundance, was vaguely open-minded. 'What is love?' asked Bletherly, 'surely that at any rate is immortal!' His remark was considered irrelevant and ignored.

Lewisham, as became the most promising student of the year, weighed the evidence—comprehensively under headings. He dismissed the mediumistic *séances* as trickery.

'Rot and imposture,' said Smithers loudly, and with an oblique glance to see if his challenge reached its mark. Its mark was a grizzled little old man with a very small face and very big gray eyes, who had been standing listlessly at one of the laboratory windows until the discussion caught him. He wore a brown velvet jacket and was reputed to be enormously rich. His name was Lagune. He was not a regular attendant, but one of those casual outsiders who are admitted to laboratories that are not completely full. He was known to be an ardent spiritualist—it was even said that he had challenged Huxley to a public discussion on materialism, and he came to the biological lectures and worked intermittently, in order, he explained, to fight disbelief with its own weapons. He rose greedily to Smithers's controversial bait.

'I say *no*!' he said, calling down the narrow laboratory and following his voice. He spoke with the ghost of a lisp. 'Pardon my interrupting, sir. The question interests me profoundly. I hope I don't intrude. Excuse me, sir. Make it personal. Am I a—fool, or an impostor?'

'Well,' parried Smithers, with all a South Kensington student's want of polish, 'that's a bit personal.'

'Assume, sir, that I am an honest observer.'

'Well?'

'I have *seen* spirits, *heard* spirits, *felt* the touch of spirits.' He opened his pale eyes very widely.

'Fool, then,' said Smithers in an undertone which did not reach the ears of the spiritualist.

'You may have been deceived,' paraphrased Lewisham.

'I can assure you . . . others can see, hear, feel. I have tested, sir. Tested! I have some scientific training and I have employed tests. Scientific and exhaustive tests! Every possible way. I ask you, sir—have you given the spirits a chance?'

'It is only paying guineas to humbugs,' said Smithers.

'There you are! Prejudice! Here is a man denies the facts and consequently *won't* see them, won't go near them.'

'But you wouldn't have every man in the three

kingdoms, who disbelieved in spirits, attend *séances*
before he should be allowed to deny?'

'Most assuredly yes. Most assuredly yes! He
knows nothing about it till then.'

The argument became heated. The little old
gentleman was soon under way. He knew a person
of the most extraordinary gifts, a medium . . .

'Paid?' asked Smithers.

'Would you muzzle the ox that treadeth out the
corn?' said Lagune promptly.

Smithers's derision was manifest.

'Would you distrust a balance because you
bought it? Come and see.' Lagune was now very
excited and inclined to gesticulate and raise his
voice. He invited the whole class incontinently to
a series of special *séances*. 'Not all at once—the
spirits—new influences.' But in sections. 'I warn
you we may get nothing. But the chances are
. . . I would rejoice infinitely . . .'

So it came about that Lewisham consented to
witness a spirit-raising. Miss Heydinger, it was
arranged, should be there, and the sceptic Smithers,
Lagune, his typewriter, and the medium would
complete the party. Afterwards there was to be
another party for the others. Lewisham was glad
he had the moral support of Smithers. 'It's an
evening wasted,' said Smithers, who had gallantly
resolved to make the running for Lewisham in the
contest for the Forbes medal. 'But I'll prove my
case. You see if I don't.' They were given an
address in Chelsea.

The house, when Lewisham found it at last,
proved a large one with such an air of mellowed
dignity that he was abashed. He hung his hat up
for himself beside a green-trimmed hat of straw in
the wide, rich-toned hall. Through an open door
he had a glimpse of a palatial study, book-shelves
bearing white busts, a huge writing-table lit by a

green-shaded electric lamp and covered thickly
with papers. The housemaid looked, he thought,
with infinite disdain at the rusty mourning and
flamboyant tie, and flounced about and led him
upstairs.

She rapped, and there was a discussion within.
'They're at it already, I believe,' she said to
Lewisham confidentially. 'Mr Lagune's always
at it.'

There were sounds of chairs being moved,
Smithers's extensive voice making a suggestion and
laughing nervously. Lagune appeared opening the
door. His grizzled face seemed smaller and his
big gray eyes larger than usual.

'We were just going to begin without you,' he
whispered. 'Come along.'

The room was furnished even more finely than
the drawing-room of the Whortley Grammar School,
hitherto the finest room (except certain of the
State Apartments at Windsor) known to Lewisham.
The furniture struck him in a general way as akin
to that in the South Kensington Museum. His
first impression was an appreciation of the vast
social superiority of the chairs; it seemed impertinent to think of sitting on anything quite so
quietly stately. He perceived Smithers standing
with an air of bashful hostility against a bookcase.
Then he was aware that Lagune was asking them
all to sit down. Already seated at the table was the
Medium, Chaffery, a benevolent-looking, faintly
shabby gentleman with bushy iron-gray side-
whiskers, a wide, thin-lipped mouth tucked in at
the corners, and a chin like the toe of a boot. He
regarded Lewisham critically and disconcertingly
over gilt glasses. Miss Heydinger was quite at her
ease and began talking at once. Lewisham's
replies were less confident than they had been in
the Gallery of Old Iron; indeed there was almost a

reversal of their positions. She led and he was abashed. He felt obscurely that she had taken an advantage of him. He became aware of another girlish figure in a dark dress on his right.

Every one moved towards the round table in the centre of the room, on which lay a tambourine and a little green box. Lagune developed unsuspected lengths of knobby wrist and finger directing his guests to their seats. Lewisham was to sit next to him, between him and the Medium ; beyond the Medium sat Smithers with Miss Heydinger on the other side of him, linked to Lagune by the type-writer. So sceptics compassed the Medium about. The company was already seated before Lewisham looked across Lagune and met the eyes of the girl next that gentleman. It was Ethel ! The close green dress, the absence of a hat, and a certain loss of colour made her seem less familiar, but did not prevent the instant recognition. And there was recognition in her eyes.

Immediately she looked away. At first his only emotion was surprise. He would have spoken but a little thing robbed him of speech. For a moment he was unable to remember her surname. More-over, the strangeness of his surroundings made him undecided. He did not know what was the proper way to address her—and he still kept to the superstition of etiquette. Besides—to speak to her would involve a general explanation to all these people. . . .

' Just leave a pin-point of gas, Mr Smithers, please,' said Lagune, and suddenly the one sur-viving jet of the gas chandelier was turned down and they were in darkness. The moment for recognition had passed.

The joining of hands was punctiliously verified, the circle was linked little finger to little finger. Lewisham's abstraction received a rebuke from

Smithers.   The Medium, speaking in an affable
voice, premised that he could promise nothing, he
had no *'directing'* power over manifestations.
Thereafter ensued a silence. . . .

For a space Lewisham was inattentive to all that
happened.

He sat in the breathing darkness, staring at the
dim elusive shape that had presented that remembered face.   His mind was astonishment mingled
with annoyance.   He had settled that this girl
was lost to him for ever.   The spell of the old
days of longing, of the afternoons that he had spent
after his arrival in London, wandering through
Clapham with a fading hope of meeting her, had not
returned to him.   But he was ashamed of his
stupid silence, and irritated by the awkwardness
of the situation.   At one moment he was on the very
verge of breaking the compact and saying 'Miss
Henderson' across the table. . . .

How was it he had forgotten that 'Henderson'?
He was still young enough to be surprised at
forgetfulness.

Smithers coughed, one might imagine with a
warning intention.

Lewisham, recalling his detective responsibility
with an effort, peered about him, but the room was
very dark.   The silence was broken ever and again
by deep sighs and a restless stirring from the
Medium.   Out of this mental confusion Lewisham's
personal vanity was first to emerge.   What did she
think of him?   Was she peering at him through the
darkness even as he peered at her?   Should he
pretend to see her for the first time when the lights
were restored?   As the minutes lengthened it
seemed as though the silence grew deeper and
deeper.   There was אָ fire in the room, and it
looked, for lack of that glow, chilly.   A curious
scepticism arose in his mind as to whether he had

actually seen Ethel or only mistaken some one else for her. He wanted the *séance* over in order that he might look at her again. The old days at Whortley came out of his memory with astonishing detail and yet astonishingly free from emotion. . . .

He became aware of a peculiar sensation down his back, that he tried to account for as a draught. . . .

Suddenly a beam of cold air came like a touch against his face, and made him shudder convulsively. Then he hoped that she had not marked his shudder. He thought of laughing a low laugh to show he was not afraid. Some one else shuddered too, and he perceived an extraordinarily vivid odour of violets. Lagune's finger communicated a nervous quivering.

What was happening?

The musical box somewhere on the table began playing a rather trivial, rather plaintive air that was strange to him. It seemed to deepen the silence about him, an accent on the expectant stillness, a thread of tinkling melody spanning an abyss.

Lewisham took himself in hand at this stage. What *was* happening? He must attend. Was he really watching as he should do? He had been wool-gathering. There were no such things as spirits, mediums were humbugs, and he was here to prove that sole remaining Gospel. But he must keep up with things—he was missing points. What was that scent of violets? And who had set the musical box going? The Medium, of course : but how? He tried to recall whether he had heard a rustling or detected any movement before the music began. He could not recollect. Come ! he must be more on the alert than this !

He became acutely desirous of a successful exposure. He figured the dramatic moment he had prepared with Smithers—Ethel a spectator. He peered suspiciously into the darkness.

Somebody shuddered again, some one opposite him this time. He felt Lagune's finger quiver still more palpably, and then suddenly the raps began, abruptly, all about him. *Rap !*—making him start violently. A swift percussive sound, tap, rap, dap, under the table, under the chair, in the air, round the cornices. The Medium groaned again and shuddered, and his nervous agitation passed sympathetically round the circle. The music seemed to fade to the vanishing point and grew louder again.

How was it done?

He heard Lagune's voice next him speaking with a peculiar quality of breathless reverence. 'The alphabet?' he asked, 'shall we—shall we use the alphabet?'

A forcible rap under the table.

'No !' interpreted the voice of the Medium.

The raps were continued everywhere.

Of course it was trickery. Lewisham endeavoured to think what the mechanism was. He tried to determine whether he really had the Medium's little finger touching his. He peered at the dark shape next him. There was a violent rapping far away behind them with an almost metallic resonance. Then the raps ceased, and over the healing silence the little jet of melody from the musical box played alone. And after a moment that ceased also. . . .

The stillness was profound. Mr Lewisham was now highly strung. Doubts assailed him suddenly, and an overwhelming apprehension, a sense of vast occurrences gathering above him. The darkness was a physical oppression. . . .

He started. Something had stirred on the table. There was the sharp ping of metal being struck. A number of little crepitating sounds like paper being smoothed. The sound of wind without the movement of air. A sense of a presence hovering over the table.

The excitement of Lagune communicated itself in convulsive tremblings; the Medium's hand quivered. In the darkness on the table something faintly luminous, a greenish-white patch, stirred and hopped slowly among the dim shapes.

The object, whatever it was, hopped higher, rose slowly in the air, expanded. Lewisham's attention followed this slavishly. It was ghostly—unaccountable—marvellous. For the moment he forgot even Ethel. Higher and higher this pallid luminosity rose overhead, and then he saw that it was a ghostly hand and arm, rising, rising. Slowly, deliberately, it crossed the table, seemed to touch Lagune, who shivered. It moved slowly round and touched Lewisham. He gritted his teeth.

There was no mistaking the touch, firm and yet soft, of finger-tips. Almost simultaneously, Miss Heydinger cried out that something was smoothing her hair, and suddenly the musical box set off again with a reel. The faint oval of the tambourine rose, jangled, and Lewisham heard it pat Smithers in the face. It seemed to pass overhead. Immediately a table somewhere beyond the Medium began moving audibly on its casters.

It seemed impossible that the Medium, sitting so still beside him, could be doing all these things—grotesquely unmeaning though they might be. After all . . .

The ghostly hand was hovering almost directly in front of Mr Lewisham's eyes. It hung with a slight quivering. Ever and again its fingers flapped down and rose stiffly again.

Noise! A loud noise it seemed. Something moving? What was it he had to do?

Lewisham suddenly missed the Medium's little finger. He tried to recover it. He could not find it. He caught, held, and lost an arm. There was an exclamation. A faint report. A curse close

to him bitten in half by the quick effort to suppress
it. Tzit ! The little pin-point of light flew up
with a hiss.

Lewisham, standing, saw a circle of blinking faces
turned to the group of two this sizzling light
revealed. Smithers was the chief figure of the
group; he stood triumphant, one hand on the gas
tap, the other gripping the Medium's wrist, and in
the Medium's hand—the incriminatory tambourine.

'How's this, Lewisham,' cried Smithers, with the
shadows on his face jumping as the gas flared.

'*Caught !*' said Lewisham loudly, rising in his
place and avoiding Ethel's eyes.

'What's this?' cried the Medium.

'Cheating,' panted Smithers.

'Not so,' cried the Medium. 'When you turned
up the light . . . put my hand up . . . caught
tambourine . . . to save head.'

'Mr Smithers,' cried Lagune. 'Mr Smithers,
this is very wrong. This—shock——'

The tambourine fell noisily to the floor. The
Medium's face changed, he groaned strangely and
staggered back. Lagune cried out for a glass of
water. Every one looked at the man, expecting
him to fall, save Lewisham. The thought of Ethel
had flashed back into his mind. He turned to see
how she took this exposure in which he was such
a prominent actor. He saw her leaning over the
table as if to pick up something that lay across it.
She was not looking at him, she was looking at
the Medium. Her face was set and white. Then,
as if she felt his glance, her eyes met his.

She started back, stood erect, facing him with a
strange hardness in her eyes.

In the moment Lewisham did not grasp the
situation. He wanted to show that he was acting
upon equal terms with Smithers in the exposure.
For the moment her action simply directed his

attention to the object towards which she had been leaning, a thing of shrivelled membrane, a pneumatic glove, lying on the table. This was evidently part of the mediumistic apparatus. He pounced and seized it.

' Look ! ' he said, holding it towards Smithers. ' Here is more ! What is this ? '

He perceived that the girl started. He saw Chaffery, the Medium, look instantly over Smither's shoulders, saw his swift glance of reproach at the girl. Abruptly the situation appeared to Lewisham ; he perceived her complicity. And he stood, still in the attitude of triumph, with the evidence against her in his hand ! But his triumph had vanished.

' Ah ! ' cried Smithers, leaning across the table to secure it. ' *Good* old Lewisham ! . . . Now we *have* it. This is better than the tambourine.'

His eyes shone with triumph. ' Do you see, Mr. Lagune ? ' said Smithers. ' The Medium held this in his teeth and blew it out. There's no denying this. This wasn't falling on your head, Mr Medium, was it ? *This*—this was the luminous hand ! '

CHAPTER XII

THAT night, as she went with him to Chelsea station, Miss Heydinger discovered an extraordinary moodiness in Lewisham. She had been vividly impressed by the scene in which they had just participated, she had for a time believed in the manifestations; the swift exposure had violently revolutionised her ideas. The details of the crisis were a little confused in her mind. She ranked Lewisham with Smithers in the scientific triumph of the evening. On the whole she felt elated. She had no objection to being confuted by Lewisham. But she was angry with the Medium. 'It is dreadful,' she said. 'Living a lie! How can the world grow better, when sane, educated people use their sanity and enlightenment to darken others? It is dreadful!

'He was a horrible man—such an oily, dishonest voice. And the girl—I was sorry for her. She must have been oh!—bitterly ashamed, or why should she have burst out crying? That *did* distress me. Fancy crying like that! It was—yes—*abandon*. But what can one do?'

She paused. Lewisham was walking along, looking straight before him, lost in some grim argument with himself.

'It makes me think of Sludge the Medium,' she said.

He made no answer.

She glanced at him suddenly. 'Have you read Sludge the Medium?'

Eigh?' he said, coming back out of infinity. 'What? I beg your pardon. Sludge, the Medium? I thought his name was—it *was*—Chaffery.'

He looked at her, clearly very anxious upon this question of fact.

'But I mean Browning's *Sludge*. You know—the poem.'

'No—I'm afraid I don't,' said Lewisham.

'I must lend it to you,' she said. 'It's splendid. It goes to the very bottom of this business.'

'Does it?'

'It never occurred to me before. But I see the point clearly now. If people, poor people, are offered money if phenomena happen, it's too much. They are *bound* to cheat. It's bribery—immorality !'

She talked in panting little sentences, because Lewisham was walking in heedless big strides. 'I wonder how much—such people—could earn honestly.'

Lewisham slowly became aware of the question at his ear. He hurried back from infinity. 'How much they could earn honestly? I haven't the slightest idea.'

He paused. 'The whole of this business puzzles me,' he said. 'I want to think.'

'It's frightfully complex, isn't it?' she said—a little staggered.

But the rest of the way to the station was silence. They parted with a hand-clasp they took a pride in—a little perfunctory so far as Lewisham was concerned on this occasion. She scrutinised his face as the train moved out of the station, and tried to account for his mood. He was staring before him at unknown things—as if he had already forgotten her.

He wanted to think ! But two heads, she thought, were better than one in a matter of opinion. It troubled her to be so ignorant of his mental states.

'How we are wrapped and swathed about—soul from soul!' she thought, staring out of the window at the dim things flying by outside.

Suddenly a fit of depression came upon her. She felt alone—absolutely alone—in a void world.

Presently she returned to external things. She became aware of two people in the next compartment eyeing her critically. Her hand went patting at her hair.

CHAPTER XIII

ETHEL HENDERSON sat at her machine before the window of Mr. Lagune's study, and stared blankly at the grays and blues of the November twilight. Her face was white, her eyelids were red from recent weeping, and her hands lay motionless in her lap. The door had just slammed behind Lagune.

'Heigh-ho!' she said. 'I wish I was dead. Oh! I wish I was out of it all.'

She became passive again. 'I wonder what I have *done*,' she said, 'that I should be punished like this.'

She certainly looked anything but a Fate-haunted soul, being indeed visibly and immediately a very pretty girl. Her head was shapely and covered with curly dark hair, and the eyebrows above her hazel eyes were clear and dark. Her lips were finely shaped, her mouth was not too small to be expressive, her chin small, and her neck white and full and pretty. There is no need to lay stress upon her nose—it sufficed. She was of a mediocre height, sturdy rather than slender, and her dress was of a pleasant, golden-brown material with the easy sleeves and graceful line of those æsthetic days And she sat at her typewriter and wished she was dead and wondered what she had *done*.

The room was lined with book-shelves and conspicuous therein were a long row of foolish pretentious volumes, the 'works' of Lagune—the witless, meandering imitation of philosophy that occupied his life. Along the cornices were busts of Plato, Socrates, and Newton. Behind Ethel was the great man's desk with its green-shaded electric light, and littered with proofs and copies of *Hesperus*, 'A Paper for Doubters,' which, with her assistance, he edited, published, compiled, wrote, and (without her help) paid for and read. A pen, flung down forcibly, quivered erect with its one surviving nib in the blotting pad. Mr Lagune had flung it down.

The collapse of the previous night had distressed him dreadfully, and ever and again before his retreat he had been breaking into passionate monologue. The ruin of a life-work, it was, no less. Surely she had known that Chaffery was a cheat. Had she not known? Silence. 'After so many kindnesses——'

She interrupted him with a wailing, 'Oh, I know —I know.'

But Lagune was remorseless and insisted she had betrayed him, worse—made him ridiculous ! Look at the 'work' he had undertaken at South Kensington—how could he go on with that now? How could he find the heart? When his own typewriter sacrificed him to her stepfather's trickery? 'Trickery !'

The gesticulating hands became active, the gray eyes dilated with indignation, the piping voice eloquent.

'If he hadn't cheated you, some one else would,' was Ethel's inadequate muttered retort, unheard by the seeker after phenomena.

It was perhaps not so bad as dismissal, but it certainly lasted longer. And at home was Chaffery, grimly malignant at her failure to secure that pneumatic glove. He had no right to blame her, he really had not; but a disturbed temper is apt to falsify the scales of justice. The tambourine, he insisted, he could have explained by saying he put up his hand to catch it and protect his head directly Smithers moved. But the pneumatic glove there was no explaining. He had made a chance for her to secure it when he had pretended to faint. It was rubbish to say any one could have been looking on the table then—rubbish.

Beside that significant wreck of a pen stood a little carriage clock in a case, and this suddenly lifted a slender voice and announced *five*. She turned round on her stool and sat staring at the clock. She smiled with the corners of her mouth down. 'Home,' she said, 'and begin again. It's like battledore and shuttlecock. . . .

'I *was* silly. . . .

'I suppose I've brought it on myself. I ought to have picked it up, I suppose. I had time. . . .

'Cheats . . . just cheats.

'I never thought I should see him again. . . .

'He was ashamed, of course. . . . He had his own friends.'

For a space she sat still, staring blankly before her. She sighed, rubbed a knuckle in a reddened eye, rose.

She went into the hall where her hat, transfixed by a couple of hat pins, hung above her jacket, assumed these garments, and let herself out into the cold gray street.

She had hardly gone twenty yards from Lagune's door before she became aware of a man overtaking her and walking beside her. That kind of thing is a common enough experience to girls who go to and from work in London, and she had had perforce to learn many things since her adventurous Whortley days. She looked stiffly in front of her. The man deliberately got in her way so that she had to stop. She lifted eyes of indignant protest.

It was Lewisham—and his face was white. He
hesitated awkwardly and then in silence held out
his hand. She took it mechanically. He found his
voice. 'Miss Henderson,' he said.

'What do you want?' she asked faintly.

'I don't know,' he said. . . . 'I want to talk to
you.'

'Yes?' Her heart was beating fast.

He found the thing unexpectedly difficult.

'May I——? Are you expecting——? Have
you far to go? I would like to talk to you. There
is a lot . . .'

'I walk to Clapham,' she said. 'If you care
. . . to come part of the way. . . '

She moved awkwardly. Lewisham took his place
at her side. They walked side by side for a moment,
their manner constrained, having so much to say
that they could not find a word to begin upon.

'Have you forgotten Whortley?' he asked
abruptly.

'No.'

He glanced at her; her face was downcast. 'Why
did you never write?' he asked bitterly.

'I wrote.'

'Again, I mean.'

'I did—in July.'

'I never had it.'

'It came back.'

'But Mrs Munday . . .'

'I had forgotten her name. I sent it to the
Grammar School.'

Lewisham suppressed an exclamation.

'I am very sorry,' she said.

They went on again in silence. 'Last night,'
said Lewisham at length. 'I have no business to
ask. But——'

She took a long breath. 'Mr Lewisham,' she said. 'That man you saw—the Medium—was my stepfather.'

'Well?'

'Isn't that enough?'

Lewisham paused. 'No,' he said.

There was another constrained silence. 'No,' he said less dubiously. 'I don't care a rap what your stepfather is. Were *you* cheating?'

Her face turned white. Her mouth opened and closed. 'Mr Lewisham,' she said deliberately, 'you may not believe it, it may sound impossible, but on my honour . . . I did not know—I did not know for certain, that is—that my stepfather . . .'

'Ah!' said Lewisham, leaping at conviction. 'Then I was right . . .'

For a moment she stared at him, and then, 'I *did* know,' she said, suddenly beginning to cry. 'How can I tell you? It is a lie. I *did* know. I *did* know all the time.'

He stared at her in white astonishment. He fell behind her one step, and then in a stride came level again. Then, a silence, a silence that seemed it would never end. She had stopped crying, she was one huge suspense, not daring even to look at his face. And at last he spoke.

'No,' he said slowly. 'I don't mind even that. I don't care—even if it was that.'

Abruptly they turned into the King's Road, with its roar of wheeled traffic and hurrying foot-passengers, and forthwith a crowd of boys with a broken-spirited Guy involved and separated them. In a busy highway of a night one must needs talk disconnectedly in shouted snatches or else hold one's peace. He glanced at her face and saw that it was set again. Presently she turned southward

out of the tumult into a street of darkness and warm
blinds, and they could go on talking again.

'I understand what you mean,' said Lewisham.
'I know I do. You knew but you did not want to
know. It was like that.'

But her mind had been active. 'At the end of
this road,' she said, gulping a sob, 'you must go
back. It was kind of you to come, Mr Lewisham.
But you were ashamed—you are sure to be ashamed.
My employer is a spiritualist, and my stepfather is
a professional Medium, and my mother is a spiritualist. You were quite right not to speak to me last
night. Quite. It was kind of you to come, but you
must go back. Life is hard enough as it is . . .
You must go back at the end of the road. Go back
at the end of the road . . .'

Lewisham made no reply for a hundred yards.
'I'm coming on to Clapham,' he said.

They came to the end of the road in silence. Then
at the kerb corner she turned and faced him. 'Go
back,' she whispered.

'No,' he said obstinately, and they stood face to
face at the cardinal point of their lives.

'Listen to me,' said Lewisham. 'It is hard to
say what I feel. I don't know myself. . . . But
I'm not going to lose you like this. I'm not going
to let you slip a second time. I was awake about
it all last night. I don't care where you are, what
your people are, nor very much whether you've
kept quite clear of this medium humbug. I don't.
You will in future. Anyhow. I've had a day and
night to think it over. I had to come and try to
find you. It's you. I've never forgotten you.
Never. I'm not going to be sent back like this.'

'It can be no good for either of us,' she said, as
resolute as he.

'I shan't leave you.'

'But what is the good? . . .'

'I'm coming,' said Lewisham, dogmatically.

And he came.

He asked her a question point blank and she would not answer him, and for some way they walked in grim silence. Presently she spoke with a twitching mouth. 'I wish you would leave me,' she said. 'You are quite different from what I am. You felt that last night. You helped find us out. . . .'

'When first I came to London I used to wander about Clapham looking for you,' said Lewisham, 'week after week.'

They had crossed the bridge and were in a narrow little street of shabby shops near Clapham Junction before they talked again. She kept her face averted and expressionless.

'I'm sorry,' said Lewisham, with a sort of stiff civility, 'if I seem to be forcing myself upon you. I don't want to pry into your affairs—if you don't wish me to. The sight of you has somehow brought back a lot of things. . . . I can't explain it. Perhaps—I had to come to find you—I kept on thinking of your face, of how you used to smile, how you jumped from the gate by the lock, and how we had tea . . . a lot of things.

He stopped again.

'A lot of things.'

'If I may come,' he said, and went unanswered. They crossed the wide streets by the Junction and went on towards the Common.

'I live down this road,' she said, stopping abruptly at a corner. 'I would rather . . .'

'But I have said nothing.'

She looked at him with her face white, unable to

speak for a space. 'It can do no good,' she said. 'I am mixed up with this. . . .'

She stopped.

He spoke deliberately. 'I shall come,' he said, 'to-morrow night.'

'No,' she said.

'But I shall come.'

'No,' she whispered.

'I shall come.' She could hide the gladness of her heart from herself no longer. She was frightened that he had come, but she was glad, and she knew he knew that she was glad. She made no further protest. She held out her hand dumbly. And on the morrow she found him awaiting her even as he had said.

CHAPTER XIV

FOR three days the Laboratory at South Kensington saw nothing of Lagune, and then he came back more invincibly voluble than ever. Every one had expected him to return apostate, but he brought back an invigorated faith, a propaganda unashamed. From some source he had derived strength and conviction afresh. Even the rhetorical Smithers availed nothing. There was a joined battle over the insufficient tea-cups, and the elderly young assistant demonstrator hovered on the verge of the discussion, rejoicing, it is supposed, over the entanglements of Smithers. For at the outset Smithers displayed an overweening confidence and civility, and at the end his ears were red and his finer manners lost to him.

Lewisham, it was remarked by Miss Heydinger, made but a poor figure in this discussion. Once or twice he seemed about to address Lagune, and thought better of it with the words upon his lips.

Lagune's treatment of the exposure was light and vigorous. 'The man Chaffery,' he said, 'has made a clean breast of it. His point of view——'

'Facts are facts,' said Smithers.

'A fact is a synthesis of impressions,' said Lagune; 'but that you will learn when you are older. The thing is that we were at cross purposes. I told Chaffery you were beginners. He treated you as beginners—arranged a demonstration.'

'It *was* a demonstration,' said Smithers.

'Precisely. If it had not been for your inter-ruptions . . .'

'Ah !'

'He forged elementary effects. . . .'

'You can't but admit that.'

'I don't attempt to deny it. But, as he explained —the thing is necessary—justifiable. Psychic phenomena are subtle, a certain training of the observation is necessary. A medium is a more subtle instrument than a balance or a borax bead, and see how long it is before you can get assured results with a borax bead ! In the elementary class, in the introductory phase, conditions are too crude. . . .'

'For honesty.'

'Wait a moment. *Is* it dishonest—rigging a demonstration?'

'Of course it is.'

'Your professors do it.'

'I deny that *in toto*,' said Smithers, and repeated with satisfaction, '*in toto*.'

'That's all right,' said Lagune, 'because I have the facts. Your chemical lecturers—you may go downstairs now and ask, if you disbelieve me— always cheat over the indestructibility of matter experiment—always. And then another—a physio-graphy thing. You know the experiment I mean? To demonstrate the existence of the earth's rotation. They use—they use——'

'Foucault's pendulum,' said Lewisham. 'They use a rubber ball with a pin-hole hidden in the hand, and blow the pendulum round the way it ought to go.'

'But that's different,' said Smithers.

'Wait a moment,' said Lagune, and produced **a**

piece of folded printed paper from his pocket. 'Here is a review from *Nature* of the work of no less a person than Professor Greenhill. And see— a convenient pin is introduced in the apparatus for the demonstration of virtual velocities! Read it— if you doubt me. I suppose you doubt me.'

Smithers abruptly abandoned his position of denial '*in toto.*' 'This isn't my point, Mr Lagune; this isn't my point,' he said. 'These things that are done in the lecture theatre are not to prove facts, but to give ideas.'

'So was my demonstration,' said Lagune.

'We didn't understand it in that light.'

'Nor does the ordinary person who goes to Science lectures understand it in that light. He is comforted by the thought that he is seeing things with his own eyes.'

'Well, I don't care,' said Smithers; 'two wrongs don't make a right. To rig demonstrations is wrong.'

'There I agree with you. I have spoken plainly with this man Chaffery. He's not a full-blown professor, you know, a highly salaried ornament of the rock of truth like your demonstration-rigging professors here, and so I can speak plainly to him without offence. He takes quite the view they would take. But I am more rigorous. I insist that there shall be no more of this. . . .'

'Next time——' said Smithers, with irony.

'There will be no next time. I have done with elementary exhibitions. You must take the word of the trained observer—just as you do in the matter of chemical analysis.'

'Do you mean you are going on with that chap when he's been caught cheating under your very nose?'

'Certainly. Why not?'

Smithers set out to explain why not, and happened on confusion. 'I still believe the man has powers,' said Lagune.

'Of deception,' said Smithers.

'Those I must eliminate,' said Lagune. 'You might as well refuse to study electricity because it escaped through your body. All new science is elusive. No investigator in his senses would refuse to investigate a compound because it did unexpected things. Either this dissolves in acid or I have nothing more to do with it—eh? That's fine research!'

Then it was the last vestiges of Smithers's manners vanished. 'I don't care *what* you say,' said Smithers. 'It's all rot—it's all just rot. Argue if you like—but have you convinced anybody? Put it to the vote?'

'That's democracy with a vengeance,' said Lagune. 'A general election of the truth half-yearly, eh?'

'That's simply wriggling out of it,' said Smithers. 'That hasn't anything to do with it at all.'

Lagune, flushed but cheerful, was on his way downstairs when Lewisham overtook him. He was pale and out of breath, but as the staircase invariably rendered Lagune breathless he did not re-mark the younger man's disturbance. 'Interesting talk,' panted Lewisham. 'Very interesting talk, sir.'

'I'm glad you found it so—very,' said Lagune.

There was a pause, and then Lewisham plunged desperately. 'There is a young lady—she is your typewriter. . . .'

He stopped from sheer loss of breath.

'Yes?' said Lagune.

'Is she a medium or anything of that sort?'

'Well,' Lagune reflected. 'She is not a medium, certainly. But—why do you ask?'

'Oh! . . . I wondered.'

'You noticed her eyes, perhaps. She is the stepdaughter of that man Chaffery—a queer character but indisputably mediumistic. It's odd the thing should have struck you. Curiously enough I myself have fancied she might be something of a psychic—judging from her face.'

'A what?'

'A psychic—undeveloped, of course. I have thought once or twice. Only a little while ago I was speaking to that man Chaffery about her.'

'Were you?'

'Yes. He, of course, would like to see any latent powers developed. But it's a little difficult to begin, you know.'

'You mean—she won't?'

'Not at present. She is a good girl, but in this matter she is—timid. There is often a sort of disinclination—a queer sort of feeling—one might almost call it modesty.'

'I see,' said Lewisham.

'One can override it usually. I don't despair.'

'No,' said Lewisham shortly. They were at the foot of the staircase now. He hesitated. 'You've given me a lot to think about,' he said, with an attempt at an off-hand manner. 'The way you talked upstairs'; and turned towards the book he had to sign.

'I'm glad you don't take up quite such an intolerant attitude as Mr Smithers,' said Lagune; 'very glad. I must lend you a book or two. If

your *cramming* here leaves you any time, that
is.'

'Thanks,' said Lewisham shortly, and walked
away from him. The studiously characteristic
signature quivered and sprawled in an unfamiliar
manner.

'I'm *damned* if he orverides it,' said Lewisham,
under his breath.

CHAPTER XV

LOVE IN THE STREETS

LEWISHAM was not quite clear what course he meant to take in the high enterprise of foiling Lagune, and indeed he was anything but clear about the entire situation. His logical processes, his emotions and his imagination seemed playing some sort of snatching game with his will. Enormous things hung imminent, but it worked out to this, that he walked home with Ethel night after night for—to be exact—seven and-sixty nights. Every week night through November and December, save once, when he had to go into the far East to buy himself an overcoat, he was waiting to walk with her home. A curious, inconclusive affair, that walk, to which he came nightly full of vague longings and which ended invariably under an odd shadow of disappointment. It began outside Lagune's most punctually at five, and ended—mysteriously —at the corner of a side road in Clapham, a road of little yellow houses with sunk basements and tawdry decorations of stone. Up that road she vanished night after night, into a gray mist and the shadow beyond a feeble yellow gas-lamp, and he would watch her vanish, and then sigh and turn back towards his lodgings.

They talked of this and that, their little superficial ideas about themselves, and of their circumstances and tastes, and always there was something,

97

something that was with them unspoken, unacknow-
ledged, which made all these things unreal and
insincere.

Yet out of their talk he began to form vague ideas
of the home from which she came. There was, of
course, no servant, and the mother was something
meandering, furtive, tearful in the face of troubles.
Sometimes of an afternoon or evening she grew
garrulous. 'Mother does talk so—sometimes.' She
rarely went out of doors. Chaffery always rose
late, and would sometimes go away for days
together. He was mean, he allowed her only a
weekly twenty-five shillings for housekeeping and
sometimes things grew unsatisfactory at the week-
end. There seemed to be little sympathy between
mother and daughter; the widow had been flighty
in a dingy fashion, and her marriage with her chief
lodger Chaffery had led to unforgettable sayings.
It was to facilitate this marriage that Ethel had been
sent to Whortley, so that was counted a mitigated
evil. But these were far-off things, remote and
unreal down the long, ill-lit vista of the suburban
street which swallowed up Ethel nightly. The
walk, her warmth and light and motion close to
him, her clear little voice, and the touch of her
hand; that was reality.

The shadow of Chaffery and his deceptions lay
indeed across all these things, sometimes faint,
sometimes dark and present. Then Lewisham
became insistent, his sentimental memories ceased,
and he asked questions that verged on gulfs of
doubt. Had she ever 'helped'? She had not, she
declared. Then she added that twice at home she
had 'sat down' to complete the circle. She would
never help again. That she promised—if it needed
promising. There had already been dreadful

trouble at home about the exposure at Lagune's. Her mother had sided with her stepfather and joined in blaming her. But was she to blame?

'Of *course* you were not to blame,' said Lewisham.

Lagune, he learnt, had been unhappy and restless for the three days after the *séance*—indulging in wearisome monologue—with Ethel as sole auditor (at twenty-one shillings a week). Then he had decided to give Chaffery a sound lecture on his disastrous dishonesty. But it was Chaffery gave the lecture. Smithers, had he only known it, had been overthrown by a better brain than Lagune's, albeit it spoke through Lagune's treble.

Ethel did not like talking of Chaffery and these other things. 'If you knew how sweet it was to forget it all,' she would say; 'to be just us two together for a little while.' And, 'What good *does* it do to keep on?' when Lewisham was pressing. Lewisham wanted very much to keep on at times, but the good of it was a little hard to demonstrate. So his knowledge of the situation remained imperfect and the weeks drifted by.

Wonderfully varied were those seven-and-sixty nights, as he came to remember in after life. There were nights of damp and drizzle, and then thick fogs, beautiful, isolating, gray-white veils, turning every yard of pavement into a private room. Grand indeed were these fogs, things to rejoice at mightily, since then it was no longer a thing for public scorn when two young people hurried along arm in arm, and one could do a thousand impudent, significant things with varying pressure and the fondling of a little hand (a hand in a greatly mended glove of cheap kid). Then indeed one seemed to be nearer that elusive something that threaded it all together. And the dangers of the street corners, the horses

looming up suddenly out of the dark, the carters
with lanterns at their horses' heads, the street lamps,
blurred, smoky orange at one's nearest, and vanishing at twenty yards into dim haze, seemed to
accentuate the infinite need of protection on the
part of a delicate young lady who had already
traversed three winters of fogs, thornily alone.
Moreover, one could come right down the quiet
street where she lived, half-way to the steps of
her house, with a delightful sense of enterprise.

The fogs passed all too soon into a hard frost,
into nights of starlight and presently moonlight,
when the lamps looked hard, flashing like rows of
yellow gems, and their reflections and the glare of
the shop windows were sharp and frosty, and even
the stars hard and bright, snapping noiselessly (if
one may say so) instead of twinkling. A jacket
trimmed with imitation astrachan replaced Ethel's
lighter coat, and a round cap of astrachan her hat,
and her eyes shone hard and bright, and her forehead
was broad and white beneath it. It was exhilarating, but one got home too soon, and so the way
from Chelsea to Clapham was lengthened, first into
a loop of side streets, and then when the first
pulverulent snows told that Christmas was at
hand, into a new loop down King's Road, and once
even through the Brompton Road and Sloane
Street, where the shops were full of decorations and
entertaining things.

And, under circumstances of infinite gravity, Mr
Lewisham secretly spent three-and-twenty shillings
out of the vestiges of that hundred pounds, and
bought Ethel a little gold ring set with pearls.
With that there must needs be a ceremonial, and on
the verge of the snowy, foggy Common she took
off her glove and the ring was placed on her finger.

Whereupon he was moved to kiss her—on the frost-pink knuckle next to an inky nail.

'It's silly of us,' she said. 'What can we do? —ever?'

'You wait,' he said, and his tone was full of vague promises.

Afterwards he thought over those promises, and another evening went into the matter more fully, telling her of all the brilliant things that he held it was possible for a South Kensington student to do and be—of head masterships, northern science schools, inspectorships, demonstratorships, yea, even professorships. And then, and then—— To all of which she lent a willing and incredulous ear, finding in that dreaming a quality of fear as well as delight.

The putting on of the pearl-set ring was mere ceremonial, of course; she could not wear it either at Lagune's or at home, so instead she threaded it on a little white satin ribbon and wore it round her neck—'next her heart.' He thought of it there 'warm next her heart.'

When he had bought the ring he had meant to save it for Christmas before he gave it to her. But the desire to see her pleasure had been too strong for him.

Christmas Eve, I know not by what deceit on her part, these young people spent together all day. Lagune was down with a touch of bronchitis and had given his typewriter a holiday. Perhaps she forgot to mention it at home. The Royal College was in vacation and Lewisham was free. He declined the plumber's invitation; 'work' kept him in London, he said, though it meant a pound or more of added expenditure. These absurd young people walked sixteen miles that Christmas Eve, and parted warm and glowing. There had been a hard frost and a little snow, the sky was a colourless gray, icicles hung from the arms of the street lamps, and the pavements were patterned out with frond-like forms that were trodden into slides as the day grew older. The Thames they knew was a wonderful sight, but that they kept until last. They went first along the Brompton Road. . . .

And it is well that you should have the picture of them right; Lewisham in the ready-made over-coat, blue cloth and velvet collar, dirty tan gloves, red tie, and bowler hat; and Ethel in a two-year-old jacket and hat of curly astrachan; both pink-cheeked from the keen air, shyly arm in arm occasionally, and very alert to miss no possible spectacle. The shops were varied and interesting along the Brompton Road, but nothing to compare with Piccadilly. There were windows in Piccadilly so full of costly little things, it took fifteen minutes to get them done, card shops, drapers' shops full of foolish, entertaining attractions. Lewisham, in spite of his old animosities, forgot to be severe on Shopping Class, Ethel was so vastly entertained by all these pretty follies.

Then up Regent Street by the place where the sham diamonds are, and the place where the girls display their long hair, and the place where the little chickens run about in the window, and so into Oxford Street, Holborn, Ludgate Hill, St Paul's Churchyard, to Leadenhall, and the markets where turkeys, geese, ducklings, and chickens— turkeys predominant, however—hang in rows of a thousand at a time.

'I *must* buy you something,' said Lewisham resuming a topic.

'No, no,' said Ethel, with her eye down a vista of innumerable birds.

'But I *must*,' said Lewisham. 'You had better choose it, or I shall get something wrong.' His mind ran on brooches and clasps.

'You mustn't waste your money, and besides, I have that ring.'

But Lewisham insisted.

'Then—if you must—I am starving. Buy me something to eat.'

An immense and memorable joke. Lewisham plunged recklessly — orientally — into an awe-inspiring place with mitred napkins. They lunched on cutlets—stripped the cutlets to the bone—and little crisp brown potatoes, and they drank between them a whole half-bottle of—some white wine or other, Lewisham selected in an off-hand way from the list. Neither of them had ever taken wine at a meal before. One and ninepence it cost him, Sir, and the name of it was Capri! It was really very passable Capri—a manufactured product, no doubt, but warming and aromatic. Ethel was aghast at his magnificence and drank a glass and a half.

Then, very warm and comfortable, they went down by the Tower, and the Tower Bridge with its crest of snow, huge pendant icicles, and the ice blocks choked in its side arches, was seasonable seeing. And as they had had enough of shops and crowds they set off resolutely along the desolate Embankment homeward.

But indeed the Thames was a wonderful sight that year! ice-fringed along either shore, and with drift-ice in the middle reflecting a luminous scarlet from the broad red setting sun, and moving steadily, incessantly seaward. A swarm of mewing gulls went to and fro, and with them mingled pigeons and crows. The buildings on the Surrey side were dim and gray and very mysterious, the moored,

ice-blocked barges silent and deserted, and here
and there a lit window shone warm. The sun sank
right out of sight into a bank of blue, and the
Surrey side dissolved in mist save for a few insoluble
spots of yellow light, that presently became many.
And after our lovers had come under Charing Cross
Bridge the Houses of Parliament rose before them
at the end of a great crescent of golden lamps,
blue and faint, half-way between the earth and sky.
And the clock on the Tower was like a November
sun.

It was a day without a flaw, or at most but the
slightest speck. And that only came at the very
end.

'Good-bye, dear,' she said. 'I have been very
happy to-day.'

His face came very close to hers. 'Good-bye,'
he said, pressing her hand and looking into her
eyes.

She glanced round, she drew nearer to him.
'*Dearest* one,' she whispered very softly, and then,
'Good-bye.'

Suddenly he became unaccountably petulant, he
dropped her hand. 'It's always like this. We are
happy. *I* am happy. And then—then you are
taken away. . . .'

There was a silence of mute interrogations.

'Dear,' she whispered, 'we must wait.'

A moment's pause. '*Wait!*' he said, and broke
off. He hesitated. 'Good-bye,' he said, as though
he was snapping a thread that held them together.

CHAPTER XVI

MISS HEYDINGER'S PRIVATE THOUGHTS

THE way from Chelsea to Clapham and the way
from South Kensington to Battersea, especially if
the former is looped about a little to make it longer,
come very near to each other. One night close
upon Christmas two friends of Lewisham's passed
him and Ethel. But Lewisham did not see them,
because he was looking at Ethel's face.

'Did you see?' said the other girl, a little
maliciously.

'Mr Lewisham—wasn't it?' said Miss Heydinger
in a perfectly indifferent tone.

Miss Heydinger sat in the room her younger
sisters called her 'Sanctum.' Her Sanctum was
only too evidently an intellectualised bedroom, and
a cheap wall-paper of silvery roses peeped coquet-
tishly from among her draped furniture. Her
particular glories were the writing-desk in the
middle and the microscope on the unsteady octag-
onal table under the window. There were book-
shelves of workmanship patently feminine in their
facile decoration and structural instability, and on
them an array of glittering poets, Shelley, Rossetti,
Keats, Browning, and odd volumes of Ruskin, South
Place Sermons, Socialistic publications in torn paper
covers, and above, science text-books and notebooks in an oppressive abundance. The autotypes
that hung about the room were eloquent of æsthetic

ambitions and of a certain impermeability to implicit meanings. There was the Mirror of Venus by Burne Jones, Rossetti's Annunciation, Lippi's Annunciation, and the Love of Life and Love and Death of Watts. And among other photographs was one of last year's Debating Society Committee. Lewisham smiling a little weakly near the centre, and Miss Heydinger out of focus in the right wing, And Miss Heydinger sat with her back to all these things, in her black horsehair arm-chair, staring into the fire, her eyes hot, and her chin on her hand.

'I might have guessed—before,' she said. 'Ever since that *séance*. It has been different . . .'

She smiled bitterly. 'Some shop girl . . .'

She mused. 'They are all alike, I suppose. They come back—a little damaged, as the woman says in *Lady Windermere's Fan*. Perhaps he will. I wonder . . .

'Why should he be so deceitful? Why should he act to me? . . .'

'Pretty, pretty, pretty—that is our business. What man hesitates in the choice? He goes his own way, thinks his own thoughts, does his own work . . .

'His dissection is getting behind—one can see he takes scarcely any notes. . . .'

For a long time she was silent. Her face became more intent. She began to bite her thumb, at first slowly, then faster. She broke out at last into words again.

'The things he might do, the great things he might do. He is able, he is dogged, he is strong. And then comes a pretty face! Oh, God! *Why* was I made with heart and brain?' She sprang to her feet, with her hands clenched and her face contorted. But she shed no tears.

Her attitude fell limp in a moment. One hand dropped by her side, the other rested on a fossil on the mantel-shelf, and she stared down into the red fire.

'To think of all we might have done! It maddens me!

'To work, and think, and learn. To hope and wait. To despise the petty arts of womanliness, to trust to the sanity of man . . .

'To awake like the foolish virgins,' she said, 'and find the hour of life is past!'

Her face, her pose, softened into self-pity.

'Futility . . .

'It's no good. . . .' Her voice broke.

'I shall never be happy. . . .'

She saw the grandiose vision of the future she had cherished, suddenly rolled aside and vanishing, more and more splendid as it grew more and more remote—like a dream at the waking moment. The vision of her inevitable loneliness came to replace it, clear and acute. She saw herself alone and small in a huge desolation—infinitely pitiful, Lewisham callously receding. With 'some shop girl.' The tears came, came faster, until they were streaming down her face. She turned, as if looking for something. She flung herself upon her knees before the little arm-chair, and began an incoherent sobbing prayer for the pity and comfort of God.

The next day one of the other girls in the biological course remarked to her friend that 'Heydinger-dingery' had relapsed. Her friend glanced down the laboratory. 'It's a bad relapse,' she said. 'Really . . . I couldn't . . . wear my hair like that.'

She continued to regard Miss Heydinger with a

critical eye. She was free to do this because Miss
Heydinger was standing, lost in thought, staring at
the December fog outside the laboratory windows.
'She looks white,' said the girl who had originally
spoken. 'I wonder if she works hard.'

'It makes precious little difference if she does,'
said her friend. 'I asked her yesterday what were
the bones in the parietal segment, and she didn't
know one. Not one.'

The next day Miss Heydinger's place was vacant.
She was ill—from overstudy—and her illness lasted
to within three weeks of the terminal examination.
Then she came back with a pallid face and a
strenuous unavailing industry.

CHAPTER XVII

IN THE RAPHAEL GALLERY

IT was nearly three o'clock, and in the Biological Laboratory the lamps were all alight. The class was busy with razors cutting sections of the root of a fern to examine it microscopically. A certain silent frog-like boy, a private student who plays no further part in this story, was working intently, looking more like a frog than usual—his expression modest with a touch of effort. Behind Miss Heydinger, jaded and untidy in her early manner again, was a vacant seat, an abandoned microscope, and scattered pencils and notebooks.

On the door of the class-room was a list of those who had passed the Christmas examination. At the head of it was the name of the aforesaid frog-like boy; next to him came Smithers and one of the girls bracketed together. Lewisham ingloriously headed the second class, and Miss Heydinger's name did not appear—there was, the list asserted, 'one failure.' So the student pays for the finer emotions.

And in the spacious solitude of the museum gallery devoted to the Raphael cartoons, sat Lewisham, plunged in gloomy meditation. A negligent hand pulled thoughtfully at the indisputable moustache, with particular attention to such portions as were long enough to gnaw.

He was trying to see the situation clearly. As

109

he was just smarting acutely under his defeat, this speaks little for the clearness of his mind. The shadow of that defeat lay across everything, blotted out the light of his pride, shaded his honour, threw everything into a new perspective. The rich prettiness of his lovemaking had fled to some remote quarter of his being. Against the frog-like youngster he felt a savage animosity. And Smithers had betrayed him. He was angry, bitterly angry with 'swats' and 'muggers' who spent their whole time grinding for these foolish chancy examinations. Nor had the practical examination been altogether fair, and one of the questions in the written portion was quite outside the lectures. Biver, Professor Biver, was an indiscriminating ass, he felt assured, and so too was Weeks, the demonstrator. But these obstacles could not blind his intelligence to the manifest cause of his overthrow, the waste of more than half his available evening, the best time for study in the twenty-four hours, day after day. And that was going on steadily, a perpetual leakage of time. To-night he would go to meet her again, and begin to accumulate to himself ignominy in the second part of the course, the botanical section, also. And so, reluctantly rejecting one cloudy excuse after another, he clearly focused the antagonism between his relations to Ethel and his immediate ambitions.

Things had come so easily to him for the last two years that he had taken his steady upward progress in life as assured. It had never occurred to him, when he went to intercept Ethel after that *séance*, that he went into any peril of that sort. Now he had had a sharp reminder. He began to shape a picture of the frog-like boy at home—he was a private student of the upper middle-class—sitting in a convenient study with a writing-table, book-shelves, and a shaded lamp—Lewisham worked at his chest of drawers, with his greatcoat on, and his feet in the lowest drawer wrapped in all his available linen—and in the midst of incredible conveniences the frog-like boy was working, working, working. Meanwhile Lewisham toiled through the foggy streets, Chelsea-ward, or, after he had left her, tramped homeward—full of foolish imaginings.

He began to think with bloodless lucidity of his entire relationship to Ethel. His softer emotions were in abeyance, but he told himself no lies. He cared for her, he loved to be with her and to talk to her and please her, but that was not all his desire. He thought of the bitter words of an orator at Hammersmith, who had complained that in our present civilisation even the elemental need of marriage was denied. Virtue had become a vice. 'We marry in fear and trembling, sex for a home is the woman's traffic, and the man comes to his heart's desire when his heart's desire is dead.' The thing which had seemed a mere flourish, came back now with a terrible air of truth. Lewisham saw that it was a case of divergent ways. On the one hand that shining staircase to fame and power, that had been his dream from the very dawn of his adolescence, and on the other hand—Ethel.

And if he chose Ethel, even then, would he have his choice? What would come of it? A few walks more or less! She was hopelessly poor, he was hopelessly poor, and this cheat of a Medium was her stepfather! After all she was not well-educated, she did not understand his work and his aims. . . .

He suddenly perceived with absolute conviction that after the *séance* he should have gone home and forgotten her. Why had he felt that irresistible

impulse to seek her out? Why had his imagination
spun such a strange web of possibilities about her?
He was involved now, foolishly involved. . . . All
his future was a sacrifice to this transitory ghost of
lovemaking in the streets. He pulled spitefully at
his moustache.

His picture began to shape itself into Ethel, and
her mysterious mother and the vague, dexterous
Chaffery holding him back, entangled in an impalpable net from that bright and glorious ascent to
performance and distinction. Leaky boots and the
splash of cabs for all his life as his portion! Already
the Forbes Medal, the immediate step, was as good
as lost. . . .

What on earth had he been thinking about? He
fell foul of his upbringing. Men of the upper or
middle classes were put up to these things by their
parents; they were properly warned against involving themselves in this love nonsense before they
were independent. It was much better. . . .

Everything was going. Not only his work—his
scientific career, but the Debating Society, the
political movement, all his work for Humanity.
. . . Why not be resolute—even now? . . . Why
not put the thing clearly and plainly to her? Or
write? If he wrote now he could get the advantage
of the evening at the Library. He must ask her
to forgo these walks home—at least until the next
examination. *She* would understand. He had a
qualm of doubt whether she would understand.
. . . He grew angry at this possibility. But it was
no good mincing matters. If once he began to
consider her—— Why should he consider her in
that way? Simply because she was unreasonable!

Lewisham had a transitory gust of anger.

Yet that abandonment of the walks insisted on

looking mean to him. And she would think it mean. Which was very much worse, somehow. *Why* mean? Why should she think it mean? He grew angry again.

The portly museum policeman who had been watching him furtively, wondering why a student should sit in front of the 'Sacrifice of Lystra' and gnaw lips and nails and moustache and scowl and glare at that masterpiece, saw him rise suddenly to his feet with an air of resolution, spin on his heel, and set off with a quick step out of the gallery. He looked neither to the right nor the left. He passed out of sight down the staircase.

'Gone to get some more moustache to eat, I suppose,' said the policeman reflectively. . . .

'One 'ud think something had bit him.'

After some pensive moments the policeman strolled along down the gallery and came to a stop opposite the cartoon.

'Figgers is a bit big for the houses,' said the policeman, anxious to do impartial justice. 'But that's Art. I lay 'e couldn't do anything . . . not arf so good.'

CHAPTER XVIII

THE FRIENDS OF PROGRESS MEET

THE next night but one after this meditation saw a new order in the world. A young lady dressed in an astrachan-edged jacket and with a face of diminished cheerfulness marched from Chelsea to Clapham alone, and Lewisham sat in the flickering electric light of the Education Library, staring blankly over a businesslike pile of books at unseen things.

The arrangement had not been effected without friction, the explanation had proved difficult. Evidently she did not appreciate the full seriousness of Lewisham's mediocre position in the list. 'But you have *passed* all right,' she said. Neither could she grasp the importance of evening study. 'Of course I don't know,' she said judicially; 'but I thought you were learning all day.' She calculated the time consumed by their walk as half an hour, 'just one half-hour,' she forgot that he had to get to Chelsea and then to return to his lodgings. Her customary tenderness was veiled by an only too apparent resentment. First at him, and then when he protested, at Fate. 'I suppose it *has* to be,' she said. 'Of course, it doesn't matter, I suppose, if we *don't* see each other quite so often,' with a quiver of pale lips.

He had returned from the parting with an uneasy mind, and that evening had gone in the composition of a letter that was to make things clearer. But his scientific studies rendered his prose style 'hard,' and things he could whisper he could not write. His justification indeed did him no sort of justice. But her reception of it made her seem a very unreasonable person. He had some violent fluctuations. At times he was bitterly angry with her for her failure to see things as he did. He would wander about the museum conducting imaginary discussions with her and making even scathing remarks. At other times he had to summon all his powers of acrid discipline and all his memories of her resentful retorts, to keep himself from a headlong rush to Chelsea and unmanly capitulation.

And this new disposition of things endured for two weeks. It did not take Miss Heydinger all that time to discover that the disaster of the examination had wrought a change in Lewisham. She perceived those nightly walks were over. It was speedily evident to her that he was working with a kind of dogged fury; he came early, he went late. The wholesome freshness of his cheek paled. He was to be seen on each of the late nights amidst a pile of diagrams and text-books in one of the less draughty corners of the Educational Library, accumulating piles of memoranda. And nightly in the Students' 'club' he wrote a letter addressed to a stationer's shop in Clapham, but that she did not see. For the most part these letters were brief, for Lewisham, South Kensington fashion, prided himself upon not being 'literary,' and some of the more despatch-like wounded a heart perhaps too hungry for tender words.

He did not meet Miss Heydinger's renewed advances with invariable kindness. Yet something of the old relations were presently restored. He would talk well to her for a time, and then snap like a dry twig. But the loaning of books was resumed, the subtle process of his æsthetic education that Miss Heydinger had devised. 'Here is a book I promised you,' she said one day, and he tried to remember the promise.

The book was a collection of Browning's Poems, and it contained *Sludge*; it also happened that it contained *The Statue and the Bust*— that stimulating lecture on half-hearted constraints. *Sludge* did not interest Lewisham, it was not at all his idea of a medium, but he read and re-read *The Statue and the Bust*. It had the profoundest effect upon him. He went to sleep—he used to read his literature in bed because it was warmer there, and over literature nowadays it did not matter as it did with science if one dozed a little—with these lines stimulating his emotion :—

'So weeks grew months, years; gleam by gleam
The glory dropped from their youth and love,
And both perceived they had dreamed a dream.'

By way of fruit it may be to such seed, he dreamed a dream that night. It concerned Ethel, and at last they were a-marrying. He drew her to his arms. He bent to kiss her. And suddenly he saw her lips were shrivelled and her eyes were dull, saw the wrinkles seaming her face ! She was old ! She was intolerably old ! He woke in a kind of horror and lay awake and very dismal until dawn, thinking of their separation and of her solitary walk through the muddy streets, thinking of his position, the leeway he had lost and the chances there were against him in the battle of the world. He perceived the colourless truth; the Career was improbable, and that Ethel should be added to it was almost hopeless. Clearly the question was

between these two. Or should he vacillate and
lose both? And then his wretchedness gave place
to that anger that comes of perpetually thwarted
desires. . . .

It was on the day after this dream that he insulted
Parkson so grossly. He insulted Parkson after a
meeting of the 'Friends of Progress' at Parkson's
rooms.

No type of English student quite realises the
noble ideal of plain living and high thinking nowadays. Our admirable examination system admits
of extremely little thinking at any level, high or
low. But the Kensington student's living is at any
rate insufficient, and he makes occasional signs of
recognition towards the cosmic process.

One such sign was the periodic gathering of these
'Friends of Progress,' an association begotten of
Lewisham's paper on Socialism. It was understood
that strenuous things were to be done to make the
world better, but so far no decisive action had been
taken.

They met in Parkson's sitting-room, because
Parkson was the only one of the Friends opulent
enough to have a sitting-room, he being a Whit-
worth Scholar and in receipt of one hundred pounds
a year. The Friends were of various ages, mostly
very young. Several smoked and others held pipes
which they had discontinued smoking—but there
was nothing to drink, except coffee, because that
was the extent of their means. Dunkerley, an
assistant master in a suburban school, and Lewisham's former colleague at Whortley, attended these
assemblies through the introduction of Lewisham.
All the Friends wore red ties except Bletherley,
who wore an orange one to show that he was aware
of Art, and Dunkerley, who wore a black one with

blue specks, because assistant masters in small private schools have to keep up appearances. And their simple procedure was that each talked as much as the others would suffer.

Usually the self-proposed 'Luther of Socialism' —ridiculous Lewisham!—had a thesis or so to maintain, but this night he was depressed and inattentive. He sat with his legs over the arm of his chair by way of indicating the state of his mind. He had a packet of Algerian cigarettes (twenty for fivepence) and appeared chiefly concerned to smoke them all before the evening was out. Bletherley was going to discourse of 'Women under Socialism,' and he brought a big American edition of Shelley's works and a volume of Tennyson with the *Princess*, both bristling with paper tongues against his marked quotations. He was all for the abolition of 'monopolies,' and the *crèche* was to replace the family. He was unctuous when he was not pretty-pretty, and his views were evidently unpopular.

Parkson was a man from Lancashire, and a devout Quaker; his third and completing factor was Ruskin, with whose work and phraseology he was saturated. He listened to Bletherley with a marked disapproval, and opened a vigorous defence of that ancient tradition of loyalty that Bletherley had called the monopolist institution of marriage. 'The pure and simple old theory—love and faithfulness,' said Parkson, 'suffices for me. If we are to smear our political movements with this sort of stuff . . .'

'Does it work?' interjected Lewisham, speaking for the first time.

'What work?'

'The pure and simple old theory. I know the

theory. I believe in the theory. Bletherley's Shelley-witted. But it's theory. You meet the inevitable girl. The theory says you may meet her anywhen. You meet too young. You fall in love. You marry—in spite of obstacles. Love laughs at locksmiths. You have children. That's the theory. All very well for a man whose father can leave him five hundred a year. But how does it work for a shopman? . . . An assistant master like Dunkerley? Or . . . Me?'

'In these cases one must exercise restraint,' said Parkson. 'Have faith. A man that is worth having is worth waiting for.'

'Worth growing old for?' said Lewisham.

'Chap ought to fight,' said Dunkerley. 'Don't see your difficulty, Lewisham. Struggle for existence keen, no doubt, tremendous, in fact—still. In it —may as well struggle. Two—join forces—pool the luck. If I saw, a girl I fancied so that I wanted to, I'd marry her to-morrow. And my market value is seventy *non res.*'

Lewisham looked round at him eagerly, suddenly interested. '*Would* you?' he said. Dunkerley's face was slightly flushed.

'Like a shot. Why not?'

'But how are you to live?'

'That comes after. If . . .'

'I can't agree with you, Mr Dunkerley,' said Parkson. 'I don't know if you have read *Sesame and Lilies*, but there you have, set forth far more fairly than any words of mine could do, an ideal of a woman's place . . .'

'All rot—*Sesame and Lilies*,' interrupted Dunkerley. 'Read bits. Couldn't stand it. Never *can* stand Ruskin. Too many prepositions. Tremendous English, no doubt, but not my style.

Sort of thing a wholesale grocer's daughter might read to get refined. *We* can't afford to get refined.'

'But would you really marry a girl . . .?' began Lewisham, with an unprecedented admiration for Dunkerley in his eyes.

'Why not?'

'On——? Lewisham hesitated.

'Forty pounds a year *res*. Whack! Yes.'

A silent youngster began to speak, cleared an accumulated huskiness from his throat and said, 'Consider the girl.'

'Why *marry*?' asked Bletherley, unregarded.

'You must admit you are asking a great thing when you want a girl . . .' began Parkson.

'Not so. When a girl's chosen a man, and he chooses her, her place is with him. What is the good of hankering. Mutual. Fight together.'

'Good!' said Lewisham, suddenly emotional. 'You talk like a man, Dunkerley. I'm hanged if you don't.'

'The place of Woman,' insisted Parkson, 'is the Home. And if there is no home——! I hold that, if need be, a man should toil seven years—as Jacob did for Rachel—ruling his passions, to make the home fitting and sweet for her . . .'

'Get the hutch for the pet animal,' said Dunkerley. 'No. I mean to marry a *woman*. Female sex always *has* been in the struggle for existence—no great damage so far—always will be. Tremendous idea —that struggle for existence. Only sensible theory you've got hold of, Lewisham. Woman who isn't fighting square side by side with a man—woman who's just kept and fed and petted is . . .' He hesitated.

A lad with a spotted face and a bulldog pipe between his teeth supplied a Biblical word.

'That's shag,' said Dunkerley. 'I was going to say " a harem of one." '

The youngster was puzzled for a moment. 'I smoke Perique,' he said.

'It will make you just as sick,' said Dunkerley.

'Refinement's so beastly vulgar,' was the belated answer of the smoker of Perique.

That was the interesting part of the evening to Lewisham. Parkson suddenly rose, got down *Sesame and Lilies,* and insisted upon reading a lengthy mellifluous extract that went like a garden roller over the debate, and afterwards Bletherley became the centre of a wrangle that left him grossly insulted and in a minority of one. The institution of marriage, so far as the South Kensington student is concerned, is in no immediate danger.

Parkson turned out with the rest of them at half-past ten, for a walk. The night was warm for February and the waxing moon bright. Parkson fixed himself upon Lewisham and Dunkerley, to Lewisham's intense annoyance—for he had a few intimate things he could have said to the man of Ideas that night. Dunkerley lived north, so that the three went up Exhibition Road to High Street, Kensington. There they parted from Dunkerley and Lewisham and Parkson turned southward again for Lewisham's new lodging in Chelsea.

Parkson was one of those exponents of virtue for whom the discussion of sexual matters has an irresistible attraction. The meeting had left him eloquent. He had argued with Dunkerley to the verge of indelicacy, and now he poured out a vast and increasingly confidential flow of talk upon Lewisham. Lewisham was distraught. He walked as fast as he could. His sole object was to get rid of Parkson. Parkson's sole object was to tell

him interesting secrets, about himself and a Certain
Person with a mind of extraordinary Purity of
whom Lewisham had heard before.

Ages passed.

Lewisham suddenly found himself being shown
a photograph under a lamp. It represented an
unsymmetrical face singularly void of expression,
the upper part of an 'art' dress, and a fringe of
curls. He perceived he was being given to understand that this was a Paragon of Purity, and that
she was the particular property of Parkson. Park-
was regarding him proudly and apparently awaiting
his verdict.

Lewisham struggled with the truth. 'It's an
interesting face,' he said.

'It is a face essentially beautiful,' said Parkson
quietly but firmly. 'Do you notice the eyes,
Lewisham?'

'Oh, yes,' said Lewisham. 'Yes. I see the
eyes.'

'They are . . . innocent. They are the eyes of
a little child.'

'Yes. They look that sort of eye. Very nice,
old man. I congratulate you. Where does she
live?'

'You never saw a face like that in London,'
said Parkson.

'*Never*,' said Lewisham decisively.

'I would not show that to every one,' said
Parkson. 'You can scarcely judge all that pure-
hearted, wonderful girl is to me.' He returned
the photograph solemnly to its envelope, regarding
Lewisham with an air of one who has performed the
ceremony of blood-brotherhood. Then, taking
Lewisham's arm affectionately—a thing Lewisham
detested—he went on to a copious outpouring on

Love—with illustrative anecdotes of the Paragon.
It was just sufficiently cognate to the matter of
Lewisham's thoughts to demand attention. Every
now and then he had to answer, and he felt an
idiotic desire—albeit he clearly perceived its idiocy
—to reciprocate confidences. The necessity of
fleeing Parkson became urgent—Lewisham's temper
under these multitudinous stresses was going.

'Every man needs a Lodestar,' said Parkson
—and Lewisham swore under his breath.

Parkson's lodgings were now near at hand to
the left, and it occurred to him this boredom would
be soonest ended if he took Parkson home. Parkson
consented mechanically, still discoursing.

'I have often seen you talking to Miss Heydinger,' he said. 'If you will pardon my saying
it . . .'

'We are excellent friends,' admitted Lewisham.
'But here we are at your diggings.'

Parkson stared at his 'diggings.' 'There's Heaps
I want to talk about. I'll come part of the way at
any rate to Battersea. Your Miss Heydinger, I
was saying . . .'

From that point onwards he made casual appeals
to a supposed confidence between Lewisham and
Miss Heydinger, each of which increased Lewisham's
exasperation. 'It will not be long before you also,
Lewisham, will begin to know the infinite purifi-
cation of a Pure Love. . . .' Then suddenly, with
a vague idea of suppressing Parkson's unendurable
chatter, as one motive at least, Lewisham rushed
into the confidential.

'I know,' he said. 'You talk to me as though
. . . I've marked out my destiny these three years.'
His confidential impulse died as he relieved
it.

'You don't mean to say Miss Heydinger——?'
asked Parkson.

'Oh, *damn* Miss Heydinger!' said Lewisham,
and suddenly, abruptly, uncivilly, he turned away
from Parkson at the end of the street and began
walking away southward, leaving Parkson in mid-
sentence at the crossing.

Parkson stared in astonishment at his receding
back and ran after him to ask for the grounds of
this sudden offence. Lewisham walked on for a
space with Parkson trotting by his side. Then
suddenly he turned. His face was quite white and
he spoke in a tired voice.

'Parkson,' he said, 'you are a fool! . . . You
have the face of a sheep, the manners of a buffalo,
and the conversation of a bore. Pewrity indeed!
. . . The girl whose photograph you showed me
has eyes that don't match. She looks as loathsome
as one would naturally expect. . . . I'm not joking
now. . . . Go away!'

After that Lewisham went on his southward way
alone. He did not go straight to his room in
Chelsea, but spent some hours in a street in
Battersea, pacing to and fro in front of a possible
house. His passion changed from savageness to a
tender longing. If only he could see her to-night!
He knew his own mind now. To-morrow he was
resolved he would fling work to the dogs and
meet her. The things Dunkerley had said had filled
his mind with wonderful novel thoughts. If only
he could see her now!

His wish was granted. At the corner of the
street two figures passed him: one of these, a
tall man in glasses and a quasi-clerical hat, with
coat collar turned up under his gray side-whiskers,
he recognised as Chaffery; the other he knew only

too well. The pair passed him without seeing him, but for an instant the lamp-light fell upon her face and showed it white and tired.

Lewisham stopped dead at the corner, staring in blank astonishment after these two figures as they receded into the haze under the lights. He was dumbfounded. A clock struck slowly. It was midnight. Presently down the road came the slamming of their door.

Long after the echo died away he stood there. 'She has been at a *séance*; she has broken her promise. She has been at a *séance*, she has broken her promise,' sang in perpetual reiteration through his brain.

And then came the interpretation. 'She has done it because I have left her. I might have told it from her letters. She has done it because she thinks I am not in earnest, that my lovemaking was just boyishness . . .

'I knew she would never understand.'

CHAPTER XIX

LEWISHAM'S SOLUTION

THE next morning Lewisham learnt from Lagune that his intuition was correct, that Ethel had at last succumbed to pressure and consented to attempt thought-reading. 'We made a good beginning,' said Lagune, rubbing his hands. 'I am sure we shall do well with her. Certainly she has powers.' I have always felt it in her face. She has powers.'

'Was much . . . pressure necessary?' asked Lewisham by an effort.

'We had—considerable difficulty. Considerable. But of course—as I pointed out to her—it was scarcely possible for her to continue as my type-writer unless she was disposed to take an interest in my investigations——'

'You did that?'

'Had to. Fortunately Chaffery—it was his idea. I must admit——'

Lagune stopped, astonished. Lewisham, after making an odd sort of movement with his hands, had turned round and was walking away down the laboratory. Lagune stared, confronted by a psychic phenomenon beyond his circle of ideas. 'Odd!' he said at last, and began to unpack his bag. Ever and again he stopped and stared at Lewisham, who was now sitting in his own place and drumming on the table with both hands.

Presently Miss Heydinger came out of the specimen room and addressed a remark to the young

man. He appeared to answer with considerable
brevity. He then stood up, hesitated for a moment
between the three doors of the laboratory, and
walked out by that opening on the back staircase.
Lagune did not see him again until the afternoon.

That night Ethel had Lewisham's company again
on her way home, and their voices were earnest
She did not go straight home, but instead they
went up under the gas lamps to the vague spaces
of Clapham Common to talk there at length. And
the talk that night was a momentous one. 'Why
have you broken your promise?' he said.

Her excuses were vague and weak. 'I thought
you did not care so much as you did,' she said.
'And when you stopped these walks—nothing
seemed to matter. Besides—it is not like *séances*
with spirits . . .'

At first Lewisham was passionate and forcible.
His anger at Lagune and Chaffery blinded him to
her turpitude. He talked her defences down.
'It is cheating,' he said. 'Well—even if what
you do is not cheating, it is delusion—unconscious
cheating. Even if there is something in it, it is
wrong. True or not, it is wrong. Why don't they
thought-read each other? Why should they want
you? Your mind is your own. It is sacred. To
probe it!—I won't have it! I won't have it! At
least you are mine to that extent. I can't think
of you like that—bandaged. And that little fool
pressing his hand on the back of your neck and asking
questions. I won't have it! I would rather kill
you than that.'

'They don't do that!

'I don't care! that is what it will come to.
The bandage is the beginning. People must not
get their living in that way anyhow. I've thought

it out. Let them thought-read their daughters
and hypnotise their aunts, and leave their typewriters alone.'

'But what am I to do?'

'That's not it. There are things one must not
suffer anyhow, whatever happens! Or else—one
might be made to do anything. Honour! Just
because we are poor—Let him dismiss you! *Let*
him dismiss you. You can get another place——'

'Not at a guinea a week.'

'Then take less.'

'But I have to pay sixteen shillings every week.'

'That doesn't matter.'

She caught at a sob. 'But to leave London—
I can't do it. I can't.'

'But how?—Leave London?' Lewisham's face
changed.

'Oh! life is *hard*,' she said. 'I can't. They—
they wouldn't let me stop in London.'

'What do you mean?'

She explained if Lagune dismissed her she was
to go into the country to an aunt, a sister of
Chaffery's who needed a companion. Chaffery
insisted upon that. 'Companion they call it. I
shall be just a servant—she has no servant. My
mother cries when I talk to her. She tells me she
doesn't want me to go away from her. But she's
afraid of him. " Why don't you do what he wants? "
she says.'

She sat staring in front of her at the gathering
night. She spoke again in an even tone.

'I hate telling you these things. It is you . . .
If you didn't mind. . . . But you make it all different. I could do it—if it wasn't for you. I was
. . . I *was* helping. . . . I had gone meaning to
help if anything went wrong at Mr Lagune's. Yes

—that night. No . . . don't! It was too hard
before to tell you. But I really did not feel it . . .
until I saw you there. Then all at once I felt shabby
and mean.'

'Well?' said Lewisham.

'That's all. I may have done thought-reading,
but I have never really cheated since—*never*. . . .
If you knew how hard it is . . .'

'I wish you had told me that before.'

'I couldn't. Before you came it was different.
He used to make fun of the people—used to imitate
Lagune and make me laugh. It seemed a sort of
joke.' She stopped abruptly. 'Why did you ever
come on with me? I told you not to—you *know*
I did.'

She was near wailing. For a minute she was
silent.

'I can't go to his sister's,' she cried. 'I may be
a coward—but I can't.'

Pause. And then Lewisham saw his solution
straight and clear. Suddenly his secret desire had
become his manifest duty.

'Look here,' he said, not looking at her and
pulling his moustache. 'I won't have you doing
any more of that damned cheating. You shan't
soil yourself any more. And I won't have you leaving
London.'

'But what am I to do?' Her voice went up.

'Well—there is one thing you can do. If you
dare.'

'What is it?'

He made no answer for some seconds. Then he
turned round and sat looking at her. Their eyes
met. . . .

The gray of his mind began to colour. Her face
was white and she was looking at him, in fear and

perplexity. A new tenderness for her sprang up
in him—a new feeling. Hitherto he had loved and
desired her sweetness and animation—but now
she was white and weary-eyed. He felt as though
he had forgotten her and suddenly remembered.
A great longing came into his mind.

'But what is the other thing I can do?'

It was strangely hard to say. There came a
peculiar sensation in his throat and facial muscles,
a nervous stress between laughing and crying.
All the world vanished before that great desire.
And he was afraid she would not dare, that she
would not take him seriously.

'What is it?' she said again.

'Don't you see that we can marry?' he said,
with the flood of his resolution suddenly strong
and steady. 'Don't you see that is the only thing
for us? The dead lane we are in! You must come
out of your cheating, and I must come out of my
. . . cramming. And we—we must marry.'

He paused and then became eloquent. 'The
world is against us, against—us. To you it offers
money to cheat—to be ignoble. For it *is* ignoble!
It offers you no honest way, only a miserable
drudgery. And it keeps you from me. And me too
it bribes with the promise of success—if I will
desert you. . . . You don't know all. . . . We may
have to wait for years—we may have to wait for
ever, if we wait until life is safe. We may be
separated. . . . We may lose one another altogether.
. . . Let us fight against it. Why should we
separate? Unless True Love is like the other
things—an empty cant. This is the only way.
We two—who belong to one another.'

She looked at him, her face perplexed with this
new idea, her heart beating very fast. 'We are so

young,' she said. 'And how are we to live? You get a guinea.'

'I can get more—I can earn more. I have thought it out. I have been thinking of it these two days. I have been thinking what we could do. I have money.'

'You have money?'

'Nearly a hundred pounds.'

'But we are so young—— And my mother . . .'

'We won't ask her. We will ask no one. This is *our* affair. Ethel! this is *our* affair. It is not a question of ways and means—even before this— I have thought. . . . Dear one!—*don't* you love me?'

She did not grasp his emotional quality. She looked at him with puzzled eyes—still practical— making the suggestion arithmetical.

'I could typewrite if I had a machine. I have heard——'

'It's not a question of ways and means. Now. Ethel—I have longed——'

He stopped. She looked at his face, at his eyes now eager and eloquent with the things that never shaped themselves into words.

'*Dare* you come with me?' he whispered.

Suddenly the world opened out in reality to her as sometimes it had opened out to her in wistful dreams. And she quailed before it. She dropped her eyes from his. She became a fellow-conspirator. 'But, how——?'

'I will think how. Trust me! Surely we know each other now—— Think! We two——'

'But I have never thought——'

'I could get apartments for us both. It would be so easy. And think of it—think—of what life would be!'

'How can I?'

'You will come?'

She looked at him, startled. 'You know,' she said, 'you must know I would like—I would love——'

'You will come.'

'But dear——! Dear, if you *make* me——

'Yes!' cried Lewisham triumphantly. 'You will come.' He glanced round and his voice dropped. 'Oh! my dearest! my dearest! . . .'

His voice sank to an inaudible whisper. But his face was eloquent. Two garrulous, home-going clerks passed opportunely to remind him that his emotions were in a public place.

CHAPTER XX

On the Wednesday afternoon following this—it was hard upon the botanical examination—Mr Lewisham was observed by Smithers in the big Education Library reading in a volume of the British Encyclopædia. Beside him were the current Whitaker's Almanac, an open notebook, a book from the Contemporary Science Series, and the Science and Art Department's Directory. Smithers, who had a profound sense of Lewisham's superiority in the art of obtaining facts of value in examinations, wondered for some minutes what valuable tip for a student in botany might be hidden in Whitaker, and on reaching his lodgings spent some time over the landlady's copy. But really Lewisham was not studying botany, but the art of marriage according to the best authorities. (The book from the Contemporary Science Series was Professor Letourneau's *Evolution of Marriage*. It was interesting certainly, but of little immediate use.)

From Whitaker Lewisham learnt that it would be possible at a cost of £2 6s. 1d. or £2 7s. 1d. (one of the items was ambiguous) to get married within the week—that charge being exclusive of vails—at the district registry office. He did little addition sums in the notebook. The church fees he found were variable, but for more personal reasons he rejected a marriage at church. Marriage by certificate at a registrar's involved an inconvenient delay.

It would have to be £2 7s. 1d. Vails—ten shillings, say

Afterwards, without needless ostentation, he produced a cheque-book and a deposit-book, and proceeded to further arithmetic. He found that he was master of £61 4s. 7d. Not a hundred as he had said, but a fine big sum—men have started great businesses on less. It had been a hundred originally. Allowing five pounds for the marriage and moving, this would leave about £56. Plenty. No provision was made for flowers, carriages, or the honeymoon. But there would be a typewriter to buy. Ethel was to do her share. . . .

'It will be a devilish close thing,' said Lewisham with a quite unreasonable exultation. For, strangely enough, the affair was beginning to take on a flavour of adventure not at all unpleasant. He leant back in his chair with the notebook closed in his hand. . . .

But there was much to see to that afternoon. First of all he had to discover the district superintendent registrar, and then to find a lodging whither he should take Ethel—their lodging, where they were to live together.

At the thought of that new life together that was drawing so near, she came into his head, vivid and near and warm. . . .

He recovered himself from a day dream. He became aware of a library attendant down the room leaning forward over his desk, gnawing the tip of a paper knife after the fashion of South Kensington library attendants, and staring at him curiously. It occurred to Lewisham that thought-reading was one of the most possible things in the world. He blushed, rose clumsily, and took the volume of the Encyclopædia back to its shelf.

He found the selection of lodgings a difficult business. After his first essay he began to fancy himself a suspicious-looking character, and that perhaps hampered him. He had chosen the district southward of the Brompton Road. It had one disadvantage—he might blunder into a house with a fellow-student. . . . Not that it mattered vitally. But the fact is, it is rather unusual for married couples to live permanently in furnished lodgings in London. People who are too poor to take a house or a flat commonly find it best to take part of a house or unfurnished apartments. There are a hundred couples living in unfurnished rooms (with 'the use of the kitchen') to one in furnished in London. The absence of furniture predicates a dangerous want of capital to the discreet landlady. The first landlady Lewisham interviewed didn't like ladies, they required such a lot of attendance, the second was of the same mind, the third told Mr Lewisham he was 'youngish to be married,' the fourth said she only 'did' for single 'gents.' The fifth was a young person with an arch manner, who liked to know all about people she took in, and subjected Lewisham to a searching cross-examination. When she had spitted him in a downright lie or so, she expressed an opinion that her rooms 'would scarcely do,' and bowed him amiably out.

He cooled his ears and cheeks by walking up and down the street for a space, and then tried again. This landlady was a terrible and pitiful person, so gray and dusty she was, and her face deep lined with dust and trouble and labour. She wore a dirty cap that was all askew. She took Lewisham up into a threadbare room on the first floor. 'There's the use of a piano,' she said, and indicated an instrument with a front of torn green silk. Lewisham opened

the keyboard and evoked a vibration of broken
strings. He took one further survey of the dismal
place. 'Eighteen shillings,' he said. 'Thank you
. . . I'll let you know.' The woman smiled with
the corners of her mouth down, and without a word
moved wearily towards the door. Lewisham felt a
transient wonder at her hopeless position, but he
did not pursue the inquiry.

The next landlady sufficed. She was a clean-
looking German woman, rather smartly dressed;
she had a fringe of flaxen curls and a voluble flow
of words, for the most part recognisably English.
With this she sketched out remarks. Fifteen
shillings was her demand for a minute bedroom and
a small sitting-room separated by folding doors
on the ground floor, and her personal services.
Coals were to be 'sixpence a kettle,' she said—a
pretty substitute for scuttle. She had not understood Lewisham to say he was married. But she
had no hesitation. 'Aayteen shillin',' she said
imperturbably. 'Paid furs day ich wik . . . See?'
Mr Lewisham surveyed the rooms again. They
looked clean, and the bonus tea vases, the rancid,
gilt-framed oleographs, two toilet tidies used as
ornaments, and the fact that the chest of drawers
had been crowded out of the bedroom into the
sitting-room, simply appealed to his sense of humour.
'I'll take 'em from Saturday next,' he said.

She was sure he would like them and proposed
to give him his book forthwith. She mentioned
casually that the previous lodger had been a captain
and had stayed three years. (One never hears by
any chance of lodgers stopping for a shorter period.)
Something happened (German) and now he kept his
carriage—apparently an outcome of his stay. She
returned with a small penny account-book, a bottle

of ink, and an execrable pen, wrote Lewisham's name on the cover of this, and a receipt for eighteen shillings on the first page. She was evidently a person of considerable business aptitude. Lewisham paid, and the transaction terminated. 'Szhure to be gomfortable,' followed him comfortingly to the street.

Then he went on to Chelsea and interviewed a fatherly gentleman at the Vestry offices. The fatherly gentleman was chubby-faced and spectacled, and his manner was sympathetic but businesslike. He 'called back' each item of the interview. 'And what can I do for you? You wish to be married ! by licence?'

'By licence.'

'By licence !'

And so forth. He opened a book and made neat entries of the particulars.

'The lady's age?'

'Twenty-one.'

'A very suitable age . . . for a lady.'

He advised Lewisham to get a ring and said he would need two witnesses.

'*Well*——' hesitated Lewisham.

'There is always some one about,' said the superintendent registrar. 'And they are quite used to it.'

Thursday and Friday Lewisham passed in exceedingly high spirits. No consciousness of the practical destruction of the Career seems to have troubled him at this time. Doubt had vanished from his universe for a space. He wanted to dance along the corridors. He felt curiously irresponsible and threw up an unpleasant sort of humour that pleased nobody. He wished Miss Heydinger many happy returns of the day, apropos of nothing, and he threw

a bun across the refreshment room at Smithers
and hit one of the Art School officials. Both were
extremely silly things to do. In the first instance he
was penitent immediately after the outrage, but in
the second he added insult to injury by going across
the room and asking in an offensively suspicious
manner if any one had seen his bun. He crawled
under a table and found it at last, rather dusty but
quite eatable, under the chair of a lady art student.
He sat down by Smithers to eat it, while he argued
with the Art official. The Art official said the
manners of the Science students were getting un-
bearable, and threatened to bring the matter before
the refreshment-room Committee. Lewisham said
it was a pity to make such a fuss about a trivial
thing, and proposed that the Art official should
throw his lunch—steak and kidney pudding—across
the room at him, Lewisham, and so get immediate
satisfaction. He then apologised to the official
and pointed out in extenuation that it was a very
long and difficult shot he had attempted. The
official then drank a crumb, or breathed some beer,
or something of that sort, and the discussion terminated. In the afternoon, however, Lewisham, to
his undying honour, felt acutely ashamed of himself.
Miss Heydinger would not speak to him.

On Saturday morning he absented himself from
the schools, pleading by post a slight indisposition,
and took all his earthly goods to the booking-office
at Vauxhall Station. Chaffery's sister lived at
Tongham, near Farnham, and Ethel, dismissed a
week since by Lagune, had started that morning
under her mother's maudlin supervision, to begin
her new slavery. She was to alight either at Farnham or Woking, as opportunity arose, and to return
to Vauxhall to meet him. So that Lewisham's vigil

on the main platform was of indefinite dura-
tion.

At first he felt the exhilaration of a great
adventure. Then, as he paced the long platform,
came a philosophical mood, a sense of entire
detachment from the world. He saw a bundle of
uprooted plants beside the portmanteau of a fellow-
passenger, and it suggested a grotesque simile.
His roots, his earthly possessions, were all downstairs in the booking-office. What a flimsy thing
he was! A box of books and a trunk of clothes,
some certificates and scraps of paper, an entry here
and an entry there, a body not over strong—and
the vast multitude of people about him—against
him—the huge world in which he found himself!
Did it matter anything to one human soul save
her if he ceased to exist forthwith? And miles away
perhaps she also was feeling little and lonely. . . .

Would she have trouble with her luggage?
Suppose her aunt were to come to Farnham Junction
to meet her? Suppose some one stole her purse?
Suppose she came too late! The marriage was to
take place at two. . . . Suppose she never came at
all! After three trains in succession had disappointed
him his vague feelings of dread gave place to a
profound depression. . . .

But she came at last, and it was twenty-three
minutes to two. He hurried her luggage downstairs, booked it with his own, and in another
minute they were in a hansom—their first experience
of that species of conveyance—on the way to the
vestry-office. They had said scarcely anything to
one another, save hasty directions from Lewisham,
but their eyes were full of excitement, and under
the apron of the cab their hands were gripped
together.

The little old gentleman was businesslike but kindly. They made their vows to him, to a little black-bearded clerk and a lady who took off an apron in the nether part of the building to attend. The little old gentleman made no long speeches. 'You are young people,' he said slowly, 'and life together is a difficult thing. . . . Be kind to each other.' He smiled a little sadly, and held out a friendly hand.

Ethel's eyes glistened and she found she could not speak.

CHAPTER XXI

HOME !

THEN a furtive payment of witnesses, and Lewisham was beside her. His face was radiant. A steady current of workers going home to their half-holiday rest poured along the street. On the steps before them lay a few grains of rice from some more public nuptials.

A critical little girl eyed our couple curiously and made some remark to her ragamuffin friend.

'Not them,' said the ragamuffin friend. 'They've only been askin' questions.'

The ragamuffin friend was no judge of faces.

They walked back through the thronged streets to Vauxhall Station, saying little to one another, and there Lewisham, assuming as indifferent a manner as he could command, recovered their possessions from the booking-office by means of two separate tickets and put them aboard a four-wheeler. His luggage went outside, but the little brown portmanteau containing Ethel's trousseau was small enough to go on the seat in front of them. You must figure a rather broken-down four-wheeler bearing the yellow-painted box and the experienced trunk and Mr Lewisham and all his fortunes, a despondent fitful horse, and a threadbare venerable driver, blasphemous *sotto voce* and flagellant, in an ancient coat with capes. When our two young people found themselves in the cab again a certain stiffness of manner between them vanished and there was more squeezing of hands. 'Ethel *Lewisham*,' said Lewisham several times, and Ethel reciprocated with 'Husbinder' and 'Hubby dear,' and took off her glove to look again in an ostentatious manner at a ring. And she kissed the ring.

They were resolved that their newly-married state should not appear, and with considerable ceremony it was arranged that he should treat her with off-hand brusqueness when they arrived at their lodging. The Teutonic landlady appeared in the passage with an amiable smile and the hope that they had had a pleasant journey, and became voluble with promises of comfort. Lewisham, having assisted the slatternly general servant to carry in his boxes, paid the cabman a florin in a resolute manner and followed the ladies into the sitting-room.

Ethel answered Madam Gadow's inquiries with admirable self-possession, followed her through the folding-doors, and displayed an intelligent interest in a new spring mattress. Presently the folding-doors were closed again. Lewisham hovered about the front room pulling his moustache and pretending to admire the oleographs, surprised to find himself trembling. . . .

The slatternly general servant reappeared with the chops and tinned salmon he had asked Madam Gadow to prepare for them. He went and stared out of the window, heard the door close behind the girl, and turned at a sound as Ethel appeared shyly through the folding-doors.

She was suddenly domestic. Hitherto he had seen her without a hat and jacket only on one indistinct dramatic occasion. Now she wore a little blouse of soft, dark red material, with a white froth about the wrists and that pretty neck of hers.

And her hair was a new wonderland of curls and soft strands. How delicate she looked and sweet as she stood hesitating there. These gracious moments in life ! He took two steps and held out his arms. She glanced at the closed door of the room and came flitting towards him. . . .

CHAPTER XXII

EPITHALAMY

For three indelible days Lewisham's existence was a fabric of fine emotions, life was too wonderful and beautiful for any doubts or forethought. To be with Ethel was perpetual delight—she astonished this sisterless youngster with a thousand feminine niceties and refinements. She shamed him for his strength and clumsiness. And the light in her eyes and the warmth in her heart that lit them!

Even to be away from her was a wonder and in its way delightful. He was no common Student, he was a man with a Secret Life. To part from her on Monday near South Kensington station and go up Exhibition Road among all the fellows who lived in sordid, lonely lodgings and were boys to his day-old experience! To neglect one's work and sit back and dream of meeting again! To slip off to the shady churchyard behind the Oratory when, or even a little before, the midday bell woke the great staircase to activity, and to meet a smiling face and hear a soft voice saying sweet foolish things! And after four another meeting and the walk home—their own home.

No little form now went from him and flitted past a gas lamp down a foggy vista, taking his desire with her. Never more was that to be. Lewisham's long hours in the laboratory were spent largely in a dreamy meditation, in—to tell the truth—the invention of foolish terms of endearment: 'Dear Wife,' 'Dear Little Wife Thing,'

'Sweetest Dearest Little Wife,' 'Dillywings.' A pretty employment! And these are quite a fair specimen of his originality during those wonderful days. A moment of heart-searching in that particular matter led to the discovery of hitherto undreamt-of kindred with Swift. For Lewisham, like Swift and most other people, had hit upon the Little Language. Indeed it was a very foolish time.

Such section cutting as he did that third day of his married life—and he did very little—was a thing to marvel at. Bindon, the botany professor, under the fresh shock of his performance, protested to a colleague in the grill room that never had a student been so foolishly overrated.

And Ethel too had a fine emotional time. She was mistress of a home—*their* home together. She shopped and was called 'Ma'am' by respectful, good-looking shopmen; she designed meals and copied out papers of notes with a rich sense of helpfulness. And ever and again she would stop writing and sit dreaming. And for four bright week-days she went to and fro to accompany and meet Lewisham and listen greedily to the latest fruits of his imagination.

The landlady was very polite and conversed entertainingly about the very extraordinary and dissolute servants that had fallen to her lot. And Ethel disguised her newly-wedded state by a series of ingenious prevarications. She wrote a letter that Saturday evening to her mother—Lewisham had helped her to write it—making a sort of proclamation of her heroic departure and promising a speedy visit. They posted the letter so that it might not be delivered until Monday.

She was quite sure with Lewisham that only the possible dishonour of mediumship could have brought their marriage about—she sank the mutual attraction beyond even her own vision. There was more than a touch of magnificence, you perceive, about this affair.

It was Lewisham had persuaded her to delay that reassuring visit until Monday night. 'One whole day of honeymoon,' he insisted, was to be theirs. In his prenuptial meditations he had not clearly focused the fact that even after marriage some sort of relations with Mr and Mrs Chaffery would still go on. Even now he was exceedingly disinclined to face that obvious necessity. He foresaw, in spite of a resolute attempt to ignore it, that there would be explanatory scenes of some little difficulty. But the prevailing magnificence carried him over this trouble.

'Let us at least have this little time for ourselves,' he said, and that seemed to settle their position.

Save for its brevity and these intimations of future trouble it was a very fine time indeed. Their midday dinner together, for example—it was a little cold when at last they came to it on Saturday —was immense fun. There was no marked subsidence of appetite; they ate extremely well in spite of the meeting of their souls, and in spite of certain shiftings of chairs and hand-claspings and similar delays. He really made the acquaintance of her hands then for the first time, plump white hands with short white fingers, and the engagement ring had come out of its tender hiding-place and acted as keeper to the wedding ring. Their eyes were perpetually flitting about the room and coming back to mutual smiles. All their movements were faintly tremulous.

She professed to be vastly interested and amused

by the room and its furniture and her position, and
he was delighted by her delight. She was particularly entertained by the chest of drawers in the
living room, and by Lewisham's witticisms at the
toilet tidies and the oleographs.

And after the chops and the most of the tinned
salmon and the very new loaf were gone they fell
to with fine effect upon a tapioca pudding. Their
talk was fragmentary. 'Did you hear her call me
Madame? *Mádáme*—so!' 'And presently I must
go out and do some shopping. There are all the
things for Sunday and Monday morning to get.
I must make a list. It will never do to let her know
how little I know about things. . . . I wish I
knew more.'

At the time Lewisham regarded her confession
of domestic ignorance as a fine basis for facetious-
ness. He developed a fresh line of thought, and
condoled with her on the inglorious circumstances
of their wedding. 'No bridesmaids,' he said; 'no
little children scattering flowers, no carriages, no
policemen to guard the wedding presents, nothing
proper—nothing right. Not even a white favour.
Only you and I.'

'Only you and I. *Oh!*'

'This is nonsense,' said Lewisham, after an
interval.

'And think what we lose in the way of speeches,'
he resumed. 'Cannot you imagine the best man
rising: " Ladies and gentlemen—the health of the
bride." That is what the best man has to do, isn't
it?'

By way of answer she extended her hand.

'And do you know,' he said, after that had
received due recognition, 'we have never been
introduced!'

'Neither have we!' said Ethel. 'Neither have we! We have never been introduced!'

For some inscrutable reason it delighted them both enormously to think that they had never been introduced. . . .

In the later afternoon Lewisham, having unpacked his books to a certain extent and so forth, was visible to all men, visibly in the highest spirits, carrying home Ethel's shopping. There were parcels and cones in blue and parcels in rough gray paper and a bag of confectionery, and out of one of the side pockets of that East End overcoat the tail of a haddock protruded from its paper. Under such magnificent sanctions and amid such ignoble circumstances did this honeymoon begin.

On Sunday evening they went for a long rambling walk through the quiet streets, coming out at last into Hyde Park. The early spring night was mild and clear and the kindly moonlight was about them. They went to the bridge and looked down the Serpentine, with the little lights of Paddington yellow and remote. They stood there, dim little figures and very close together. They whispered and became silent.

Presently it seemed that something passed and Lewisham began talking in his magnificent vein. He likened the Serpentine to Life, and found Meaning in the dark banks of Kensington Gardens and the remote bright lights. 'The long struggle,' he said, 'and the lights at the end'—though he really did not know what he meant by the lights at the end. Neither did Ethel, though the emotion was indisputable. 'We are Fighting the World,' he said, finding great satisfaction in the thought. 'All the world is against us—and we are fighting it all.'

'We will not be beaten,' said Ethel.

'How could we be beaten—together?' said Lewisham. 'For you I would fight a dozen worlds.'

It seemed a very sweet and noble thing to them under the sympathetic moonlight, almost indeed too easy for their courage, to be merely fighting the world.

'You 'aven't bin married ver' long,' said Madam Gadow, with an insinuating smile, when she readmitted Ethel on Monday morning after Lewisham had been swallowed up by the Schools.

'No, I haven't *very* long,' admitted Ethel.

'You are ver' 'appy,' said Madam Gadow, and sighed.

'*I* was ver' 'appy,' said Madam Gadow.

CHAPTER XXIII

MR CHAFFERY AT HOME

THE golden mists of delight lifted a little on Monday, when Mr and Mrs G. E. Lewisham went to call on his mother-in-law and Mr Chaffery. Mrs Lewisham went in evident apprehension, but clouds of glory still hung about Lewisham's head, and his manner was heroic. He wore a cotton shirt and linen collar, and a very nice black satin tie that Mrs Lewisham had bought on her own responsibility during the day. She naturally wanted him to look all right.

Mrs Chaffery appeared in the half light of the passage as the top of a grimy cap over Ethel's shoulder and two black sleeves about her neck. She emerged as a small, middle-aged woman, with a thin little nose between silver-rimmed spectacles, a weak mouth and perplexed eyes, a queer little dust-lined woman with the oddest resemblance to Ethel in her face. She was trembling visibly with nervous agitation.

She hesitated, peering, and then kissed Mr Lewisham effusively. 'And this is Mr Lewisham!' she said as she did so.

She was the third thing feminine to kiss Lewisham since the promiscuous days of his babyhood. 'I was so afraid—There!' She laughed hysterically.

'You'll excuse my saying that it's comforting to see you—honest like and young. Not but what Ethel . . . *He* has been something dreadful,' said

150

Mrs Chaffery. 'You didn't ought to have written about that mesmerising. And of all letters that which Jane wrote—there ! But he's waiting and listening——'

'Are we to go downstairs, Mums?' asked Ethel.

'He's waiting for you there,' said Mrs Chaffery. She held a dismal little oil lamp, and they descended a tenebrous spiral structure into an underground breakfast-room lit by gas that shone through a partially frosted globe with cut-glass stars. That descent had a distinctly depressing effect upon Lewisham. He went first. He took a deep breath at the door. What on earth was Chaffery going to say? Not that he cared, of course.

Chaffery was standing with his back to the fire, trimming his finger-nails with a pocket-knife. His gilt glasses were tilted forward so as to make an inflamed knob at the top of his long nose, and he regarded Mr and Mrs Lewisham over them with—Lewisham doubted his eyes for a moment—but it was positively a smile, an essentially waggish smile.

'You've come back,' he said quite cheerfully over Lewisham to Ethel. There was a hint of falsetto in his voice.

'She has called to see her mother,' said Lewisham. 'You, I believe, are Mr Chaffery?'

'I would like to know who the Deuce *you* are?' said Chaffery, suddenly tilting his head back so as to look through his glasses instead of over them, and laughing genially. 'For thorough-going Cheek, I'm inclined to think you take the Cake. Are you the Mr Lewisham to whom this misguided girl refers in her letter?'

'I am.'

'Maggie,' said Mr Chaffery to Mrs Chaffery,

'there is a class of being upon whom delicacy is lost—to whom delicacy is practically unknown. Has your daughter got her marriage lines?'

'Mr Chaffery!' said Lewisham, and Mrs Chaffery exclaimed, 'James! How *can* you?'

Chaffery shut his penknife with a click and slipped it into his vest-pocket. Then he looked up again, speaking in the same equal voice. 'I presume we are civilised persons prepared to manage our affairs in a civilised way. My stepdaughter vanishes for two nights and returns with an alleged husband. I, at least, am not disposed to be careless about her legal position.'

'You ought to know her better——' began Lewisham.

'Why argue about it?' said Chaffery gaily, pointing a lean finger at Ethel's gesture, 'when she has 'em in her pocket? She may just as well show me now. I thought so. Don't be alarmed at my handling them. Fresh copies can always be got at the nominal price of two and seven. Thank you . . . Lewisham, George Edgar. One-and-twenty. And . . . You—one-and-twenty! I never did know your age, my dear, exactly, and now your mother won't say. Student! Thank you. I am greatly obliged. Indeed I am greatly relieved. And now, what have you got to say for yourselves in this remarkable affair?'

'You had a letter,' said Lewisham.

'I had a letter of excuses—the personalities I overlook. . . . Yes, sir—they were excuses. You young people wanted to marry—and you seized an occasion. You did not even refer to the fact that you wanted to marry in your letter. Pure modesty!

But now you have come here married. It disorganises this household, it inflicts endless bother on people, but never you mind that! I'm not blaming *you*. Nature's to blame! Neither of you know what you are in for yet. You will. You're married and that is the great essential thing. . . . (Ethel, my dear, just put your husband's hat and stick behind the door.) And you, sir, are so good as to disapprove of the way in which I earn my living?'

'Well,' said Lewisham. 'Yes—I'm bound to say I do.'

'You are really *not* bound to say it. The modesty of inexperience would excuse you.'

'Yes, but it isn't right—it isn't straight.'

'Dogma,' said Chaffery. 'Dogma!'

'What do you mean by dogma?' asked Lewisham.

'I mean, dogma. But we must argue this out in comfort. It is our supper hour, and I'm not the man to fight against accomplished facts. We have intermarried. There it is. You must stop to supper—and you and I must thresh these things out. We've involved ourselves with each other and we've got to make the best of it. Your wife and mine will spread the board, and we will go on talking. Why not sit in that chair instead of leaning on the back? This is a home—*domus*—not a debating society—humble in spite of my manifest frauds. . . . That's better. And in the first place I hope—I do so hope'—Chaffery was suddenly very impressive—'that you're not a Dissenter.'

'Eh!' said Lewisham, and then, 'No! I am *not* a Dissenter.'

'That's better,' said Mr Chaffery. 'I'm glad of that. I was just a little afraid——. Something in your manner. I can't stand Dissenters. I've a peculiar dislike to Dissenters. To my mind it's the great drawback of this Clapham. **You** see . . . I have invariably found them deceitful—invariably.'

He grimaced and dropped his glasses with a click against his waistcoat buttons. 'I'm very glad of that,' he said, replacing them. 'The Dissenter, the Nonconformist Conscience, the Puritan, you know, the Vegetarian and Total Abstainer, and all that sort of thing, I cannot away with them. I have cleared my mind of cant and formulæ. I've a nature essentially Hellenic. Have you ever read Matthew Arnold?'

'Beyond my scientific reading——'

'Ah! you *should* read Matthew Arnold—a mind of singular clarity. In him you would find a certain quality that is sometimes a little wanting in your scientific men. They are apt to be a little too phenomenal, you know, a little too objective. Now I seek after noumena. Noumena, Mr Lewisham! If you follow me——?'

He paused, and his eyes behind the glasses were mildly interrogative. Ethel re-entered without her hat and jacket, and with a noisy square black tray, a white cloth, some plates and knives and glasses, and began to lay the table.

'*I* follow you,' said Lewisham, reddening. He had not the courage to admit ignorance of this remarkable word. 'You state your case.'

'I seek after *noumena*,' repeated Chaffery, with great satisfaction, and gesticulated with his hand, waving away everything but that. 'I cannot do with surfaces and appearances. I am one of those nympholepts, you know, nympholepts. . . . Must pursue the truth of things! the elusive fundamental. . . . I make a rule, I never tell myself lies—never. There are few who can say that. To my mind—truth begins at home. And for the most part—stops there. Safest and seemliest! *you* know. With most men—with your typical Dissenter *par excellence* —it's always gadding abroad, calling on the neighbours. You see my point of view?'

He glanced at Lewisham, who was conscious of an unwonted opacity of mind. He became wary, as wary as he could manage to be on the spur of the moment.

'It's a little surprising, you know,' he said very carefully, 'if I may say so—and considering what happened—to hear *you* . . .'

'Speaking of truth? Not when you understand my position. Not when you see where I stand. That is what I am getting at. That is what I am naturally anxious to make clear to you now that we have intermarried, now that you are my step-son-in-law. You're young, you know, you're young, and you're hard and fast. Only years can give a mine *tone*—mitigate the varnish of education. I gather from this letter—and your face—that you are one of the party that participated in that little affair at Lagune's.'

He stuck out a finger at a point he had just seen. 'By the bye!—That accounts for Ethel,' he said.

Ethel rapped down the mustard on the table. 'It does,' she said, but not very loudly.

'But you had met before?' said Chaffery.

'At Whortley,' said Lewisham.

'I see,' said Chaffery.

'I was in—— I was one of those who arranged the exposure,' said Lewisham. 'And now you have raised the matter, I am bound to say——'

'I knew,' interrupted Chaffery. 'But what a shock that was for Lagune!' He looked down at his toes for a moment with the corners of his mouth tucked in. 'The hand dodge wasn't bad, you know,' he said, with a queer sidelong smile.

Lewisham was very busy for a moment trying to get this remark in focus. 'I don't see it in the same light as you do,' he explained at last.

'Can't get away from your moral bias, eh?—Well, well. We'll go into all that. But apart from its moral merits—simply as an artistic trick—it was not bad.'

'I don't know much about tricks——'

'So few who undertake exposures do. You admit you never heard or thought of that before—the bladder, I mean. Yet it's as obvious as tin-tacks that a medium who's hampered at his hands will do all he can with his teeth, and what *could* be so self-evident as a bladder under one's lapel? What could be? Yet I know psychic literature pretty well and it's never been suggested yet! Never. It's a perpetual surprise to me how many things are *not* thought of by investigators. For one thing, they never count the odds against them, and that puts them wrong at the start. Look at it! I am by nature tricky. I spend all my leisure standing or sitting about and thinking up or practising new little tricks, because it amuses me immensely to do so. The whole thing amuses me. Well—what is the result of these meditations? Take one thing: I know eight and forty ways of making raps—of which at least ten are original. Ten original ways of making raps.' His manner was very impressive. 'And some of them simply tremendous raps.' There !'

A confirmatory rap exploded—as it seemed between Lewisham and Chaffery.

'*Eh ?*' said Chaffery.

The mantelpiece opened a dropping fire, and the

table went off under Lewisham's nose like a cracker.

'You see?' said Chaffery, putting his hands under the tail of his coat. The whole room seemed snapping its fingers at Lewisham for a space.

'Very well, and now take the other side. Take the severest test I ever tried. Two respectable professors of physics—not Newtons, you understand, but good, worthy, self-important professors of physics—a lady anxious to prove there's a life beyond the grave, a journalist who wants stuff to write—a person, that is, who gets his living by these researches just as I do—undertook to test me. Test *me*! . . . Of course they had their other work to do, professing physics, professing religion, organising research, and so forth. At the outside they don't think an hour a day about it, and most of them had never cheated anybody in their existence, and couldn't, for example, travel without a ticket for a three-mile journey and not get caught, to save their lives. . . . Well—you see the odds?'

He paused. Lewisham appeared involved in some interior struggle.

'You know,' explained Chaffery, 'it was quite an accident you got me—quite. The thing slipped out of my mouth. Or your friend with the flat voice wouldn't have had a chance. Not a chance.'

Lewisham spoke like a man who is lifting a weight. 'All *this*, you know, is off the question. I'm not disputing your ability. But the thing is . . . it isn't right.'

'We're coming to that,' said Chaffery.

'It's evident we look at things in a different light.'

'That's it. That's just what we've got to discuss. Exactly!'

'Cheating is cheating. You can't get away from that. That's simple enough.'

'Wait till I've done with it,' said Chaffery, with a certain zest. 'Of course, it's imperative you should understand my position. It isn't as though I hadn't one. Ever since I read your letter I've been thinking over that. Really!—a justification! In a way you might almost say I had a mission. A sort of prophet. You really don't see the beginning of it yet.'

'Oh, but hang it!' protested Lewisham.

'Ah! you're young, you're crude. My dear young man, you're only at the beginning of things. You really must concede a certain possibility of wider views to a man more than twice your age. But here's supper. For a little while at any rate we'll call a truce.'

Ethel had come in again bearing an additional chair, and Mrs Chaffery appeared behind her, crowning the preparations with a jug of small beer. The cloth, Lewisham observed, as he turned towards it, had several undarned holes and discoloured places, and in the centre stood a tarnished cruet which contained mustard, pepper, vinegar, and three ambiguous dried-up bottles. The bread was on an ample board with a pious rim, and an honest wedge of cheese loomed disproportionate on a little plate. Mr and Mrs Lewisham were seated facing one another, and Mrs Chaffery sat in the broken chair because she understood its ways.

'This cheese is as nutritious and unattractive and indigestible as Science,' remarked Chaffery, cutting and passing wedges. 'But crush it—so—under your fork, add a little of this good Dorset butter, a dab of mustard, pepper—the pepper is very necessary—and some malt vinegar, and crush

together. You get a compound called Crab and by
no means disagreeable. So the wise deal with the
facts of life, neither bolting nor rejecting, but
adapting.'

'As though pepper and mustard were not facts.'
said Lewisham, scoring his solitary point that
evening.

Chaffery admitted the collapse of his image in
very complimentary terms, and Lewisham could not
avoid a glance across the table at Ethel. He remembered that Chaffery was a slippery scoundrel whose
blame was better than his praise, immediately
afterwards.

For a time the Crab engaged Chaffery, and the
conversation languished. Mrs Chaffery asked Ethel
formal questions about their lodgings, and Ethel's
answers were buoyant. 'You must come and have
tea one day,' said Ethel, not waiting for Lewisham's
endorsement, 'and see it all.'

Chaffery astonished Lewisham by suddenly dis-
playing a complete acquaintance with his status as
a South Kensington teacher in training. 'I suppose
you have some money beyond that guinea,' said
Chaffery off-handedly.

'Enough to go on with,' said Lewisham, reddening.

'And you look to them at South Kensington to
do something for you—a hundred a year or so,
when your scholarship is up?'

'Yes,' said Lewisham, a little reluctantly. 'Yes.
A hundred a year or so. That's the sort of idea.
And there's lots of places beyond South Kensington,
of course, even if they don't put me up
there.'

'I see,' said Chaffery; 'but it will be a pretty
close shave for all that—one hundred a year. Well,
well—there's many a deserving man has to do

with less,' and after a meditative pause he asked Lewisham to pass the beer.

'Hev you a mother living, Mr Lewisham?' said Mrs Chaffery suddenly, and pursued him through the tale of his connections. When he came to the plumber, Mrs Chaffery remarked with an unexpected air of consequence, that most families have their poor relations. Then the air of consequence vanished again into the past from which it had arisen.

Supper finished, Chaffery poured the residuum of the beer into his glass, produced a Broseley clay of the longest sort, and invited Lewisham to smoke. 'Honest smoking,' said Chaffery, tapping the bowl of his clay, and added : 'In this country—cigars— sound cigars—and honesty rarely meet.'

Lewisham fumbled in his pocket for his Algerian cigarettes, and Chaffery having regarded them unfavourably through his glasses, took up the thread of his promised apologia. The ladies retired to wash up the supper things.

'You see,' said Chaffery, opening abruptly so soon as the clay was drawing, 'about this cheating—— I do not find life such a simple matter as you do.'

'*I* don't find life simple,' said Lewisham, 'but I do think there's a Right and a Wrong in things. And I don't think you have said anything so far to show that spiritualistic cheating is Right.'

'Let us thresh the matter out,' said Chaffery, crossing his legs; 'let us thresh the matter out. Now'—he drew at his pipe—'I don't think you fully appreciate the importance of Illusion in life, the Essential Nature of Lies and Deception of the body politic. You are inclined to discredit one particular form of Imposture, because it is not generally admitted—carries a certain discredit, and

—witness the heel edges of my trouser legs, witness yonder viands—small rewards.'

'It's not that,' said Lewisham.

'Now I am prepared to maintain,' said Chaffery, proceeding with his proposition, 'that Honesty is essentially an anarchistic and disintegrating force in society, that communities are held together and the progress of civilisation made possible only by vigorous and sometimes even violent Lying; that the Social Contract is nothing more or less than a vast conspiracy of human beings to lie to and humbug themselves and one another for the general Good. Lies are the mortar that bind the savage individual man into the social masonry. There is the general thesis upon which I base my justification. My mediumship, I can assure you, is a particular instance of the general assertion. Were I not of a profoundly indolent, restless, adventurous nature, and horribly averse to writing, I would make a great book of this and live honoured by every profound duffer in the world.'

'But how are you going to prove it?'

'Prove it ! It simply needs pointing out. Even now there are men—Bernard Shaw, Ibsen, and such like—who have seen bits of it in a new-gospel-grubbing sort of fashion. What is man? Lust and greed tempered by fear and an irrational vanity.'

'I don't agree with that,' said Mr Lewisham.

'You will as you grow older,' said Chaffery. 'There's truths you have to grow into. But about this matter of Lies—let us look at the fabric of society, let us compare the savage. You will discover the only essential difference between savage and civilised is this : The former hasn't learnt to shirk the truth of things, and the latter has. Take the most obvious difference—the clothing of the

civilised man, his invention of decency. What *is*
clothing? The concealment of essential facts.
What is decorum? Suppression! I don't argue
against decency and decorum, mind you, but there
they are—essentials to civilisation and essentially
" *suppressio veri.*" And in the pockets of his clothes
our citizen carries money. The pure savage has
no money. To him a lump of metal is a lump of
metal—possibly ornamental—no more. That's right.
To any lucid-minded man it's the same or different
only through the gross folly of his fellows. But to
the common civilised man the universal exchange-
ability of this gold is a sacred and fundamental
fact. Think of it! Why should it be? There isn't
a why! I live in perpetual amazement at the
gullibility of my fellow-creatures. Of a morning
sometimes, I can assure you, I lie in bed fancying
that people may have found out this swindle in
the night, expect to hear a tumult downstairs and
see your mother-in-law come rushing into the room
with a rejected shilling from the milkman. " What's
this? " says he. " This Muck for milk? " But
it never happens. Never. If it did, if people
suddenly cleared their minds of this cant of money,
what would happen? The true nature of man
would appear. I should whip out of bed, seize
some weapon, and after the milkman forthwith.
It's becoming to keep the peace, but it's necessary
to have milk. The neighbours would come pouring
out—also after milk. Milkman, suddenly enlight-
ened, would start clattering up the street. After
him! Clutch—tear! Got him! Over goes the
cart! Fight if you like, but don't upset the can!
. . . Don't you see it all—perfectly reasonable every
bit of it. I should return, bruised and bloody, with
the milk-can under my arm. Yes—*I* should have

the milk-can—I should keep my eye on that. . . .
But why go on? You of all men should know that
life is a struggle for existence, a fight for food.
Money is just the lie that mitigates our fury.'

'No,' said Lewisham; 'no! I'm not prepared
to admit that.'

'What *is* money?'

Mr Lewisham dodged. 'You state your case
first,' he said. 'I really don't see what all this
has to do with cheating at a *séance*.'

'I weave my defence from this loom, though.
Take some aggressively respectable sort of man—
a bishop, for example.'

'Well,' said Lewisham, 'I don't much hold with
bishops.'

'It doesn't matter. Take a professor of science,
walking the earth. Remark his clothing, making a
decent citizen out of him, concealing the fact that
physically he is a flabby, pot-bellied degenerate.
That is the first Lie of his being. No fringes round
his trousers, my boy. Notice his hair, groomed and
clipped, the tacit lie that its average length is half
an inch, whereas in nature he would wave a few
score yard-long hairs of ginger gray to the winds of
heaven. Notice the smug suppressions of his face.
In his mouth are Lies in the shape of false teeth.
Then on the earth somewhere poor devils are toiling
to get him meat and corn and wine. He is clothed
in the lives of bent and thwarted weavers, his way
is lit by phossy jaw, he eats from lead-glazed
crockery—all his ways are paved with the lives
of men. . . . Think of the chubby, comfortable
creature! And, as Swift has it—to think that such
a thing should deal in pride! . . . He pretends
that his blessed little researches are in some way a
fair return to these remote beings for their toil,

their suffering; pretends that he and his parasitic
career are payment for their thwarted desires.
Imagine him bullying his gardener over some trans-
planted geraniums, the thick mist of lies they stand
in, so that the man does not immediately, with the
edge of a spade, smite down his impertinence to
the dust from which it rose. . . . And his case is
the case of all comfortable lives. What a lie and
sham all civility is, all good breeding, all culture
and refinement, while one poor ragged wretch
drags hungry on the earth!'

'But this is Socialism!' said Lewisham. '*I*——'

'No Ism,' said Chaffery, raising his rich voice.
'Only the ghastly truth of things—the truth that
the warp and the woof of the world of men is
Lying. Socialism is no remedy, no *ism* is a remedy;
things are so.'

'I don't agree——' began Lewisham.

'Not with the hopelessness, because you are
young, but with the description you do.'

'Well—within limits.'

'You agree that most respectable positions in the
world are tainted with the fraud of our social
conditions. If they were not tainted with fraud
they would not be respectable. Even your own
position—— Who gave you the right to marry
and prosecute interesting scientific studies while
other young men rot in mines?'

'I admit——'

'You can't help admitting. And here is my
position. Since all ways of life are tainted with
fraud, since to live and speak the truth is beyond
human strength and courage—as one finds it—is it
not better for a man that he engage in some straight-
forward comparatively harmless cheating, than if
he risk his mental integrity in some ambiguous

position and fall at last into self-deception and self-righteousness? That is the essential danger. That is the thing I always guard against. Heed that! It is the master sin. Self-righteousness.'

Mr Lewisham pulled at his moustache.

'You begin to take me. And after all, these worthy people do not suffer so greatly. If I did not take their money some other impostor would. Their huge conceit of intelligence would breed perhaps some viler swindle than my facetious rappings. That's the line our doubting bishops take, and why shouldn't I? For example, these people might give it to Public Charities, minister to the fattened secretary, the prodigal younger son. After all, at worst, I am a sort of latter-day Robin Hood; I take from the rich according to their incomes. I don't give to the poor certainly, I don't get enough. But—there are other good works. Many a poor weakling have I comforted with Lies, great thumping, silly Lies, about the grave! Compare me with one of those rascals who disseminate phossy jaw and lead poisons, compare me with a millionaire who runs a music-hall with an eye to feminine talent, or an underwriter, or the common stockbroker. Or any sort of lawyer. . . .

'There are bishops,' said Chaffery, 'who believe in Darwin and doubt Moses. Now, I hold myself better than they—analogous perhaps but better— for I do at least invent something of the tricks I play—I do do that.'

'That's all very well,' began Lewisham.

'I might forgive them their dishonesty,' said Chaffery, 'but the stupidity of it, the mental self-abnegation—Lord! If a solicitor doesn't swindle in the proper shabby-magnificent way, they chuck him for unprofessional conduct.' He paused. He became meditative, and smiled faintly.

'Now, some of *my* dodges,' he said, with a sudden change of voice, turning towards Lewisham, his eyes smiling over his glasses and an emphatic hand patting the table-cloth; 'some of *my* dodges are *damned* ingenious, you know—*damned* ingenious—and well worth double the money they bring me—double.'

He turned towards the fire again, pulling at his smouldering pipe and eyeing Lewisham over the corner of his glasses.

'One or two of my little things would make Maskelyne sit up,' he said presently. 'They would set that mechanical orchestra playing out of pure astonishment. I really must explain some of them to you—now we have intermarried.'

It took Mr Lewisham a minute or so to re-form the regiment of his mind disordered by its head-long pursuit of Chaffery's flying arguments. 'But on your principles you might do almost anything !' he said.

'Precisely !' said Chaffery.

'But——'

'It is rather a curious method,' protested Chaffery; 'to test one's principles of action by judging the resultant actions on some other principle, isn't it ?'

Lewisham took a moment to think. 'I suppose that is so,' he said, in the manner of a man convinced against his will.

He perceived his logic insufficient. He suddenly thrust the delicacies of argument aside. Certain sentences he had brought ready for use in his mind came up and he delivered them abruptly. 'Anyhow,' he said, 'I don't agree with this cheating. In spite of what you say, I hold to what I said in my letter. Ethel's connection with all these things is at an end. I shan't go out of my way to expose you, of course, but if it comes in my way I shall speak my mind of all these spiritualistic phenomena. It's just as well that we should know clearly where we are.'

'That is clearly understood, my dear step-son-in-law,' said Chaffery. 'Our present object is discussion.'

'But Ethel——'

'Ethel is yours,' said Chaffery. 'Ethel is yours,' he repeated after an interval, and added pensively —'to keep.'

'But talking of Illusion,' he resumed, dismissing the sordid with a sign of relief, 'I sometimes think with Bishop Berkeley, that all experience is probably something quite different from reality. That consciousness is *essentially* hallucination. I, here, and you, and our talk—it is all Illusion. Bring your Science to bear—what am I? A cloudy multitude of atoms, an infinite interplay of little cells. Is this hand that I hold out me? This head? Is the surface of my skin any more than a rude average boundary? You say it is my mind that is me? But consider the war of motives. Suppose I have an impulse that I resist—it is *I* resist it—the impulse is outside me, eh? But suppose that impulse carries me and I do the thing—that impulse is part of me, is it not? Ah! My brain reels at these mysteries! Lord! what flimsy fluctuating things we are—first this, then that, a thought, an impulse, a deed and a forgetting, and all the time madly cocksure we are ourselves. And as for you—you who have hardly learned to think for more than five or six short years, there you sit, assured, coherent,

there you sit in all your inherited original sin—
Hallucinatory Windlestraw !—judging and condemn-
ing. *You* know Right from Wrong ! My boy, so
did Adam and Eve . . . *so soon as they'd had
dealings with the father of lies !*'

At the end of the evening whisky and hot water
were produced, and Chaffery, now in a mood of
great urbanity, said he had rarely enjoyed any one's
conversation so much as Lewisham's, and insisted
upon every one having whisky. Mrs Chaffery and
Ethel added sugar and lemon. Lewisham felt an
instantaneous mild surprise at the sight of Ethel
drinking grog.

At the door Mrs Chaffery kissed Lewisham an
effusive good-bye and told Ethel she really believed
it was all for the best.

On the way home Lewisham was thoughtful and
preoccupied. The problem of Chaffery assumed
enormous proportions. At times indeed even that
good man's own philosophical sketch of himself as
a practical exponent of mental sincerity touched
with humour and the artistic spirit, seemed plausible.
Lagune was an undeniable ass, and conceivably
psychic research was an incentive to trickery. Then
he remembered the matter in his relation to
Ethel. . . .

'Your stepfather is a little hard to follow,' he
said at last, sitting on the bed and taking off one
boot. 'He's dodgy—he's so confoundedly dodgy.
One doesn't know where to take hold of him. He's
got such a break he's clean bowled me again and
again.'

He thought for a space, and then removed his
boot and sat with it on his knee. 'Of course ! . . .
all that he said was wrong—quite wrong. Right is

right and cheating is cheating, whatever you say about it.'

'That's what I feel about him,' said Ethel at the looking-glass. 'That's exactly how it seems to me.'

CHAPTER XXIV

THE CAMPAIGN OPENS

ON Saturday Lewisham was first through the folding doors. In a moment he reappeared with a document extended. Mrs Lewisham stood arrested with her dress skirt in her hand, astonished at the astonishment on his face. '*I* say!' said Lewisham; 'just look here!'

She looked at the book that he held open before her, and perceived that its vertical ruling betokened a sordid import, that its list of items in an illegible mixture of English and German was lengthy. '1 kettle of coals 6d.' occurred regularly down that portentous array and buttoned it all together. It was Madam Gadow's first bill. Ethel took it out of his hand and examined it closer. It looked no smaller closer. The overcharges were scandalous. It was curious how the humour of calling a scuttle 'kettle' had evaporated.

That document, I take it, was the end of Mr Lewisham's informal honeymoon. It's advent was the snap of that bright Prince Rupert's drop; and in a moment—Dust. For a glorious week he had lived in the persuasion that life was made of love and mystery, and now he was reminded with singular clearness that it was begotten of a struggle for existence and the Will to Live. 'Confounded imposition!' fumed Mr Lewisham, and the breakfast table was novel and ominous, mutterings towards anger on the one hand and a certain consternation on the other. 'I must give her a talking to this afternoon,' said Lewisham at his watch, and after he had bundled his books into the shiny black bag, he gave the first of his kisses that was not a distinct and self-subsisting ceremony. It was usage and done in a hurry, and the door slammed as he went his way to the schools. Ethel was not coming that morning, because by special request and because she wanted to help him she was going to copy out some of his botanical notes which had fallen into arrears.

On his way to the schools Lewisham felt something suspiciously near a sinking of the heart. His pre-occupation was essentially arithmetical. The thing that engaged his mind to the exclusion of all other matters is best expressed in the recognised business form.

Dr.	£	s.	d.	Cr.	£	s.	d.
Mr. L, ⎧	13	10	4½	By 'bus fares to South Kensington (late).........			2
Cash in hand ⎨				By 6 lunches at the Students' Club.		5	2½
Mrs. L. ⎩		11	7	By 2 packets of cigarettes (to smoke after dinner).			6
....				By marriage and elopement.	4	18	10
At Bank	45	0	0	By necessary subsequent additions to bride's trousseau..........		16	1
To Scholarship	1	1	0	By housekeeping expenses...........	1	1	4½
				By " A few little things " bought by housekeeper		15	3½
				By Madam Cadow for coal, lodging and attendance (as per account rendered).	1	15	0
				By missing.......,...			4
				By balance..........	50	11	2
	£60	3	11½		£60	3	11½

From this it will be manifest to the most un-business like that, disregarding the extraordinary expenditure on the marriage, and the by no means final 'few little things' Ethel had bought, out-goings exceeded income by two pounds and more, and a brief excursion into arithmetic will demonstrate that in five-and-twenty weeks the balance of the account would be nothing.

But that guinea a week was not to go on for five-and-twenty weeks, but simply for fifteen, and then the net outgoings will be well over three guineas, reducing the 'law' accorded our young people to two-and-twenty weeks. These details are tiresome and disagreeable, no doubt, to the refined reader, but just imagine how much more disagreeable they were to Mr Lewisham, trudging meditative to the schools. You will understand his slipping out of the laboratory, and betaking himself to the Educational Reading-room, and how it was that the observant Smithers, grinding his lecture notes against the now imminent second examination for the 'Forbes,' was presently perplexed to the centre of his being by the spectacle of Lewisham, intent upon a pile of current periodicals, the *Educational Times*, the *Journal of Education*, *the Schoolmaster*, *Science and Art*, *The University Correspondent*, *Nature*, *The Athenæum*, *The Academy*, and *The Author*.

Smithers remarked the appearance of a note-book, the jotting down of memoranda. He edged into the bay nearest Lewisham's table and approached him suddenly from the flank. 'What are *you* after?' said Smithers in a noisy whisper and with a detective eye on the papers. He perceived Lewisham was scrutinising the advertisement column, and his perplexity increased.

'Oh—nothing,' said Lewisham blandly, with his hand falling casually over his memoranda; 'what's your particular little game?'

'Nothing much,' said Smithers, 'just mooching round. You weren't at the meeting last Friday?'

He turned a chair, knelt on it, and began whispering over the back about Debating Society politics. Lewisham was inattentive and brief. What had he to do with these puerilities. At last Smithers went away foiled, and met Parkson by the entrance. Parkson, by the bye, had not spoken to Lewisham since their painful misunderstanding. He made a wide detour to his seat at the end table, and so, and by a singular rectitude of bearing and a dignified expression, showed himself aware of Lewisham's offensive presence.

Lewisham's investigations were two-fold. He wanted to discover some way of adding materially to that weekly guinea by his own exertions, and he wanted to learn the conditions of the market for typewriting. For himself he had a vague idea, an idea subsequently abandoned, that it was possible to get teaching work in evening classes during the month of March. But, except by reason of sudden death, no evening class in London changes its staff after September until July comes round again. Private tuition, moreover, offered many attractions to him, but no definite proposals. His ideas of his own possibilities were youthful, or he would not have spent time in noting the conditions of application for a vacant professorship in physics at the Melbourne University. He also made a note of the vacant editorship of a monthly magazine devoted to social questions. He would not have minded doing that sort of thing at all, though the proprietor might.   There was also a vacant curatorship in the Museum of Eton College.

The typewriting business was less varied and more definite.   Those were the days before the violent competition of the half-educated had brought things down to an impossible tenpence the thousand words, and the prevailing price was as high as one and six.   Calculating that Ethel could do a thousand words in an hour and that she could work five or six hours in the day, it was evident that her contributions to the household expenses would be by no means despicable; thirty shillings a week perhaps.   Lewisham was naturally elated at this discovery.   He could find no advertisements of authors or others seeking typewriting, but he saw that a great number of typewriters advertised themselves in the literary papers.   It was evident Ethel also must advertise.   ' " Scientific phraseology a speciality " might be put,' meditated Lewisham. He returned to his lodgings in a hopeful mood with quite a bundle of memoranda of possible employments.   He spent five shillings in stamps on the way.

After lunch, Lewisham—a little short of breath —asked to see Madam Gadow.   She came up in the most affable frame of mind; nothing could be farther from the normal indignation of the British landlady.   She was very voluble, gesticulatory, and lucid, but unhappily bi-lingual, and at all the crucial points German.   Mr Lewisham's natural politeness restrained him from too close a pursuit across the boundary of the two imperial tongues. Quite half an hour's amicable discussion led at last to a reduction of sixpence, and all parties professed themselves satisfied with this result.

Madam Gadow was quite cool even at the end.

Mr Lewisham was flushed in the face, red-eared, and his hair slightly disordered, but that sixpence was at any rate an admission of the justice of his claim. 'She was evidently trying it on,' he said almost apologetically to Ethel. 'It was absolutely necessary to present a firm front to her. I doubt if we shall have any trouble again. . . .

'Of course, what she says about kitchen coals is perfectly just.'

Then the young couple went for a walk in Kensington Gardens, and—the spring afternoon was so warm and pleasant—sat on two attractive green chairs near the bandstand, for which Lewisham had subsequently to pay twopence. They had what Ethel called a 'serious talk.' She was really wonderfully sensible, and discussed the situation exhaustively. She was particularly insistent upon the importance of economy in her domestic disbursements and deplored her general ignorance very earnestly. It was decided that Lewisham should get a good elementary text-book of domestic economy for her private study. At home Mrs Chaffery guided her house by the oracular items of *Inquire Within upon Everything*, but Lewisham considered that work unscientific.

Ethel was also of opinion that much might be learnt from the sixpenny ladies' papers—the penny ones had hardly begun in those days. She had bought such publications during seasons of affluence, but chiefly, as she now deplored, with an eye to the trimming of hats and such-like vanities. The sooner the typewriter came the better. It occurred to Lewisham with unpleasant suddenness that he had not allowed for the purchase of a typewriter in his estimate of their resources. It brought their 'law' down to twelve or thirteen weeks.

They spent the evening in writing and copying
a number of letters, addressing envelopes and
enclosing stamps.   There were optimistic moments.

'Melbourne's a fine city,' said Lewisham, 'and
we should have a glorious voyage out.'   He read
the application for the Melbourne professorship out
loud to her, just to see how it read, and she was
greatly impressed by the list of his accomplishments
and successes.   'I did not know you knew *half*
those things,' she said, and became depressed at
her relative illiteracy.   It was natural after such
encouragement, to write to the scholastic agents in
a tone of assured consequence.

The advertisement for typewriting in the
Athenæum troubled his conscience a little.   After he
had copied out his draft with its 'Scientific phraseology a speciality,' fine and large, he saw the notes
she had written out for him.   Her handwriting was
still round and boyish, even as it had appeared in
the Whortley avenue, but her punctuation was
confined to the erratic comma and the dash, and
there was a disposition to spell the imperfectly
legible along the line of least resistance.   However,
he dismissed that matter with a resolve to read over
and correct anything in that way that she might
have sent her to do.   It would not be a bad idea,
he thought parenthetically, if he himself read up
some sound authority on the punctuation of
sentences.

They sat at this business quite late, heedless of
the examination in botany that came on the morrow.
It was very bright and cosy in their little room with
their fire burning, the gas lit and the curtains drawn,
and the number of applications they had written
made them hopeful.   She was flushed and enthusiastic, now flitting about the room, now coming

close to him and leaning over him to see what he had done. At Lewisham's request she got him the envelopes from the chest of drawers. 'You *are* a help to a chap,' said Lewisham, leaning back from the table. 'I feel I could do anything for a girl like you—anything.'

'*Really!*' she cried. 'Really! Am I really a help?'

Lewisham's face and gesture were all assent. She gave a little cry of delight, stood for a moment, and then by way of practical demonstration of her unflinching helpfulness, hurried round the table towards him with arms extended. 'You dear!' she cried.

Lewisham, partially embraced, pushed his chair back with his disengaged arm, so that she might sit on his knee. . . .

Who could doubt that she was a help?

CHAPTER XXV

THE FIRST BATTLE

LEWISHAM'S inquiries for evening teaching and private tuition were essentially provisional measures. His proposals for a more permanent establishment displayed a certain defect in his sense of proportion. That Melbourne professorship, for example, was beyond his merits, and there were aspects of things that would have affected the welcome of himself and his wife at Eton College. At the outset he was inclined to regard the South Kensington scholar as the intellectual salt of the earth, to overrate the abundance of 'decent things' yielding from one hundred and fifty to three hundred a year, and to disregard the competition of such inferior enterprises as the universities of Oxford, Cambridge, and the literate North. But the scholastic agents to whom he went on the following Saturday did much in a quiet way to disabuse his mind.

Mr Blendershin's chief assistant in the grimy little office in Oxford Street cleared up the matter so vigorously that Lewisham was angered. 'Head Master of an endowed school, perhaps!' said Mr Blendershin's chief assistant. 'Lord!—why not a bishopric? I say'—as Mr Blendershin entered smoking an assertive cigar—'one-and-twenty, *no* degree, *no* games, two years' experience as junior —wants a head-mastership of an endowed school!' He spoke so loudly that it was inevitable the selection of clients in the waiting-room should hear, and he pointed with his pen.

'Look here!' said Lewisham hotly; 'if I knew the ways of the market I shouldn't come to you.'

Mr Blendershin stared at Lewisham for a moment. 'What's he done in the way of certificates?' asked Mr Blendershin of the assistant.

The assistant read a list of 'ologies and 'ographies. 'Fifty resident,' said Mr Blendershin concisely— 'that's *your* figure. Sixty, if you're lucky.'

'*What?*' said Mr Lewisham.

'Not enough for you?'

'Not nearly.'

'You can get a Cambridge graduate for eighty resident—and grateful,' said Mr Blendershin.

'But I don't want a resident post,' said Lewisham.

'Precious few non-resident shops,' said Mr Blendershin. 'Precious few. They want you for dormitory supervision—and they're afraid of your taking pups outside.'

'Not married by any chance?' said the assistant suddenly, after an attentive study of Lewisham's face.

'Well—er.' Lewisham met Mr Blendershin's eye. 'Yes,' he said.

The assistant was briefly unprintable. 'Lord! you'll have to keep that dark,' said Mr Blendershin. But you have got a tough bit of hoeing before you. If I was you I'd go on and get my degree now you're so near it. You'll stand a better chance.'

Pause.

'The fact is,' said Lewisham slowly and looking at his boot toes, 'I must be doing *something* while I am getting my degree.'

The assistant whistled softly.

'Might get you a visiting job, perhaps,' said Mr Blendershin speculatively. 'Just read me those items again, Binks.' He listened attentively.

'Objects to religious teaching !—Eh?' He stopped
the reading by a gesture. 'That's nonsense. You
can't have everything, you know. Scratch that out.
You won't get a place in any middle-class school
in England if you object to religious teaching.
It's the mothers—bless 'em ! Say nothing about
it. Don't believe—who does? There's hundreds
like you, you know—hundreds. Parsons—all sorts.
Say nothing about it——'

'But if I'm asked?'

'Church of England. Every man in this country
who has not dissented belongs to the Church of
England. It'll be hard enough to get you anything
without that.'

'But——' said Mr Lewisham. 'It's lying.'

'Legal fiction,' said Mr Blendershin. 'Every one
understands. If you don't do that, my dear chap,
we can't do anything for you. It's journalism, or
London docks. Well, considering your experience
—say docks.'

Lewisham's face flushed irregularly. He did not
answer. He scowled and tugged at the still by no
means ample moustache.

'Compromise, you know,' said Mr Blendershin,
watching him kindly. 'Compromise.'

For the first time in his life Lewisham faced the
necessity of telling a lie in cold blood. He glissaded
from the austere altitudes of his self-respect and his
next words were already disingenuous.

'I won't promise to tell lies if I'm asked,' he said
aloud. 'I can't do that.'

'Scratch it out,' said Blendershin to the clerk.
'You needn't mention it. Then you don't say you
can teach drawing.'

'I can't,' said Lewisham.

'You just give out the copies,' said Blendershin,

'and take care they don't see you draw, you know.'

'But that's not teaching drawing——'

'It's what's understood by it in *this* country,' said Blendershin. 'Don't you go corrupting your mind with pedagogueries. They're the ruin of assistants. Put down drawing. Then there's shorthand——'

'Here, I say!' said Lewisham.

'There's shorthand, French, book-keeping, commercial geography, land measuring——'

'But I can't teach any of those things!'

'Look here,' said Blendershin, and paused. 'Has your wife or you a private income?'

'No,' said Lewisham.

'Well?'

A pause of further moral descent, and a whack against an obstacle. 'But they will find me out.' said Lewisham.

Blendershin smiled. 'It's not so much ability as willingness to teach, you know. And *they* won't find you out. The sort of schoolmaster we deal with can't find anything out. He can't teach any of these things himself—and consequently he doesn't believe they *can* be taught. Talk to him of pedagogics and he talks of practical experience. But he puts 'em on his prospectus, you know, and he wants 'em on his time-table. Some of these subjects —there's commercial geography, for instance. What *is* commercial geography?'

'Barilla,' said the assistant, biting the end of his pen, and added pensively, '*and* blethers.'

'Fad,' said Blendershin. 'Just fad. Newspapers talk rot about commercial education, Duke of Devonshire catches on and talks ditto—pretends he thought it himself—much *he* cares—parents get hold of it—schoolmasters obliged to put something

down, consequently assistants must. **And that's**
the end of the matter !'

'*All* right,' said Lewisham, catching his breath
in a faint sob of shame. 'Stick 'em down. But
mind—a non-resident place.'

'Well,' said Blendershin, 'your science may pull
you through. But I tell you it's hard. Some
grant-earning grammar school may want that.
And that's about all, I think. Make a note of the
address. . . .'

The assistant made a noise, something between a
whistle and the word 'Fee.' Blendershin glanced
at Lewisham and nodded doubtfully.

'Fee for booking,' said the assistant; 'half a
crown. Postage—in advance—half a crown.'

But Lewisham remembered certain advice Dunkerley had given him in the old Whortley days.
He hesitated. 'No,' he said. 'I don't pay that.
If you get me anything there's the commission—if
you don't——'

'We lose,' supplied the assistant.

'And you ought to,' said Lewisham. 'It's a
fair game.'

'Living in London?' asked Blendershin.

'Yes,' said the clerk.

'That's all right,' said Mr Blendershin. 'We
won't say anything about the postage in that case.
Of course it's the off season, and you mustn't expect
anything at present very much. Sometimes there's
a shift or so at Easter. . . . There's nothing more.
. . . Afternoon. Any one else, Binks?'

Messrs Maskelyne, Smith, and Thrums did a
higher class of work than Blendershin, whose
specialities were lower class private establishments
and the cheaper sort of endowed schools. Indeed,
so superior were Maskelyne, Smith, and Thrums that

they enraged Lewisham by refusing at first to put
him on their books. He was interviewed briefly by
a young man dressed and speaking with offensive
precision, whose eye adhered rigidly to the waterproof collar throughout the interview.

'Hardly our line,' he said, and pushed Lewisham
a form to fill up. 'Mostly upper class and good
preparatory schools here, you know.'

As Lewisham filled up the form with his multitudinous ''ologies' and ''ographies,' a youth of
ducal appearance entered and greeted the precise
young man in a friendly way. Lewisham, bending
down to write, perceived that this professional rival
wore a very long frock coat, patent leather boots,
and the most beautiful gray trousers. His con-
ceptions of competition enlarged. The precise young
man by a motion of his eyes directed the new-
comer's attention to Lewisham's waterproof collar,
and was answered by raised eyebrows and a faint
tightening of the mouth. 'That bounder at Castleford has answered me,' said the new-comer in a fine
rich voice. 'Is he any bally good?'

When the bounder at Castleford had been discussed Lewisham presented his paper, and the
precise young man with his eye still fixed on the
waterproof collar took the document in the manner
of one who reaches across a gulf. 'I doubt if we
shall be able to do anything for you,' he said
reassuringly. 'But an English mastership may
chance to be vacant. Science doesn't count for
much in *our* sort of schools, you know. Classics
and good games—that's our sort of thing.'

'I see,' said Lewisham.

'Good games, good form, you know, and all that
sort of thing.'

'I see,' said Lewisham.

'You don't happen to be a public-school boy?'
asked the precise young man.

'No,' said Lewisham.

'Where were you educated?'

Lewisham's face grew hot. 'Does that matter?'
he asked, with his eye on the exquisite gray
trousering.

'In our sort of school—decidedly. It's a question
of tone, you know.'

'I see,' said Lewisham, beginning to realise new
limitations. His immediate impulse was to escape
the eye of the nicely dressed assistant master.
'You'll write, I suppose, if you have anything,'
he said, and the precise young man responded with
alacrity to his doorward motion.

'Often get that kind of thing?' asked the nicely
dressed young man when Lewisham had departed.

'Rather. Not quite so bad as that, you know.
That waterproof collar—did you notice it? Ugh!
And—" I see." And the scowl and the clumsiness
of it. Of course *he* hasn't any decent clothes—he'd
go to a new shop with one tin box! But that sort
of thing—and board school teachers—they're getting
everywhere! Only the other day—Rowton was
here.'

'Not Rowton of Pinner?'

'Yes, Rowton of Pinner. And he asked right
out for a board schoolmaster. He said, " I want
some one who can teach arithmetic." '

He laughed. The nicely dressed young man
meditated over the handle of his cane. 'A bounder
of that kind can't have a particularly nice time,'
he said, 'anyhow. If he does get into a decent
school, he must get tremendously cut by all the
decent men.'

'Too thick-skinned to mind that sort of thing,

I fancy,' said the scholastic agent. 'He's a new type. This South Kensington place and the polytechnics are turning him out by the hundred. . . .'

Lewisham forgot his resentment at having to profess a religion he did not believe, in this new discovery of the scholastic importance of clothing. He went along with an eye to all the shop windows that afforded a view of his person. Indisputably his trousers *were* ungainly, flapping abominably over his boots and bagging terribly at the knees, and his boots were not only worn and ugly but extremely ill blacked. His wrists projected offensively from his coat sleeves, he perceived a huge asymmetry in the collar of his jacket, his red tie was askew and ill tied, and that waterproof collar ! It was shiny, slightly discoloured, suddenly clammy to the neck. What if he did happen to be well equipped for science teaching? That was nothing. He speculated on the cost of a complete outfit. It would be difficult to get such gray trousers as those he had seen for less than sixteen shillings, and he reckoned a frock coat at forty shillings at least— possibly even more. He knew good clothes were very expensive. He hesitated at Poole's door and turned away. The thing was out of the question. He crossed Leicester Square and went down Bedford Street disliking every well-dressed person he met.

Messrs Danks & Wimbourne inhabited a bank-like establishment near Chancery Lane, and without any conversation presented him with forms to fill up. Religion? asked the form. Lewisham paused and wrote 'Church of England.'

Thence he went to the College of Pedagogues in Holborn. The College of Pedagogues presented itself as a long-bearded, corpulent, comfortable person with a thin gold watch chain and fat hands. He wore gilt glasses and had a kindly confidential manner that did much to heal Lewisham's wounded feelings. The 'ologies and 'ographies were taken down with polite surprise at their number. 'You ought to take one of our diplomas,' said the stout man. 'You would find no difficulty. No competition. And there are prizes—several prizes—in money.'

Lewisham was not away that the waterproof collar had found a sympathetic observer.

'We give courses of lectures, and have an examination in the theory and practice of education. It is the only examination in the theory and practice of education for men engaged in middle and upper-class teaching in this country. Except the Teacher's Diploma. And so few come—not two hundred a year. Mostly governesses. The men prefer to teach by rule of thumb, you know. English characteristic—rule of thumb. It doesn't do to say anything, of course—but there's bound to be—something happen—something a little disagreeable —somewhen, if things go on as they do. American schools keep on getting better—German too. What used to do won't do now. I tell this to you, you know, but it doesn't do to tell every one. It doesn't do. It doesn't do to do anything. So much has to be considered. However. . . . But you'd do well to get a diploma and make yourself efficient. Though that's looking ahead.'

He spoke of looking ahead with an apologetic laugh as though it was an amiable weakness of his. He turned from such abstruse matters and furnished Lewisham with the particulars of the college diplomas, and proceeded to other possibilities.

'There's private tuition,' he said. 'Would you mind a backward boy? Then we are occasionally asked for visiting masters. Mostly by girls' schools. But that's for older men—married men, you know.'

'I am married,' said Lewisham.

'*Eh?*' said the College of Pedagogues, startled.

'I *am* married,' said Lewisham.

'Dear me,' said the College of Pedagogues gravely, and regarding Mr Lewisham over gold-rimmed glasses. 'Dear me! And I am more than twice your age, and I am not married at all. One-and-twenty! Have you—have you been married long?'

'A few weeks,' said Lewisham.

'That's very remarkable,' said the College of Pedagogues. 'Very interesting. . . . *Really!* Your wife must be a very courageous young person. . . . Excuse me! You know——. You will really have a hard fight for a position. However—it certainly makes you eligible for girls' schools; it does do that. To a certain extent, that is.'

The evidently enhanced respect of the College of Pedagogues pleased Lewisham extremely. But his encounter with the Medical, Scholastic, and Clerical Agency that holds by Waterloo Bridge was depressing again, and after that he set out to walk home. Long before he reached home he was tired, and his simple pride in being married and in active grapple with an unsympathetic world had passed. His surrender on the religious question had left a rankling bitterness behind it; the problem of the clothes was acutely painful. He was still far from a firm grasp of the fact that his market price was under rather than over one hundred pounds a year, but that persuasion was gaining ground in his mind.

The day was a grayish one, with a dull cold wind,

and a nail in one of his boots took upon itself to be objectionable. Certain wild shots and disastrous lapses in his recent botanical examination, that he had managed to keep out of his mind hitherto, forced their way on his attention. For the first time since his marriage he harboured premonitions of failure.

When he got in he wanted to sit down at once in the little creaky chair by the fire, but Ethel came flitting from the newly bought typewriter with arms extended and prevented him. 'Oh!—it *has* been dull,' she said.

He missed the compliment. '*I* haven't had such a giddy time that you should grumble,' he said, in a tone that was novel to her. He disengaged himself from her arms and sat down. He noticed the expression of her face.

'I'm rather tired,' he said by way of apology. 'And there's a confounded nail I must hammer down in my boot. It's tiring work hunting up these agents, but of course it's better to go and see them. How have you been getting on?'

'All right,' she said, regarding him. And then, 'You *are* tired. We'll have some tea. And—let me take off your boot for you, dear. Yes—I will.'

She rang the bell, bustled out of the room, called for tea at the staircase, came back, pulled out Madam Gadow's ungainly hassock and began unlacing his boot. Lewisham's mood changed. 'You *are* a trump, Ethel,' he said; 'I'm hanged if you're not.' As the laces flicked he bent forward and kissed her ear. The unlacing was suspended and there were reciprocal endearments. . . .

Presently he was sitting in his slippers, with a cup of tea in his hand, and Ethel, kneeling on the hearthrug with the firelight on her face, was telling him of an answer that had come that afternoon to her advertisement in the *Athenæum*.

'That's good,' said Lewisham.

'It's a novelist,' she said, with the light of pride in her eyes, and handed him the letter. 'Lucas Holderness, the author of *The Furnace of Sin* and other stories.'

'That's first-rate,' said Lewisham, with just a touch of envy, and bent forward to read by the firelight.

The letter was from an address in Judd Street, Euston Road, written on good paper and in a fair round hand, such as one might imagine a novelist using. 'Dear Madam,' said the letter; 'I propose to send you, by registered letter, the MS. of a three-volume novel. It is about 90,000 words—but you must count the exact number.'

'How I shall count I don't know,' said Ethel.

'I'll show you a way,' said Lewisham. 'There's no difficulty in that. You count the words on three or four pages, strike an average, and multiply.'

'But of course, before doing so I must have a satisfactory guarantee that my confidence in putting my work in your hands will not be misplaced and that your execution is of the necessary high quality.'

'Oh !' said Lewisham; 'that's a bother.'

'Accordingly I must ask you for references.'

'That's a downright nuisance,' said Lewisham. 'I suppose that ass, Lagune. . . . But what's this? " Or, failing references, for a deposit . . ." That's reasonable, I suppose.'

It was such a moderate deposit too—merely a guinea. Even had the doubt been stronger, the aspect of helpful, hopeful little Ethel eager for work might well have thrust it aside. 'Sending him a cheque will show him we have a banking account behind us,' said Lewisham—his banking was still sufficiently recent for pride. 'We will send him a cheque. That'll settle *him* all right.'

That evening, after the guinea cheque had been despatched, things were further brightened by the arrival of a letter of atrociously jellygraphed advices from Messrs Danks & Wimborne. They all referred to resident vacancies for which Lewisham was manifestly unsuitable, nevertheless their arrival brought an encouraging assurance of things going on, of shifting and unstable places in the defences of the beleaguered world. Afterwards, with occasional endearments for Ethel, he set himself to a revision of his last year's notebooks, for now the botany was finished, the advanced zoological course —the last lap, as it were, for the Forbes medal— was beginning. She got her best hat from the next room to make certain changes in the arrangement of its trimmings. She sat in the little chair, while Lewisham, with documents spread before him, sat at the table.

Presently she looked up from an experimental arrangement of her cornflowers, and discovered Lewisham, no longer reading, but staring blankly at the middle of the table-cloth, with an extraordinary misery in his eyes. She forgot the cornflowers and stared at him.

'Penny,' she said after an interval.

Lewisham started and looked up. *'Eh?'*

'Why were you looking so miserable?' she asked.

'Was I looking miserable?'

'Yes. And *cross* !'

'I was thinking just then that I would like to boil a bishop or so in oil.'

'My dear !'

'They know perfectly well the case against what they teach, they know it's neither madness nor wickedness nor any great harm to others, not to believe, they know perfectly well that a man may be as honest as the day, and right—right and decent in every way—and not believe in what they teach. And they know that it only wants the edge off a man's honour, for him to profess anything in the way of belief. Just anything. And they won't say so. I suppose they want the edge off every man's honour. If a man is well off they will truckle to him no end, though he laughs at all their teaching. They'll take gold plate from company promoters and rent from insanitary houses. But if a man is poor and doesn't profess to believe in what some of them scarcely believe themselves, they wouldn't lift a finger to help him against the ignorance of their followers. Your stepfather was right enough there. They know what's going on. They know that it means lying and humbug for any number of people, and they don't care. Why should they? *They've* got it down all right. They're spoilt and why shouldn't we be?'

Lewisham having selected the bishops as scapegoats for his turpitude, was inclined to ascribe even the nail in his boot to their agency.

Mrs Lewisham looked puzzled. She realised his drift.

'You're not,' she said, and dropped her voice, 'an *infidel*?'

Lewisham nodded gloomily. 'Aren't you?' he said.

'Oh, no,' said Mrs Lewisham.

'But you don't go to church, you don't——'

'No, I don't,' said Mrs Lewisham; and then with more assurance. 'But I'm not an infidel.'

'Christian?'

'I suppose so.'

'But a Christian—— What do you believe?'

'Oh! to tell the truth, and do right, and not hurt or injure people and all that.'

'That's not a Christian. A Christian is one who believes.'

'It's what *I* mean by a Christian,' said Mrs Lewisham.

'Oh! at that rate any one's a Christian,' said Lewisham. 'We all think it's right to do right and wrong to do wrong.'

'But we don't all do it,' said Mrs Lewisham, taking up the cornflowers again.

'No,' said Lewisham, a little taken aback by the feminine method of discussion. 'We don't all do it—certainly.' He stared at her for a moment —her head was a little on one side and her eyes on the cornflower—and his mind was full of a strange discovery. He seemed on the verge of speaking, and turned to his notebook again

Very soon the centre of the table-cloth resumed its sway.

The following day Mr Lucas Holderness received his cheque for a guinea. Unhappily it was crossed. He meditated for some time and then took pen and ink and improved Lewisham's careless 'one' to 'five' and touched up his unticked figure one to correspond.

You perceive him, a lank, cadaverous, good-looking man with long black hair and a semi-clerical costume of quite painful rustiness. He made the emendations with grave carefulness. He took the cheque round to his grocer. His grocer looked at it suspiciously.

'You pay it in,' said Mr Lucas Holderness, 'if you've any doubts about it. Pay it in. *I* don't know the man or what he is. He may be a swindler for all I can tell. *I* can't answer for him. Pay it in and see. Leave the change till then. I can wait. I'll call round in a few days' time.'

'All right, wasn't it?' said Mr Lucas Holderness in a casual tone two days later.

'Quite, sir,' said his grocer, with enhanced respect, and handed him his four pounds thirteen and sixpence change.

Mr Lucas Holderness, who had been eyeing the grocer's stock with a curious intensity, immediately became animated and bought a tin of salmon. He went out of the shop with the rest of the money in his hand, for the pockets of his clothes were old and untrustworthy. At the baker's he bought a new roll.

He bit a huge piece of the roll directly he was out of the shop, and went on his way gnawing. It was so large a piece that his gnawing mouth was contorted into the ugliest shapes. He swallowed by an effort, stretching his neck each time. His eyes expressed an animal satisfaction. He turned the corner of Judd Street biting again at the roll, and the reader of this story, like the Lewishams, hears of him no more.

CHAPTER XXVI

THE GLAMOUR FADES

AFTER all, the rosy lovemaking and marrying and
Epithalamy are no more than the dawn of things,
and to follow comes all the spacious interval of
white laborious light. Try as we may to stay those
delightful moments, they fade and pass remorse-
lessly; there is no returning, no recovering, only—
for the foolish—the vilest peep-shows and imitations
in dens and darkened rooms. We go on—we grow.
At least we age. Our young couple, emerging
presently from an atmosphere of dusk and morning
stars, found the sky gathering grayly overhead and
saw one another for the first time clearly in the
light of every day.

It might perhaps witness better to Lewisham's
refinement if one could tell only of a moderated
and dignified cooling, of pathetic little concealments
of disappointment and a decent maintenance of
the sentimental atmosphere. And so at last day-
light. But our young couple were too crude for
that. The first intimations of their lack of identity
have already been described, but it would be
tedious and pitiful to tell of all the little intensifi-
cations, shade by shade, of the conflict of their
individualities. They fell out, dear lady! they came
to conflict of words. The stress of perpetual worry
was upon them, of dwindling funds and the anxious
search for work that would not come. And on

Ethel lay long, vacant, lonely hours in dull surroundings. Differences arose from the most indifferent things; one night Lewisham lay awake in unfathomable amazement because she had convinced him she did not care a rap for the Welfare of Humanity, and deemed his Socialism a fancy and an indiscretion. And one Sunday afternoon they started for a walk under the pleasantest auspices, and returned flushed and angry, satire and retort flying free—on the score of the social conventions in Ethel's novelettes. For some inexplicable reason Lewisham saw fit to hate her novelettes very bitterly. These encounters indeed were mere skirmishes for the most part, and the silences and embarrassments that followed ended sooner or later in a 'making up,' tacit or definite, though once or twice this making up only reopened the healing wound. And always each skirmish left its scar, effaced from yet another line of their lives the lingering tints of romantic colour.

There came no work, no added income for either of them, saving two trifles, for five long months. Once Lewisham won twelve shillings in the prize competition of a penny weekly, and three times came infinitesimal portions of typewriting from a poet who had apparently seen the *Athenæum* advertisement. His name was Edwin Peak Baynes and his handwriting was sprawling and unformed. He sent her several short lyrics on scraps of paper with instructions that he desired 'three copies of each written beautifully in different styles' and '*not* fastened with metal fasteners but with silk thread of an appropriate colour.' Both of our young people were greatly exercised by these instructions. One fragment was called 'Bird Song,' one 'Cloud Shadows,' and one 'Eryngium,' but Lewisham thought they might be spoken of collectively as Bosh. By way of payment, this poet sent, in contravention of the postal regulations, half a sovereign stuck into a card, asking her to keep the balance against future occasions. In a little while, greatly altered copies of these lyrics were returned by the poet in person, with this enigmatical instruction written across the cover of each : 'This style I like, only if possible more so.'

Lewisham was out, but Ethel opened the door, so this endorsement was unnecessary. 'He's really only a boy,' said Ethel, describing the interview to Lewisham, who was curious. They both felt that the youthfulness of Edwin Peak Baynes detracted something from the reality of this employment.

From his marriage until the final examination in June, Lewisham's life had an odd amphibious quality. At home were Ethel and the perpetual aching pursuit of employment, the pelting irritations of Madame Gadow's persistent overcharges, and so forth, and amid such things he felt extraordinarily grown up; but intercalated with these experiences were those intervals at Kensington, scraps of his adolescence, as it were, lying amidst the new matter of his manhood, intervals during which he was simply an insubordinate and disappointing student with an increasing disposition to gossip. At South Kensington he dwelt with theories and ideals as a student should; at the little rooms in Chelsea— they grew very stuffy as the summer came on, and the accumulation of the penny novelettes Ethel favoured made a litter—there was his particular private concrete situation, and ideals gave place to the real.

It was a strangely narrow world, he perceived dimly, in which his manhood opened. The only visitors were the Chafferys. Chaffery would come to share their supper, and won upon Lewisham in spite of his roguery by his incessantly entertaining monologue and by his expressed respect for and envy of Lewisham's scientific attainments. Moreover, as time went on Lewisham found himself more and more in sympathy with Chaffery's bitterness against those who order the world. It was good to hear him on bishops and that sort of people. He said what Lewisham wanted to say beautifully. Mrs Chaffery was perpetually flitting—out of the house as Lewisham came home, a dim, black, nervous, untidy little figure. She came because Ethel, in spite of her expressed belief that love was 'all in all,' found married life a little dull and lonely while Lewisham was away. And she went hastily when he came, because of a certain irritability that the struggle against the world was developing. He told no one at Kensington about his marriage, at first because it was such a delicious secret and then for quite other reasons. So there was no over-lapping. The two worlds began and ended sharply at the wrought-iron gates. But the day came when Lewisham passed those gates for the last time and his adolescence ended altogether.

In the final examination of the biological course, the examination that signalised the end of his income of a weekly guinea, he knew well enough that he had done badly. The evening of the last day's practical work found him belated, hot-headed, beaten, with ruffled hair and red ears. He sat to the last moment doggedly struggling to keep cool and to mount the ciliated funnel of an earthworm's nephridium. But ciliated funnels come not to those who have shirked the laboratory practice. He rose, surrendered his paper to the morose elderly young assistant demonstrator who had welcomed him so flatteringly eight months before, and walked down the laboratory to the door where the rest of his fellow-students clustered.

Smithers was talking loudly about the 'twistiness' of the identification, and the youngster with the big ears was listening attentively.

'Here's Lewisham! How did *you* get on, Lewisham?' asked Smithers, not concealing his assurance.

'Horribly,' said Lewisham shortly, and pushed past.

'Did you spot D?' clamoured Smithers.

Lewisham pretended not to hear.

Miss Heydinger stood with her hat in her hand and looked at Lewisham's hot eyes. He was for walking past her, but something in her face penetrated even his disturbance. He stopped.

'Did you get out the nephridium?' he said as graciously as he could.

She shook her head. 'Are you going downstairs?' she asked.

'Rather,' said Lewisham, with a vague intimation in his manner of the offence Smithers gave him.

He opened the glass door from the passage to the staircase. They went down one tier of that square spiral in silence.

'Are you coming up again next year,' asked Miss Heydinger.

'No,' said Lewisham. 'No, I shall not come here again. Ever.'

Pause. 'What will you do?' she asked.

'I don't know. I have to get a living somehow. It's been bothering me all the session.'

'I thought——' She stopped. 'Will you go down to your uncle's again?' she said.

'No. I shall stop in London. It's no good going

out of things into the country. And besides—I've quarrelled rather with my uncle.'

'What do you think of doing?—teaching?'

'I suppose it will be teaching. I'm not sure. Anything that turns up.'

'I see,' she said.

They went on down in silence for a time.

'I suppose you will come up again?' he asked.

'I may try the botanical again—if they can find room. And, I was thinking—sometimes one hears of things. What is your address? So that if I heard of anything.'

Lewisham stopped on the staircase and thought. 'Of course,' he said. He made no effort to give her the address, and she demanded it again at the foot of the stairs.

'That confounded nephridium——!' he said. 'It has put everything out of my head.'

They exchanged addresses on leaflets torn from Miss Heydinger's little notebook.

She waited at the Book in the hall while he signed his name. At the iron gates of the Schools she said : 'I am going through Kensington Gardens.'

He was now feeling irritated about the addresses, and he would not see the implicit invitation. 'I am going towards Chelsea.'

She hesitated a moment, looking at him—puzzled. 'Good-bye, then,' she said.

'Good-bye,' he answered, lifting his hat.

He crossed the Exhibition Road slowly with his packed glazed bag, now seamed with cracks, in his hand. He went thoughtfully down to the corner of the Cromwell Road and turned along that to the right so that he could see the red pile of the Science Schools rising fair and tall across the gardens of the Natural History Museum. He looked back towards it regretfully.

He was quite sure that he had failed in this last examination. He knew that any career as a scientific man was now closed to him for ever, and he remembered now how he had come along this very road to that great building for the first time in his life, and all the hopes and resolves that had swelled within him as he had drawn near. That dream of incessant unswerving work! Where might he have reached if only he had had singleness of purpose to realise that purpose? . . .

And in these gardens it was that he and Smithers and Parkson had sat on a seat hard by the fossil-tree and discoursed of Socialism together before the great paper was read. . . .

'Yes,' he said, speaking aloud to himself; 'yes —*that's* all over too. Everything's over.'

Presently the corner of the Natural History Museum came between him and his receding Alma Mater. He sighed and turned his face towards the stuffy little rooms at Chelsea, and the still unconquered world.

CHAPTER XXVII

CONCERNING A QUARREL

IT was late in September that this particular quarrel occurred. Almost all the roseate tints seemed gone by this time, for the Lewishams had been married six months. Their financial affairs had changed from the catastrophic to the sordid; Lewisham had found work. An army crammer named Captain Vigours wanted some one energetic for his mathematical duffers and to teach geometrical drawing and what he was pleased to call 'Sandhurst Science.' He paid no less than two shillings an hour for his uncertain demands on Lewisham's time. Moreover, there was a class in lower mathematics beginning at Walham Green where Lewisham was to show his quality. Fifty shillings a week or more seemed credible—more might be hoped for. It was now merely a case of tiding over the interval until Vigours paid. And meanwhile the freshness of Ethel's blouses departed, and Lewisham refrained from the repair of his boot which had cracked across the toe.

The beginning of the quarrel was trivial enough. But by the end they got to generalities. Lewisham had begun the day in a bad temper and under the cloud of an overnight passage of arms—and a little incident that had nothing to do with their ostensible difference lent it a warmth of emotion quite beyond its merits. As he emerged through the folding doors

he saw a letter lying among the sketchily laid breakfast things, and Ethel's attitude suggested the recoil
of a quick movement; the letter suddenly dropped.
Her eyes met his and she flushed. He sat down
and took the letter—a trifle awkwardly perhaps. It
was from Miss Heydinger. He hesitated with it
half-way to his pocket, then decided to open it.
It displayed an ample amount of reading, and he
read. On the whole he thought it rather a dull
sort of letter, but he did not allow this to appear.
When it was read he put it carefully in his pocket.

That formally had nothing to do with the quarrel.
The breakfast was already over when the quarrel
began. Lewisham's morning was vacant, and he
proposed to occupy it in the revision of certain
notes bearing upon 'Sandhurst Science. Unhappily
the search for his notebook brought him into
collision with the accumulation of Ethel's novelettes.

'These things are everywhere,' he said, after a
gust of vehement handling. 'I *wish* you'd tidy
them up sometimes.'

'They were tidy enough till you began to throw
them about,' Ethel pointed out.

'Confounded muck! it's only fit to be burnt,'
Lewisham remarked to the universe, and pitched
one viciously into the corner.

'Well, you tried to write one, anyhow,' said
Ethel, recalling a certain 'Mammoth' packet of
note-paper that had come on an evil end before
Lewisham found his industrial level. This reminiscence always irritated him exceedingly.

'Eh?' he said sharply.

'You tried to write one,' repeated Ethel—a little
unwillingly.

'You don't mean me to forget that.'

'It's you reminded me.'

He stared hostility for a space.

'Well, the things make a beastly litter anyhow, there isn't a tidy corner anywhere in the room. There never is.'

'That's just the sort of thing you always say.'

'Well—*is* there?'

'Yes, there is.'

'*Where?*'

Ethel professed not to hear. But a devil had possession of Lewisham for a time. 'It isn't as though you had anything else to do,' he remarked, wounding dishonourably.

Ethel turned. 'If I *put* those things away,' she said, with tremendous emphasis on the '*put*,' 'you'd only say I'd hidden them. What *is* the good of trying to please you?'

The spirit of perversity suggested to Lewisham, 'None apparently.'

Ethel's cheeks glowed and her eyes were bright with unshed tears. Abruptly she abandoned the defensive and blurted out the thing that had been latent so long between them. Her voice took a note of passion. 'Nothing I can do ever does please you, since that Miss Heydinger began to write to you.'

There was a pause, a gap. Something like astonishment took them both. Hitherto it had been a convention that she knew nothing of the existence of Miss Heydinger. He saw a light. 'How did you know?' he began, and perceived that line was impossible. He took the way of the natural man; he ejaculated an 'Ugh!' of vast disgust, he raised his voice. 'You *are* unreasonable!' he cried in angry remonstrance. 'Fancy saying that! As though you ever tried to please me! Just as though it wasn't all the other way about!' He stopped—struck by a momentary perception of injustice. He plunged at the point he had shirked.

'How did you know it *was* Miss Heydinger——?'

Ethel's voice took upon itself the quality of tears. 'I wasn't *meant* to know, was I?' she said.

'But how?'

'I suppose you think it doesn't concern me? I suppose you think I'm made of stone.'

'You mean—you think——?'

'Yes—I *do*.'

For a brief interval Lewisham stared at the issue she had laid bare. He sought some crushing proposition, some line of convincing reasoning, with which to overwhelm and hide this new aspect of things. It would not come. He found himself fenced in on every side. A surging, irrational rage seized upon him.

'Jealousy!' he cried. 'Jealousy! Just as though—— Can't I have letters about things you don't understand—that you *won't* understand? If I asked you to read them you wouldn't—— It's just because——'

'You never give me a *chance* to understand.'

'Don't I?'

'No!'

'Why!—At first I was always trying. Socialism, religion—all those things. But you don't care—you won't care. You won't have that I've thought over these things at all, that I care for these things! It wasn't any *good* to argue. You just care for me in a way—and all the rest of me—doesn't matter! And because I've got a friend . . .'

'Friend!'

'Yes—*friend*!'

'Why!—you hide her letters!'

'Because I tell you you wouldn't understand

what they are about. But, pah! I won't argue. I
won't! You're jealous and there's the end of the
matter!'

'Well, who *wouldn't* be jealous?'

He stared at her as if he found the question hard
to see. The theme was difficult—invincibly difficult.
He surveyed the room for a diversion. The notebook he had disinterred from her novelettes lay
upon the table and reminded him of his grievance of
ruined hours. His rage exploded. He struck out
abruptly towards fundamental things. He gesticulated forcibly. 'This can't go on!' he cried, 'this
can't go on! How can I work? How can I do
anything?'

He made three steps and stood in a clear space.

'I won't *stand* it—I won't go on at this! Quarrels
—bickerings—discomfort. Look there! I meant
to work this morning. I meant to look up notes!
Instead of which you start a quarrel——'

The gross injustice raised Ethel's voice to an
outcry. '*I* didn't start the quarrel——'

The only response to this was to shout, and
Lewisham shouted. 'You start a quarrel!' he
repeated. 'You make a shindy! You spring a
dispute—jealousy!—on me! How can I do anything? How can one stop in a house like this?
I shall go out. Look here!—I shall go out. I shall
go to Kensington and work there!'

He perceived himself wordless, and Ethel was
about to speak. He glared about him, seeking a
prompt climax. Instant action was necessary. He
perceived Huxley s *Vertebrata* upon the side-table.
He clutched it, swayed it through a momentous
arc, hurled it violently into the empty fireplace.

For a second he seemed to be seeking some other
missile. He perceived his hat on the chest of

drawers, seized it and strode tragically from the room.

He hesitated with the door half closed, then opened it wide and slammed it vehemently. Thereby the world was warned of the justice of his rage, and so he passed with credit into the street.

He went striding heedless of his direction through the streets dotted with intent people hurrying to work, and presently habit turned his feet towards the Brompton Road. The eastward trend of the morning traffic caught him. For a time, save for a rebellious ingredient of wonder at the back of his mind, he kept his anger white and pure. Why had he married her? was the text to which he clung. Why in the name of destiny had he married her? But anyhow he had said the decisive thing. He would not stand it! It must end. Things were intolerable and they must end. He meditated devastating things that he might presently say to her in pursuance of this resolution. He contemplated acts of cruelty. In such ways he would demonstrate clearly that he would not stand it. He was very careful to avoid inquiring what it was he would not stand.

How in the name of destiny had he come to marry her? The quality of his surroundings mingled in some way with the quality of his thoughts. The huge distended buildings of corrugated iron in which the Art Museum (of all places!) culminates, the truncated Oratory all askew to the street, seemed to have a similar quarrel with fate. How in the name of destiny? After such high prolusions!

He found that his thoughts had carried him past the lodge of the museum. He turned back irritably and went through the turnstile   He entered the

museum and passed beneath the gallery of Old
Iron on his way to the Education Library. The
vacant array of tables, the bays of attendant books
had a quality of refuge. . . .

So much for Lewisham in the morning. Long
before midday all the vigour of his wrath was
gone, all his passionate conviction of Ethel's
unworthiness. Over a pile of neglected geological
works he presented a face of gloom. His memory
presented a picture of himself as noisy, overbearing,
and unfair. What on earth had it all been about?

By two o'clock he was on his way to Vigours',
and his mood was acute remorse. Of the transition
there can be no telling in words, for thoughts are
more subtle than words and emotions infinitely
vaguer. But one thing at least is definite, that a
memory returned.

It drifted into him, through the glass roof of the
Library far above. He did not perceive it as a
memory at first, but as an irritating obstacle to
attention. He struck the open pages of the book
before him with his flat hand. 'Damn that infernal
hurdy-gurdy!' he whispered.

Presently he made a fretful movement and put
his hands over his ears.

Then he thrust his books from him, got up, and
wandered about the Library. The organ came to
an abrupt end in the middle of a bar, and vanished
in the circumambient silence of space.

Lewisham, standing in a bay, closed a book with
a snap and returned to his seat.

Presently he found himself humming a languid
tune, and thinking again of the quarrel that he had
imagined banished from his mind. What in the
name of destiny had it all been about? He had a
curious sense that something had got loose, was

sliding about in his mind. And as if by way of answer emerged a vision of Whortley—a singularly vivid vision. It was moonlight and a hill-side, the little town lay lit and warm below, and the scene was set to music, a lugubriously sentimental air For some reason this music had the quality of a barrel organ—though he knew that properly it came from a band—and it associated with itself a mystical formula of words, drawing words :—

'Sweet dreamland fa—ces passing to and fro,
Bring back to mem'ry, days of long ago—oh !'

This air not only reproduced the picture with graphic vividness, but it trailed after it an enormous cloud of irrational emotion, emotion that had but a moment before seemed gone for ever from his being.

He recalled it all ! He had come down that hill-side and Ethel had been with him. . . .

Had he really felt like that about her?

'Pah !' he said suddenly, and reverted to his books.

But the tune and the memory had won their footing, they were with him through his meagre lunch of milk and scones—he had resolved at the outset he would not go back to her for the midday meal—and on his way to Vigours' they insisted on attention. It may be that lunching on scone and milk does in itself make for milder ways of thinking. A sense of extraordinary contradiction, of infinite perplexity, came to him.

'But then,' he asked, 'how the devil did we get to *this*?'

Which is indeed one of the fundamental questions of matrimony.

The morning tumults had given place to an almost scientific calm. Very soon he was grappling manfully with the question. There was no disputing it, they had quarrelled. Not once but several times lately they had quarrelled. It was real quarrelling;—they had stood up against one another, striking, watching to strike, seeking to wound. He tried to recall just how things had gone—what he had said and what she had replied. He could not do it. He had forgotten phrases and connections. It stood in his memory not as a sequence of events but as a collection of disconnected static sayings; each saying blunt, permanent, inconsecutive like a graven inscription. And of the scene there came only one picture—Ethel with a burning face and her eyes shining with tears.

The traffic of a cross street engaged him for a space. He emerged on the farther side full of the vivid contrast of their changed relations. He made a last effort to indict her, to show that for the transition she was entirely to blame. She had quarrelled with him, she had quarrelled deliberately because she was jealous. She was jealous of Miss Heydinger because she was stupid. But now these accusations faded like smoke as he put them forth. But the picture of two little figures back there in the moonlit past did not fade. It was in the narrows of Kensington High Street that he abandoned her arraignment. It was beyond the Town Hall that he made the new step. Was it, after all, just possible that in some degree he himself rather was the chief person to blame?

It was instantly as if he had been aware of that all the time.

Once he had made that step, he moved swiftly. Not a hundred paces before the struggle was over, and he had plunged headlong into the blue abyss of remorse. And all these things that had been so dramatic and forcible, all the vivid brutal things he had said, stood no longer graven inscriptions but in letters of accusing flame. He tried to imagine he had not said them, that his memory played him a trick, tried to suppose he had said something similar perhaps but much less forcible. He attempted with almost equal futility to minimise his own wounds. His endeavour served only to measure the magnitude of his fall.

He had recovered everything now, he saw it all. He recalled Ethel, sunlit in the avenue, Ethel, white in the moonlight before they parted outside the Frobisher house, Ethel as she would come out of Lagune's house greeting him for their nightly walk, Ethel new wedded, as she came to him through the folding doors radiant in the splendour his emotions threw about her. And at last Ethel angry, dishevelled and tear-stained in that ill-lit, untidy little room. All to the cadence of a hurdy-gurdy tune! From that to this! How had it been possible to get from such an opalescent dawning to such a dismal day? What was it had gone? He and she were the same two persons who walked so brightly in his awakened memory; he and she who had lived so bitterly through the last few weeks of misery!

His mood sank for a space to the quality of groaning. He implicated her now at most as his partner in their failure—'What a mess we have made of things!' was his new motif. What a mess!'

He knew love now for what it was, knew it for something more ancient and more imperative than reason. He knew now that he loved her, and his recent rage, his hostility, his condemnation of her seemed to him the reign of some exterior influence in his mind. He thought incredulously of the long decline in tenderness that had followed the first days of their delight in each other, the diminution of endearment, the first yielding to irritability, the evenings he had spent doggedly working, resisting all his sense of her presence. 'One cannot always be lovemaking,' he had said, and so—they were slipping apart. Then in countless little things he had not been patient, he had not been fair. He had wounded her by harshness, by unsympathetic criticism, above all by his absurd secrecy about Miss Heydinger's letters. Why on earth had he kept those letters from her? as though there was something to hide! What was there to hide? What possible antagonism could there be? Yet it was by such little things that their love was now like some once valued possession that had been in brutal hands, it was scratched and clipped and tarnished, it was on its way to being altogether destroyed. Her manner had changed towards him, a gulf was opening that he might never be able to close again.

'No, it *shall* not be!' he said, 'it shall not be!'

But how to get back to the old footing? how to efface the things he had said, the things that had been done?

Could they get back?

For a moment he faced a new possibility. Suppose they could not get back! Suppose the mischief was done! Suppose that when he slammed the door behind him it locked, and was locked against him for ever!

'But we *must*!' said Lewisham, 'we must!'

He perceived clearly that this was no business of reasoned apologies. He must begin again, he must get back to emotion, he must thrust back the overwhelming pressure of everyday stresses and necessities that was crushing all the warmth and colour from their lives. But how? How?

He must make love to her again. But how to begin—how to mark the change? There had been making-up before, sullen concessions and treaties. But this was different. He tried to imagine something he might say, some appeal that he might make. Everything he thought of was cold and hard, or pitiful and undignified, or theatrical and foolish. Suppose the door *was* closed! If already it was too late! In every direction he was confronted by the bristling memories of harsh things. He had a glimpse of how he must have changed in her eyes, and things became intolerable for him. For now he was assured he loved her still with all his heart.

And suddenly came a florist's window, and in the centre of it a glorious heap of roses.

They caught his eye before they caught his mind. He saw white roses, virginal white, roses of cream and pink and crimson, the tints of flesh and pearl, rich, a mass of scented colour, visible odours, and in the midst of them a note of sullen red. It was as it were the very colour of his emotion. He stopped abruptly. He turned back to the window and stared frankly. It was gorgeous, he saw, but why so particularly did it appeal to him?

Then he perceived as though it was altogether self-evident what he had to do. This was what he wanted. This was the note he had to strike. Among other things because it would repudiate the accursed worship of pinching self-restraint that was one of the incessant stresses between them. They would come to her with a pure unexpectedness, they would flame upon her.

Then, after the roses, he would return.

Suddenly the gray trouble passed from his mind; he saw the world full of colour again. He saw the scene he desired bright and clear, saw Ethel no longer bitter and weeping, but glad as once she had always seemed glad. His heart-beats quickened. It was giving had been needed, and he would give.

Some weak voice of indiscreet discretion squeaked and vanished. He had, he knew, a sovereign in his pocket. He went in.

He found himself in front of a formidable young lady in black, and unprepared with any formula. He had never bought flowers before. He looked about him for an inspiration. He pointed at the roses. 'I want those roses,' he said. . . .

He emerged again with only a few small silver coins remaining out of the sovereign he had changed. The roses were to go to Ethel, properly packed; they were to be delivered according to his express direction at six o'clock.

'Six o'clock,' Lewisham had reiterated very earnestly.

'We quite understand,' the young lady in black had said, and had pretended to be unable to conceal a smile. 'We're *quite* accustomed to sending out flowers.'

CHAPTER XXVIII

THE COMING OF THE ROSES

AND the roses miscarried !

When Lewisham returned from Vigours' it was already nearly seven. He entered the house with a beating heart. He had expected to find Ethel excited, the roses displayed. But her face was white and jaded. He was so surprised by this that the greeting upon his lips died away ! He was balked ! He went into the sitting-room and there were no roses to be seen. Ethel came past him and stood with her back to him looking out of the window. The suspense was suddenly painful. . . .

He was obliged to ask, though he was certain of the answer, 'Has nothing come?'

Ethel looked at him. 'What did you think had come?'

'Oh ! nothing.'

She looked out of the window again. 'No,' she said slowly, 'nothing has come.'

He tried to think of something to say that might bridge the distance between them, but he could think of nothing. He must wait until the roses came. He took out his books and a gaunt hour passed to supper time. Supper was a chilly ceremonial set with necessary over-polite remarks. Disappointment and exasperation darkened Lewisham's soul. He began to feel angry with everything—even with her—he perceived she still judged him angry and that made him angry with her. He was resuming his books and she was helping Madam Gadow's servant to clear away, when they heard a rapping at the street door. 'They have come at last,' he said to himself, brightening, and hesitated whether he should bolt or witness her reception of them. The servant was a nuisance. Then he heard Chaffery's voice, and whispered a soft 'damn!' to himself.

The only thing to do now if the roses came was to slip out into the passage, intercept them and carry them into the bedroom by the door between that and the passage. It would be undesirable for Chaffery to witness that phase of sentiment. He might flash some dart of ridicule that would stick in their memory for ever.

Lewisham tried to show that he did not want a visitor. But Chaffery was in high spirits and could have warmed a dozen cold welcomes. He sat down without any express invitation in the chair that he preferred.

Before Mr and Mrs Chaffery the Lewishams veiled whatever trouble might be between them beneath an insincere cordiality, and Chaffery was soon talking freely, unsuspicious of their crisis. He produced two cigars. 'I had a wild moment,' he said. ' " For once," said I, " the honest shall smoke the admirable —or the admirable shall smoke the honest," whichever you like best. Try one? No? Those austere principles of yours! There will be more pleasure then. But really, I would as soon you smoked it as I. For to-night I radiate benevolence.'

He cut the cigar with care, he lit it with ceremony, waiting until nothing but honest wood was burning on the match, and for fully a minute he was silent, evolving huge puffs of smoke. And then he spoke again, punctuating his words by varied and beautiful spirals. 'So far,' he said, 'I have only trifled with knavery.'

As Lewisham said nothing he resumed after a pause.

'There are three sorts of men in the world, my boy, three and no more—and of women only one. There are happy men and there are knaves and fools. Hybrids I don't count. And to my mind knaves and fools are very much alike.'

He paused again.

'I suppose they are,' said Lewisham flatly, and frowned at the fireplace.

Chaffery eyed him. 'I am talking wisdom. To-night I am talking a particular brand of wisdom. I am broaching some of my oldest and finest, because —as you will find one day—this is a special occasion. And you are distrait!'

Lewisham looked up. 'Birthday?' he said.

'You will see. But I was making golden observations about knaves and fools. I was early convinced of the absolute necessity of righteousness if a man is to be happy. I know it as surely as there is a sun in the heavens. Does that surprise you?'

'Well, it hardly squares——'

'No. I know. I will explain all that. But let me tell you the happy life. Let me give you that, as if I lay on my deathbed and this was a parting gift. In the first place, mental integrity. Prove all things, hold fast to that which is right. Let the world have no illusions for you, no surprises. Nature is full of cruel catastrophes, man is a physically degenerate ape, every appetite, every instinct, needs the curb; salvation is not in the nature of things but whatever salvation there may be is in the nature of man; face all these painful things. I hope you follow that?'

'Go on,' said Lewisham, with the debating-society taste for a thesis prevailing for a minute over that matter of the roses.

'In youth, exercise and learning; in adolescence, ambition, and in early manhood, love—no footlight passion.' Chaffery was very solemn and insistent, with a lean, extended finger, upon this point.

'Then marriage, young and decent, and then children and stout honest work for them, work, too, for the State in which they live; a life of self-devotion, indeed, and for sunset a decent pride—that is the happy life. Rest assured that is the happy life; the life Natural Selection has been shaping for man since life began. So a man may go happy from the cradle to the grave—at least —passably happy. And to do this needs just three things—a sound body, a sound intelligence, and a sound will. . . . A sound will.'

Chaffery paused on the repetition.

'No other happiness endures. And when all men are wise, all men will seek that life. Fame! Wealth! Art!—the Red Indians worship lunatics, and we are still by way of respecting the milder sorts. But I say that all men who do not lead that happy life are knaves and fools. The physical cripple, you know, poor devil, I count a sort of bodily fool.'

'Yes,' weighed Lewisham, 'I suppose he is.'

'Now a fool fails of happiness because of his insufficient mind, he miscalculates, he stumbles and hobbles, some cant or claptrap whirls him away; he gets passion out of a book and a wife out of the stews, or he quarrels on a petty score; threats frighten him, vanity beguiles him, he fails by blindness. But the knave who is not a fool fails against the light. Many knaves are fools also—*most* are —but some are not. I know—I am a knave but no fool. The essence of your knave is that he lacks the will, the motive capacity to seek his own greater good. The knave abhors persistence. Strait is the way and narrow the gate; the knave cannot keep to it and the fool cannot find it.'

Lewisham lost something of what Chaffery was saying by reason of a rap outside. He rose, but

Ethel was before him. He concealed his anxiety as well as he could, and was relieved when he heard the front door close again and her footsteps pass into the bedroom by the passage door. He reverted to Chaffery.

'Has it ever occurred to you,' asked Chaffery, apparently apropos of nothing, 'that intellectual conviction is no motive at all? Any more than a railway map will run a train a mile.'

'Eh?' said Lewisham. 'Map—run a train a mile —of course, yes. No, it won't.'

'That is precisely my case,' said Chaffery. 'That is the case of your pure knave everywhere. We are not fools—because we know. But yonder runs the highway, windy, hard, and austere, a sort of dry happiness that will endure; and here is the pleasant byway—lush, my boy, lush, as the poets have it, and with its certain man-trap among the flowers . . .'

Ethel returned through the folding doors. She glanced at Lewisham, remained standing for a while, sat down in the basket-chair as if to resume some domestic needlework that lay upon the table, then rose and went back into the bedroom.

Chaffery proceeded to expatiate on the transitory nature of passion and all glorious and acute experiences. Whole passages of that discourse Lewisham did not hear, so intent was he upon those roses. Why had Ethel gone back into the bedroom? Was it possible——? Presently she returned, but she sat down so that he could not see her face.

'If there is one thing to set against the wholesome life it is adventure,' Chaffery was saying. 'But let every adventurer pray for an early death, for with adventure come wounds, and with wounds come sickness, and—except in romances—sickness affects the nervous system. Your nerve goes. Where are you, then, my boy?'

'Ssh! what's that?' said Lewisham.

It was a rap at the house door. Heedless of the flow of golden wisdom, he went out at once and admitted a gentleman friend of Madam Gadow, who passed along the passage and vanished down the staircase. When he returned Chaffery was standing to go.

'I could have talked with you longer,' he said, 'but you have something on your mind, I see. I will not worry you by guessing what. Some day you will remember . . .' He said no more, but laid his hand on Lewisham's shoulder.

One might almost fancy he was offended at something.

At any other time Lewisham might have been propitiatory, but now he offered no apology. Chaffery turned to Ethel and looked at her curiously for a moment. 'Good-bye,' he said, holding out his hand to her.

On the doorstep Chaffery regarded Lewisham with the same curious look, and seemed to weigh some remark. 'Good-bye,' he said at last, with something in his manner that kept Lewisham at the door for a moment looking after his stepfather's receding figure. But immediately the roses were uppermost again.

When he re-entered the living-room he found Ethel sitting idly at her typewriter, playing with the keys. She got up at his return and sat down in the arm-chair with a novelette that hid her face. He stared at her, full of questions. After all, then, they had not come. He was intensely disappointed now, he was intensely angry with the ineffable young shop-woman in black. He looked at his watch and then again, he took a book and pretended to read and found himself composing a scathing speech of remonstrance to be delivered on the morrow at the flower-shop. He put his book down, went to his black bag, opened and closed it aimlessly. He glanced covertly at Ethel and found her looking covertly at him. He could not quite understand her expression.

He fidgeted into the bedroom and stopped as dead as a pointer.

He felt an extraordinary persuasion of the scent of roses. So strong did it seem that he glanced outside the room door, expecting to find a box there, mysteriously arrived. But there was no scent of roses in the passage.

Then he saw close by his foot an enigmatical pale object, and stooping, picked up the creamy petal of a rose. He stood with it in his hand, perplexed beyond measure. He perceived a slight disorder of the valence of the dressing-table and linked it with this petal by a swift intuition.

He made two steps, lifted the valence, and behold ! there lay his roses crushed together !

He gasped like a man who plunges suddenly into cold water. He remained stooping with the valence raised.

Ethel appeared in the half doorway and her expression was unfamiliar. He stared at her white face.

'Why on earth did you put my roses here?' he asked.

She stared back at him. Her face reflected his astonishment.

'Why did you put my roses here?' he asked again.

'Your roses !' she cried. 'What ! Did *you* send those roses?'

CHAPTER XXIX

THORNS AND ROSE PETALS

He remained stooping and staring up at her, realising the implication of her words only very slowly.

Then it grew clear to him.

As she saw understanding dawning in his face, she uttered a cry of consternation. She came forward and sat down upon the little bedroom chair. She turned to him and began a sentence. 'I,' she said, and stopped, with an impatient gesture of her hands. *'Oh !'*

He straightened himself and stood regarding her. The basket of roses lay overturned between them.

'You thought these came from some one else?' he said, trying to grasp this inversion of the universe.

She turned her eyes. 'I did not know,' she panted. 'A trap. . . . Was it likely—they came from you?'

'You thought they came from some one else,' he said.

'Yes,' she said, 'I did.'

'Who?'

'Mr Baynes.'

'That boy !'

'Yes—that boy.'

'Well !'

Lewisham looked about him—a man in the presence of the inconceivable

'You mean to say you have been carrying on with that youngster behind my back?' he asked.

She opened her lips to speak and had no words to say.

His pallor increased until every tinge of colour had left his face. He laughed and then set his teeth. Husband and wife looked at one another.

'I never dreamt,' he said in even tones.

He sat down on the bed, thrusting his feet among the scattered roses with a sort of grim satisfaction. 'I never dreamt,' he repeated, and the flimsy basket kicked by his swinging foot hopped indignantly through the folding doors into the living-room and left a trail of blood-red petals.

They sat for perhaps two minutes and when he spoke again his voice was hoarse. He reverted to a former formula. 'Look here,' he said, and cleared his throat. 'I don't know whether you think I'm going to stand this, but I'm not.'

He looked at her. She sat staring in front of her, making no attempt to cope with disaster.

'When I say I'm not going to stand it,' explained Lewisham, 'I don't mean having a row or anything of that sort. One can quarrel and be disappointed over—other things—and still go on. But this is a different thing altogether.

'Of all dreams and illusions! . . . Think what I have lost in this accursed marriage. And *now* . . . You don't understand—you won't understand.'

'Nor you,' said Ethel, weeping but neither looking at him nor moving her hands from her lap where they lay helplessly. '*You* don't understand.'

'I'm beginning to.'

He sat in silence, gathering force. 'In one year,' he said, 'all my hopes, all my ambitions have gone. I know I have been cross and irritable—I know that. I've been pulled two ways. But . . . I bought you these roses.'

She looked at the roses, and then at his white

face, made an imperceptible movement towards him, and became impassive again.

'I do think one thing. I have found out you are shallow, you don't think, you can't feel things that I think and feel. I have been getting over that. But I did think you were loyal——'

'I *am* loyal,' she cried.

'And you think—Bah !—you poke my roses under the table !'

Another portentous silence. Ethel stirred and he turned his eyes to watch what she was about to do. She produced her handkerchief and began to wipe her dry eyes rapidly, first one and then the other. Then she began sobbing. 'I'm . . . as loyal as you . . . anyhow,' she said.

For a moment Lewisham was aghast. Then he perceived he must ignore that argument.

'I would have stood it—I would have stood anything if you had been loyal—if I could have been sure of you. I am a fool, I know, but I would have stood the interruption of my work, the loss of any hope of a Career, if I had been sure you were loyal. I . . . I cared for you a great deal.'

He stopped. He had suddenly perceived the pathetic. He took refuge in anger.

'And you have deceived me ! How long, how much, I don't care. You have deceived me. And I tell you'—he began to gesticulate—'I'm not so much your slave and fool as to stand that ! No woman shall make me *that* sort of fool, whatever else—— So far as I am concerned, this ends things. This ends things. We are married—but I don't care if we were married five hundred times. I won't stop with a woman who takes flowers from another man——'

'I *didn't*,' said Ethel.

Lewisham gave way to a transport of anger. He caught up a handful of roses and extended them, trembling. 'What's *this*?' he asked. His finger bled from a thorn, as once it had bled from a blackthorn spray.

'I *didn't* take them,' said Ethel. 'I couldn't help it if they were sent.'

'Ugh!' said Lewisham. 'But what is the good of argument and denial? You took them in, you had them. You may have been cunning, but you have given yourself away. And our life and all this'—he waved an inclusive hand at Madam Gadow's furniture—'is at an end.'

He looked at her and repeated with bitter satisfaction, 'at an end.'

She glanced at his face and his expression was remorseless. 'I will not go on living with you,' he said, lest there should be any mistake. 'Our life is at an end.'

Her eyes went from his face to the scattered roses. She remained staring at these. She was no longer weeping, and her face, save about the eyes, was white.

He presented it in another form. 'I shall go away.

'We never ought to have married,' he reflected. 'But . . . I never expected *this*!'

'I didn't know,' she cried out, lifting up her voice. 'I *didn't* know. How could *I* help! *Oh!*'

She stopped and stared at him with hands clenched, her eyes haggard with despair.

Lewisham remained impenetrably malignant.

'I don't *want* to know,' he said, answering her dumb appeal. 'That settles everything. *That!*' He indicated the scattered flowers. 'What does it matter to me what has happened or hasn't happened? Anyhow—oh! I don't mind. I'm glad. See? It settles things.

'The sooner we part the better. I shan't stop with you another night. I shall take my box and

my portmanteau into that room and pack. I shall
stop in there to-night, sleep in a chair or *think*.
And to-morrow I shall settle up with Madam
Gadow and go. You can go back . . . to your
cheating.'

He stopped for some seconds. She was deadly
still. 'You wanted to, and now you may. You
wanted to, before I got work. You remember?
You know your place is still open at Lagune's. I
don't care. I tell you I don't care *that*. Not that !
You may go your own way—and I shall go mine.
See? And all this rot—this sham of living together
when neither cares for the other—I don't care for
you *now*, you know, so you needn't think it—will
be over and done with. As for marriage—I don't
care *that* for marriage—it can't make a sham and
a blunder anything but a sham.

'It's a sham, and shams have to end, and that's
the end of the matter.'

He stood up resolutely. He kicked the scattered
roses out of his way and dived beneath the bed for
his portmanteau. Ethel neither spoke nor moved,
but remained watching his movements. For a time
the portmanteau refused to emerge, and he marred
his stern resolution by a half audible, 'Come here
—damn you !' He swung it into the living-room
and returned for his box. He proposed to pack
in that room.

When he had taken all his personal possessions
out of the bedroom, he closed the folding doors
with an air of finality. He knew from the sounds
that followed that she flung herself upon the bed,
and that filled him with grim satisfaction.

He stood listening for a space, then set about
packing methodically. The first rage of discovery
had abated, he knew quite clearly that he was
inflicting grievous punishment and that gratified
him. There was also indeed a curious pleasure in

the determination of a long and painful period of
vague misunderstanding by this unexpected crisis.
He was acutely conscious of the silence on the other
side of the folding doors, he kept up a succession
of deliberate little noises, beat books together and
brushed clothes, to intimate the resolute prosecution
of his preparations.

That was about nine o'clock. At eleven he was
still busy. . . .

Darkness came suddenly upon him. It was
Madam Gadow's economical habit to turn off all
her gas at that hour unless she chanced to be entertaining friends.

He felt in his pocket for matches and he had
none. He whispered curses. Against such emer-
gencies he had bought a brass lamp and in the
bedroom there were candles. Ethel had a candle
alight, he could see the bright yellow line that
appeared between the folding doors. He felt his
way presently towards the mantel, receiving a blow
in the ribs from a chair on the way, and went
carefully amidst Madam Gadow's once amusing
ornaments.

There were no matches on the mantel. Going
to the chest of drawers he almost fell over his
open portmanteau. He had a silent ecstasy of rage.
Then he kicked against the basket in which the roses
had come. He could find no matches on the chest
of drawers.

Ethel must have the matches in the bedroom,
but that was absolutely impossible. He might
even have to ask her for them, for at times she
pocketed matches. . . . There was nothing for it
but to stop packing. Not a sound came from the
other room.

He decided he would sit down in the arm-chair
and go to sleep. He crept very carefully to the
chair and sat down. Another interval of listening

and he closed his eyes and composed himself for slumber.

He began to think over his plans for the morrow. He imagined the scene with Madam Gadow, and then his departure to find bachelor lodgings once more. He debated in what direction he should go to get suitable lodgings. Possible difficulties with his luggage, possible annoyances of the search loomed gigantic. He felt greatly irritated at these minor difficulties. He wondered if Ethel also was packing. What particularly would she do? He listened but he could hear nothing. She was very still. She was really very still! What could she be doing? He forgot the bothers of the morrow in this new interest. Presently he rose very softly and listened. Then he sat down again impatiently. He tried to dismiss his curiosity about the silence by recapitulating the story of his wrongs.

He had some difficulty in fixing his mind upon this theme, but presently his memories were flowing freely. Only it was not wrongs now that he could recall. He was pestered by an absurd idea that he had again behaved unjustly to Ethel, that he had been headlong and malignant. He made strenuous efforts to recover his first heat of jealousy —in vain. Her remark that she had been as loyal as he, became an obstinate headline in his mind. Something arose within him that insisted upon Ethel's possible fate if he should leave her. What particularly would she do? He knew how much her character leant upon his. Good Heavens! What might she not do?

By an effort he succeeded in fixing his mind on Baynes. That helped him back to the harsher footing. However hard things might be for her she deserved them. She deserved them!

Yet presently he slipped again, slipped back to the remorse and regrets of the morning time. He clutched at Baynes as a drowning man clutches at a rope, and recovered himself. For a time he meditated on Baynes. He had never seen the poet, so his imagination had scope. It appeared to him as an exasperating obstacle to a tragic avenging of his honour that Baynes was a mere boy—possibly even younger than himself.

The question, 'What will become of Ethel?' rose to the surface again. He struggled against its possibilities. No! That was not it! That was her affair.

He felt inexorably kept to the path he had chosen, for all the waning of his rage. He had put his hand to the plough. 'If you condone this,' he told himself, 'you might condone anything. There are things one *must* not stand.' He tried to keep to that point of view—assuming for the most part out of his imagination what it was he was not standing. A dim sense came to him of how much he was assuming. At any rate she must have flirted! . . . He resisted this reviving perception of justice as though it was some unspeakably disgraceful craving. He tried to imagine her with Baynes.

He determined he would go to sleep.

But his was a waking weariness. He tried counting. He tried to distract his thoughts from her by going over the atomic weights of the elements. . . .

He shivered, and realised that he was cold and sitting cramped on an uncomfortable horsehair chair. He had dozed. He glanced for the yellow line between the folding doors. It was still there but it seemed to quiver. He judged the candle must be flaring. He wondered why everything was so still.

Now why should he suddenly feel afraid.

He sat for a long time trying to hear some movement, his head craning forward in the darkness. . . .

A grotesque idea came into his head that all that had happened a very long time ago. He dismissed that. He contested an unreasonable persuasion that some irrevocable thing had passed. But why was everything so still?

He was invaded by a prevision of unendurable calamity.

Presently he rose and crept very slowly and with infinite precautions against noise, towards the folding doors. He stood listening with his ear near the yellow chink.

He could hear nothing, not even the measured breathing of a sleeper.

He perceived that the doors were not shut but slightly ajar. He pushed against the inner one very gently and opened it silently. Still there was no sound of Ethel. He opened the door still wider and peered into the room. The candle had burnt down and was flaring in its socket. Ethel was lying half undressed upon the bed, and in her hand and close to her face was a rose.

He stood watching her, fearing to move. He listened hard, and his face was very white. Even now he could not hear her breathing.

After all, it was probably all right. She was just asleep. He would slip back before she woke. If she found him——

He looked at her again. There was something in her face——

He came nearer, no longer heeding the sounds he made. He bent over her. Even now she did not seem to breathe.

He saw that her eyelashes were still wet, the pillow by her cheek was wet. Her white, tear-stained face hurt him. . . .

She was intolerably pitiful to him. He forgot everything but that and how he had wounded her that day. And then she stirred and murmured indistinctly a foolish name she had given him.

He forgot that they were going to part for ever. He felt nothing but a great joy that she could stir and speak. His jealousy flashed out of being. He dropped upon his knees.

'Dear,' he whispered. 'Is it all right? I . . . I could not hear you breathing. I could not hear you breathing.'

She started and was awake.

'I was in the other room,' said Lewisham in a voice full of emotion. 'Everything was so quiet. I was afraid—I did not know what had happened. Dear—Ethel dear. Is it all right?'

She sat up quickly and scrutinised his face. 'Oh! let me tell you,' she wailed. 'Do let me tell you. It's nothing. It's nothing. You wouldn't hear me. You wouldn't hear me. It wasn't fair—before you had heard me. . . .'

His arms tightened about her. 'Dear,' he said, 'I knew it was nothing. I knew. I knew.'

She spoke in sobbing sentences. 'It was so simple. Mr Baynes . . . something in his manner . . . I knew he might be silly. . . . Only I did so want to help you.' She paused. Just for one instant she saw one untellable indiscretion as it were in a lightning flash. A chance meeting it was, a 'silly' thing or so said, a panic, retreat. She would have told it—had she known how. But she could not do it. She hesitated. She abolished it—untold. She went on : 'And then, I thought he had sent the roses and I was frightened. . . . I was frightened.'

'Dear one,' said Lewisham. 'Dear one! I have been cruel to you. I have been unjust. I understand. I do understand. Forgive me. Dearest —forgive me.'

'I did so want to do something for you. It was all I could do—that little money. And then you were angry. I thought you didn't love me any more because I did not understand your work. . . . And that Miss Heydinger—Oh! it was hard.'

'Dear one,' said Lewisham, 'I do not care your little finger for Miss Heydinger.'

'I know how I hamper you. But if you will help me. Oh! I would work, I would study. I would do all I could to understand.'

'Dear,' whispered Lewisham. '*Dear.*'

'And to have *her*——'

'Dear,' he vowed, 'I have been a brute. I will end all that. I will end all that.'

He took her suddenly into his arms and kissed her.

'Oh, I *know* I'm stupid,' she said.

'You're not. It's I have been stupid. I have been unkind, unreasonable. All to-day . . . I've been thinking about it. Dear! I don't care for anything—— It's *you*. If I have you nothing else matters. . . . Only I get hurried and cross. It's the work and being poor. Dear one, we *must* hold to each other. All to-day—— It's been dreadful . . .'

He stopped. They sat clinging to one another.

'I do love you,' she said presently, with her arms about him. 'Oh! I do—*do*—love you.'

He drew her closer to him.

He kissed her neck. She pressed him to her.

Their lips met.

The expiring candle streamed up into a tall flame, flickered, and was suddenly extinguished. The air was heavy with the scent of roses.

CHAPTER XXX

A WITHDRAWAL

On Tuesday Lewisham returned from Vigours' at five—at half-past six he would go on to his science class at Walham Green—and discovered Mrs Chaffery and Ethel in tears. He was fagged and rather anxious for some tea, but the news they had for him drove tea out of his head altogether.

'He's gone,' said Ethel.

'Who's gone? What! Not Chaffery?'

Mrs Chaffery, with a keen eye to Lewisham's behaviour, nodded tearfully over an experienced handkerchief.

Lewisham grasped the essentials of the situation forthwith, and trembled on the brink of an expletive. Ethel handed him a letter.

For a moment Lewisham held this in his hand, asking questions. Mrs Chaffery had come upon it in the case of her eight-day clock when the time to wind it came round. Chaffery, it seemed, had not been home since Saturday night. The letter was an open one addressed to Lewisham, a long, rambling, would-be clever letter, oddly inferior in style to Chaffery's conversation. It had been written some hours before Chaffery's last visit; his talk then had been perhaps a sort of codicil.

'The inordinate stupidity of that man Lagune is driving me out of the country,' Lewisham saw. 'It has been at last a definite stumbling block—even a legal stumbling block, I fear. I am off. I skedaddle. I break ties. I shall miss our long

232

refreshing chats—you had found me out and I could open my mind. I am sorry to part from Ethel also, but thank Heaven she has you to look to! And indeed they both have you to look to, though the " both " may be a new light to you.'

Lewisham growled, went from page 1 to page 3—conscious of their both looking to him now—even intensely—and discovered Chaffery in a practical vein.

'There is but little light and portable property in that house in Clapham that has escaped my lamentable improvidence, but there are one or two things; the iron-bound chest, the bureau with a broken hinge, and the large air pump, distinctly pawnable if only you can contrive to get them to a pawnshop. You have more Will power than I—I never could get the confounded things downstairs. That iron-bound box was originally mine, before I married your mother-in-law, so that I am not altogether regardless of your welfare and the necessity of giving some equivalent. Don't judge me too harshly.'

Lewisham turned over sharply, without finishing that page.

'My life at Clapham,' continued the letter, 'has irked me for some time, and to tell you the truth, the spectacle of your vigorous young happiness—you are having a very good time, you know, fighting the world—reminded me of the passing years. To be frank in self-criticism, there is more than a touch of the New Woman about me, and I feel I have still to live my own life. What a beautiful phrase that is—to live one's own life!—redolent of honest scorn for moral plagiarism. No *Imitatio Christi* in that. . . . I long to see more of men and cities. . . . I begin late, I know, to live my own life, bald as I am and gray-whiskered; but better late than never. Why should the educated girl have the monopoly of the game? And after all, the whiskers will dye. . . .

'There are things—I touch upon them lightly—that will presently astonish Lagune. Lewisham became more attentive. 'I marvel at that man, grubbing hungry for marvels amidst the almost incredibly marvellous. What can be the nature of a man who gapes after Poltergeists with the miracle of his own silly existence (inconsequent, reasonless, unfathomably weird) nearer to him than breathing and closer than hands and feet. What is *he* for, that he should wonder at Poltergeists? I am astonished these by no means flimsy psychic phenomena do not turn upon their investigators, and that a Research Society of eminent illusions and hallucinations does not pursue Lagune with sceptical inquiries. Take his house—expose the alleged man of Chelsea! *A priori* they might argue that a thing so vain, so unmeaning, so strongly beset by cackle, could only be the diseased imagining of some hysterical phantom. Do *you* believe that such a thing as Lagune exists? I must own to the gravest doubts. But happily his banker is of a more credulous type than I. . . . Of all that Lagune will tell you soon enough.'

Lewisham read no more. 'I suppose he thought himself clever when he wrote that rot,' said Lewisham bitterly, throwing the sheets forcibly athwart the table. 'The simple fact is, he's stolen, or forged, or something—and bolted.'

There was a pause. 'What will become of Mother?' said Ethel.

Lewisham looked at Mother and thought for a moment. Then he glanced at Ethel.

'We're all in the same boat,' said Lewisham.

'I don't want to give any trouble to a single human being,' said Mrs Chaffery.

'I think you might get a man his tea, Ethel,'

said Lewisham, sitting down suddenly; 'anyhow.'
He drummed on the table with his fingers. 'I have
to get to Walham Green by a quarter to seven.'

'We're all in the same boat,' he repeated, after
an interval, and continued drumming. He was
chiefly occupied by the curious fact that they were
all in the same boat. What an extraordinary
faculty he had for acquiring responsibility! He
looked up suddenly and caught Mrs Chaffery's
tearful eye directed to Ethel and full of distressful
interrogation, and his perplexity was suddenly
changed to pity. 'It's all right, Mother,' he said.
'I'm not going to be unreasonable. I'll stand by you.'

'Ah!' said Mrs Chaffery. 'As if I didn't know!'
and Ethel came and kissed him.

He seemed in imminent danger of universal
embraces.

'I wish you'd let me have my tea,' he said. And
while he had his tea he asked Mrs Chaffery questions and tried to get the new situation into focus.

But even at ten o'clock when he was returning
hot and jaded from Walham Green he was still
trying to get the situation into focus. There were
vague ends and blank walls of interrogation in the
matter, that perplexed him.

He knew that his supper would be only the
prelude to an interminable 'talking over,' and
indeed he did not get to bed until nearly two. By
that time a course of action was already agreed upon.
Mrs Chaffery was tied to the house in Clapham by
a long lease and thither they must go. The ground
floor and first floor were let unfurnished, and the
rent of these practically paid the rent of the house.
The Chafferys occupied basement and second floor.
There was a bedroom on the second floor formerly
let to the first floor tenants, that he and Ethel
could occupy, and in this an old toilet table could
be put for such studies as were to be prosecuted at

home. Ethel could have her typewriter in the subterranean breakfast-room. Mrs Chaffery and Ethel must do the catering and the bulk of the housework, and as soon as possible, since letting lodgings would not square with Lewisham's professional pride, they must get rid of the lease that bound them and take some smaller and more suburban residence. If they did that without leaving any address it might save their feelings from any return of the prodigal Chaffery.

Mrs Chaffery's frequent and pathetic acknowledgments of Lewisham's goodness only partly relieved his disposition to a philosophical bitterness. And the practical issues were complicated by excursions upon the subject of Chaffery, what he might have done, and where he might have gone, and whether by any chance he might not return.

When at last Mrs Chaffery, after a violent and tearful kissing and blessing of them both—they were 'good dear children,' she said—had departed, Mr and Mrs Lewisham returned into their sitting-room. Mrs Lewisham's little face was enthusiastic. 'You're a Trump,' she said, extending the willing arms that were his reward. 'I know,' she said, 'I know, and all to-night I have been loving you. Dear! Dear! Dear. . . .'

The next day Lewisham was too full of engagements to communicate with Lagune, but the following morning he called and found the psychic investigator busy with the proofs of *Hesperus*. He welcomed the young man cordially nevertheless, conceiving him charged with the questions that had been promised long ago—it was evident he knew nothing of Lewisham's marriage. Lewisham stated his case with some bluntness.

'He was last here on Saturday,' said Lagune. 'You have always been inclined to suspicion about him. Have you any grounds?'

'You'd better read this,' said Lewisham, repressing a grim smile, and he handed Lagune Chaffery's letter.

He glanced at the little man ever and again to see if he had come to the personal portion and for the rest of the time occupied himself with an envious inventory of the writing appointments about him. No doubt the boy with the big ears had had the same sort of thing. . . .

When Lagune came to the question of his real identity he blew out his cheeks in the most astonishing way, but made no other sign.

'Dear, dear!' he said at last. 'My bankers!'

He looked at Lewisham with the exaggerated mildness of his spectacled eye. 'What do you think it means?' he asked. 'Has he gone mad? We have been conducting some experiments involving—considerable mental strain. He and I and a lady. Hypnotic——'

'I should look at my cheque-book if I were you.'

Lagune produced some keys and got out his cheque-book. He turned over the counterfoils. 'There's nothing wrong here,' he said, and handed the book to Lewisham.

'Um,' said Lewisham. 'I suppose this—— I say, is *this* right?'

He handed back the book to Lagune, open at the blank counterfoil of a cheque that had been removed. Lagune stared and passed his hand over his forehead in a confused way. 'I can't see this,' he said.

Lewisham had never heard of post hypnotic suggestion and he stood incredulous. 'You can't see that?' he said. 'What nonsense!'

'I can't see it,' repeated Lagune.

For some seconds Lewisham could not get away from stupid repetitions of his inquiry. Then he hit upon a collateral proof. 'But look here! Can you see *this* counterfoil?'

'Plainly,' said Lagune.

'Can you read the number?'

'Five thousand two hundred and seventy-nine.'

'Well, and this?'

'Five thousand two hundred and eighty-one.'

'Well—where's five thousand two hundred and eighty?'

Lagune began to look uncomfortable. 'Surely,' he said, 'he has not. Will you read it out—the cheque, the counterfoil I mean, that I am unable to see.'

'It's blank,' said Lewisham, with an irresistible grin.

'Surely,' said Lagune, and the discomfort of his expression deepened. 'Do you mind if I call in a servant to confirm——'

Lewisham did not mind, and the same girl who had admitted him to the *séance* appeared. When she had given her evidence she went again. As she left the room by the door behind Lagune her eyes met Lewisham's, and she lifted her eyebrows, depressed her mouth and glanced at Lagune with a meaning expression.

'I'm afraid,' said Lagune, 'that I have been shabbily treated. Mr Chaffery is a man of indisputable powers—indisputable powers; but I am afraid—I am very much afraid he has abused the conditions of the experiment. All this—and his insults—touch me rather nearly.'

He paused. Lewisham rose. 'Do you mind if you come again?' asked Lagune, with gentle politeness.

Lewisham was surprised to find himself sorry.

'He was a man of extraordinary gifts,' said Lagune. 'I had come to rely upon him. . . . My cash balance has been rather heavy lately. How he came to know of that I am unable to say. Without supposing, that is, that he had very remarkable gifts.'

When Lewisham saw Lagune again he learnt the particulars of Chaffery's misdeed and the additional fact that the 'lady' had also disappeared. 'That's a good job,' he remarked selfishly. 'There's no chance of *his* coming back.' He spent a moment trying to imagine the 'lady'; he realised more vividly than he had ever done before the narrow range of his experience, the bounds of his imagination. These people also—with gray hair and truncated honour—had their emotions! Even it may be glowing! He came back to facts. Chaffery had induced Lagune when hypnotised to sign a blank cheque as an 'autograph.' 'The strange thing is,' explained Lagune, 'it's doubtful if he's legally accountable. The law is so peculiar about hypnotism, and I certainly signed the cheque, you know.'

The little man, in spite of his losses, was now almost cheerful again on account of a curious side issue. 'You may say it is coincidence,' he said, 'you may call it a fluke, but I prefer to look for some other interpretation. Consider this. The amount of my balance is a secret between me and my bankers. He never had it from *me*, for I did not know it—I hadn't looked at my pass-book for months. But he drew it all in one cheque, within seventeen and sixpence of the total. And the total was over five hundred pounds!'

He seemed quite bright again as he culminated.

'Within seventeen and sixpence,' he said. 'Now how do you account for that, eh? Give me a materialistic explanation that will explain away all that. You can't. Neither can I.'

'I think I can,' said Lewisham.

'Well—what is it?'

Lewisham nodded towards a little drawer of the bureau. 'Don't you think—perhaps'—a little ripple of laughter passed across his mind—'he had a skeleton key?'

Lagune's face lingered amusingly in Lewisham's mind as he returned to Clapham. But after a time that amusement passed away. He declined upon the extraordinary fact that Chaffery was his father-in-law, Mrs Chaffery his mother-in-law, that these two and Ethel constituted his family, his clan, and that grimy graceless house up the Clapham hill-side was to be his home. Home! His connection with these things as a point of worldly departure was as inexorable now as though he had been born to it. And a year ago, except for a fading reminiscence of Ethel, none of these people had existed for him. The ways of Destiny! The happenings of the last few months, foreshortened in perspective, seemed to have almost a pantomimic rapidity. The thing took him suddenly as being laughable; and he laughed.

His laugh marked an epoch. Never before had Lewisham laughed at any fix in which he had found himself. The enormous seriousness of adolescence was coming to an end; the days of his growing were numbered. It was a laugh of infinite admissions.

CHAPTER XXXI

IN BATTERSEA PARK

Now although Lewisham had promised to bring things to a conclusion with Miss Heydinger, he did nothing in the matter for five weeks, he merely left that crucial letter of hers unanswered. In that time their removal from Madam Gadow's into the gaunt house at Clapham was accomplished—not without polyglot controversy—and the young couple settled themselves into the little room on the second floor even as they had arranged. And there it was that suddenly the world was changed—was astonishingly transfigured—by a whisper.

It was a whisper between sobs and tears, with Ethel's arms about him and Ethel's hair streaming down so that it hid her face from him. And he too had whispered, dismayed perhaps a little, and yet feeling a strange pride, a strange novel emotion, feeling altogether different from the things he had fancied he might feel when this thing that he had dreaded should come. Suddenly he perceived finality, the advent of the solution, the reconciliation of the conflict that had been waged so long. Hesitations were at an end;—he took his line.

Next day he wrote a note and two mornings later he started for his mathematical duffers an hour before it was absolutely necessary, and instead of going directly to Vigours', went over the bridge to Battersea Park. There waiting for him by a seat where once they had met before, he found Miss Heydinger pacing. They walked up and down side by side, speaking for a little while about indifferent topics, and then they came upon a pause. . . .

'You have something to tell me?' said Miss Heydinger abruptly.

Lewisham changed colour a little. 'Oh, yes,' he said; 'the fact is——' He affected ease. 'Did I ever tell you I was married?'

'*Married ?*'

'Yes.'

'Married !'

'Yes,' a little testily.

For a moment neither spoke. Lewisham stood without dignity staring at the dahlias of the London County Council, and Miss Heydinger stood regarding him.

'And that is what you have to tell me?'

Mr Lewisham turned and met her eyes. 'Yes !' he said. 'That is what I have to tell you.'

Pause. 'Do you mind if I sit down?' asked Miss Heydinger in an indifferent tone.

'There is a seat yonder,' said Lewisham, 'under the tree.'

They walked to the seat in silence.

'Now,' said Miss Heydinger quietly. 'Tell me whom you have married.'

Lewisham answered sketchily. She asked him another question and another. He felt stupid and answered with a halting truthfulness.

'I might have known,' she said, 'I might have known. Only I would not know. Tell me some more. Tell me about her.'

Lewisham did. The whole thing was abominably disagreeable to him, but it had to be done, he had promised Ethel it should be done. Presently Miss Heydinger knew the main outline of his story, knew all his story except the emotion that made it credible. 'And you were married—before the second examination?' she repeated.

'Yes,' said Lewisham.

'But why did you not tell me of this before?' asked Miss Heydinger.

'I don't know,' said Lewisham. 'I wanted to— that day, in Kensington Gardens. But I didn't. I suppose I ought to have done so.'

'I think you ought to have done so.'

'Yes, I suppose I ought. . . . But I didn't. Somehow—it has been hard. I didn't know what you would say. The thing seemed so rash, you know, and all that.'

He paused blankly.

'I suppose you had to do it,' said Miss Heydinger presently, with her eyes on his profile.

Lewisham began the second and more difficult part of his explanation. 'There's been a difficulty,' he said, 'all the way along—I mean—about you, that is. It's a little difficult——. The fact is, my wife, you know——. She looks at things differently from what we do.'

'We?'

'Yes—it's odd, of course. But she has seen your letters——'

'You didn't show her——?'

'No. But, I mean, she knows you write to me, and she knows you write about Socialism and Literature and—things we have in common—things she hasn't.'

'You mean to say she doesn't understand these things?'

'She's not thought about them. I suppose there's a sort of difference in education——'

'And she objects——?'

'No,' said Lewisham, lying promptly. 'She doesn't *object* . . .'

'Well?' said Miss Heydinger, and her face was white.

'She feels that—— She feels—she does not say,

of course, but I know she feels that it is something she ought to share. I know—how she cares for me. And it shames her—it reminds her—— Don't you see how it hurts her?'

'Yes. I see. So that even that little——' Miss Heydinger's breath seemed to catch and she was abruptly silent.

She spoke at last with an effort. 'That it hurts *me*,' she said, and grimaced and stopped again.

'No,' said Lewisham, 'that is not it.' He hesitated.

'I *knew* this would hurt you.'

'You love her. You can sacrifice——'

'No. It is not that. But there is a difference. Hurting *her*—she would not understand. But you —somehow it seems a natural thing for me to come to you. I seem to look to you—— For her I am always making allowances——'

'You love her.'

'I wonder if it *is* that makes the difference. Things are so complex. Love means anything— or nothing. I know you better than I do her, you know me better than she will ever do. I could tell you things I could not tell her. I could put all myself before you—almost—and know you would understand—— Only——'

'You love her.'

'Yes,' said Lewisham lamely and pulling at his moustache. 'I suppose . . . that must be it.'

For a space neither spoke. Then Miss Heydinger said '*Oh!*' with extraordinary emphasis.

'To think of this end to it all! That all your promise. . . . What is it she gives that I could not have given?

'Even now! Why should I give up that much of you that is mine? If she could take it—— But she cannot take it. If I let you go—you will do nothing. All this ambition, all these interests will dwindle and die, and she will not mind. She will

not understand. She will think that she still has
you. Why should she covet what she cannot possess?
Why should she be given the thing that is mine
—to throw aside?'

She did not look at Lewisham, but before her,
her face a white misery.

'In a way—I had come to think of you as something belonging to me. . . . I shall—still.'

'There is one thing,' said Lewisham, after a
pause; 'it is a thing that has come to me once or
twice lately. Don't you think that perhaps you
overestimate the things I might have done? I
know we've talked of great things to do. But I've
been struggling for half a year and more to get the
sort of living almost any one seems able to get. It
has taken me all my time. One can't help thinking
after that, perhaps the world is a stiffer sort of
affair . . .'

'No,' she said decisively. 'You could have done
great things.

'Even now,' she said, 'you may do great
things—— If only I might see you sometimes,
write to you sometimes—— You are so capable
and—weak. You must have somebody—— That
is your weakness. You fail in your belief. You
must have support and belief—unstinted support
and belief. Why could I not be that to you? It
is all I want to be. At least—all I want to be
now. Why need she know? It robs her of nothing.
I want nothing—she has. But I know of my own
strength too I can do nothing. I know that with
you. . . . It is only knowing hurts her. Why
should she know?'

Mr Lewisham looked at her doubtfully. That
phantom greatness of his, it was that lit her eyes.
In that instant at least he had no doubts of the
possibility of his Career. But he knew that in
some way the secret of his greatness and this

admiration went together. Conceivably they were one and indivisible. Why indeed need Ethel know? His imagination ran over the things that might be done, the things that might happen, and touched swiftly upon complication, confusion, discovery.

'The thing is, I must simplify my life. I shall do nothing unless I simplify my life. Only people who are well off can be—complex. It is one thing or the other——'

He hesitated and suddenly had a vision of Ethel weeping as once he had seen her weep with the light on the tears in her eyes.

'No,' he said almost brutally. 'No. It's like this—— I can't do anything underhand. I mean—— I'm not so amazingly honest—now. But I've not that sort of mind. She would find me out. It would do no good and she would find me out. My life's too complex. I can't manage it and go straight. I—you've overrated me. And besides—— Things have happened. Something——' He hesitated and then snatched at his resolve. 'I've got to simplify—and that's the plain fact of the case. I'm sorry, but it is so.'

Miss Heydinger made no answer. Her silence astonished him. For nearly twenty seconds perhaps they sat without speaking. With a quick motion she stood up and at once he stood up before her. Her face was flushed, her eyes downcast.

'Good-bye,' she said suddenly in a low tone, and held out her hand.

'But,' said Lewisham, and stopped. Miss Heydinger's colour left her.

'Good-bye,' she said, looking him suddenly in the eyes and smiling awry. 'There is no more to say, is there? Good-bye.'

He took her hand. 'I hope I didn't——'

'Good-bye,' she said impatiently, and suddenly disengaged her hand and turned away from him. He made a step after her.

'Miss Heydinger,' he said, but she did not stop. 'Miss Heydinger.' He realised that she did not want to answer him again. . . .

He remained motionless, watching her retreating figure. An extraordinary sense of loss came into his mind, a vague impulse to pursue her and pour out vague passionate protestations. . . .

Not once did she look back. She was already remote when he began hurrying after her. Once he was in motion he quickened his pace and gained upon her. He was within thirty yards of her as she drew near the gates.

His pace slackened. Suddenly he was afraid she might look back. She passed out of the gates, out of his sight. He stopped, looking where she had disappeared. He sighed and took the pathway to his left that led back to the bridge and Vigours.

Half-way across the bridge came another crisis of indecision. He stopped, hesitating. An impertinent thought obtruded. He looked at his watch and saw that he must hurry if he would catch the train for Earl's Court and Vigours. He said Vigours might go to the devil.

But in the end he caught his train.

CHAPTER XXXII

THE CROWNING VICTORY

THAT night about Seven Ethel came into their room with a waste-paper basket she had bought for him, and found him sitting at the little toilet table at which he was to 'write.' The outlook was, for a London outlook, spacious, down a long slope of roofs towards the Junction, a huge sky of blue passing upward to the darkling zenith and downward into a hazy bristling mystery of roofs and chimneys, from which emerged signal lights and steam puffs, gliding chains of lit window carriages and the vague vistas of streets. She showed him the basket and put it beside him, and then her eye caught the yellow document in his hand. 'What is that you have there?'

He held it out to her, 'I found it—lining my yellow box. I had it at Whortley.'

She took it and perceived a chronological scheme. It was headed 'SCHEMA,' there were memoranda in the margin, and all the dates had been altered by a hasty hand.

'Hasn't it got yellow?' she said.

That seemed to him the wrong thing for her to say. He stared at the document with a sudden accession of sympathy. There was an interval. He became aware of her hand upon his shoulder, that she was bending over him. 'Dear,' she whispered, with a strange change in the quality of her

248

voice. He knew she was seeking to say something that was difficult to say.

'Yes?' he said presently.

'You are not grieving?'

'What about?'

'*This*.'

'No !'

'You are not—you are not even sorry?' she said.

'No—not even sorry.'

'I can't understand that. It's so much——'

'I'm glad,' he proclaimed. '*Glad*.'

'But—the trouble—the expense—everything—and your work?'

'Yes,' he said, 'that's just it.'

She looked at him doubtfully. He glanced up at her, and she questioned his eyes. He put his arm about her, and presently and almost absent-mindedly she obeyed his pressure and bent down and kissed him.

'It settles things,' he said, holding her. 'It joins us. Don't you see? Before. . . . But now it's different. It's something we have between us. It's something that. . . . It's the link we needed. It will hold us together, cement us together. It will be our life. This will be my work now. The other . . .'

He faced a truth. 'It was just . . . vanity !'

There was still a shade of doubt in her face, a wistfulness.

Presently she spoke.

'Dear,' she said.

'Yes?'

She knitted her brows. 'No !' she said. 'I can't say it.'

In the interval she came into a sitting position on his knees.

He kissed her hand, but her face remained grave, and she looked out upon the twilight. 'I know I'm stupid,' she said. 'The things I say . . . aren't the things I feel.'

He waited for her to say more.

'It's no good,' she said.

He felt the onus of expression lay on him. He too found it a little difficult to put into words. 'I think I understand,' he said, and wrestled with the impalpable. The pause seemed long and yet not altogether vacant. She lapsed abruptly into the prosaic. She started from him.

'If I don't go down, Mother will get supper . . .'

At the door she stopped and turned a twilight face to him. For a moment they scrutinised one another. To her he was no more than a dim out-line. Impulsively he held out his arms. . . .

Then at the sound of a movement downstairs she freed herself and hurried out. He heard her call 'Mother! You're not to lay supper. 'You're to rest.'

He listened to her footsteps until the kitchen had swallowed them up. Then he turned his eyes to the Schema again and for a moment it seemed but a little thing.

He picked it up in both hands and looked at it as if it was the writing of another man, and indeed it was the writing of another man. 'Pamphlets in the Liberal Interest,' he read, and smiled.

Presently a train of thought carried him off. His attitude relaxed a little, the Schema became for a time a mere symbol, a point of departure, and he stared out of the window at the darkling night. For a long time he sat pursuing thoughts that were half emotions, emotions that took upon themselves the shape and substance of ideas. The deepening current stirred at last among the roots of speech.

'Yes, it was vanity,' he said. 'A boy's vanity. For me—anyhow. I'm too two-sided. . . . Two-sided? . . . Commonplace!

'Dreams like mine—abilities like mine. Yes—any man! And yet . . . The things I meant to do!'

His thoughts went to his Socialism, to his red-hot ambition of world mending. He marvelled at the vistas he had discovered since those days.

'Not for us—— Not for us.

'We must perish in the wilderness. Some day. Somewhen. But not for us. . . .

'Come to think, it is all the Child. The future is the Child. The Future. What are we—any of us—but servants or traitors to that? . . .

.   .   .   .

'Natural Selection—it follows . . . this way is happiness . . . must be. There can be no other.'

He sighed. 'To last a lifetime, that is.

'And yet—it is almost as if Life had played me a trick—promised so much—given so little! . . .

'No! One must not look at it in that way! That will not do! That will *not* do.

'Career. In itself it is a career—the most important career in the world. Father! Why should I want more?

'And . . Ethel! No wonder she seemed shallow. . . . She has been shallow. No wonder she was restless. Unfulfilled. . . . What had she to do? She was drudge, she was toy . . .

'Yes. This is life. This alone is life! For this we were made and born. All these other things—all other things—they are only a sort of play . . .

'Play!'

His eyes came back to the Schema. His hands shifted to the opposite corner and he hesitated. The vision of that arranged Career, that ordered sequence of work and successes, distinctions, and yet further distinctions, rose brightly from the symbol. Then he compressed his lips and tore the yellow sheet in half, tearing very deliberately. He doubled the halves and tore again, doubled again very carefully and neatly until the Schema was torn into numberless little pieces. With it he seemed to be tearing his past self.

'Play,' he whispered, after a long silence.

'It is the end of adolescence,' he said; 'the end of empty dreams. . . .'

He became very still, his hands resting on the table, his eyes staring out of the blue oblong of the window. The dwindling light gathered itself together and became a star.

He found he was still holding the torn fragments. He stretched out his hand and dropped them into that new waste-paper basket Ethel had bought for him.

Two pieces fell outside the basket. He stooped, picked them up, and put them carefully with their fellows.